A SONG
FOR
THE DEAD

BOOKS BY D.K. HOOD

Her Bleeding Heart

Chase Her Shadow

Now You See Me

Their Wicked Games

Where Hidden Souls Lie

D.K. HOOD

A SONG FOR THE DEAD

bookouture

Published by Bookouture in 2024

An imprint of Storyfire Ltd.
Carmelite House
50 Victoria Embankment
London EC4Y 0DZ

www.bookouture.com

ISBN: 978-1-83790-509-6
eBook ISBN: 978-1-83790-508-9

To Wendy, a beautiful lady with a heart of gold. This one is for you.

PROLOGUE

SATURDAY

Dark shadows surrounded Freya Richardson as she left the beauty parlor and headed down Main. The cold night air penetrated her coat, sending a shiver crawling down her spine. Cleaning the beauty parlor after closing had seemed like a good idea at the time, well, before her truck had died. Walking home alone at night was fast becoming a nightmare. On her way to work, Main was usually busy with people dropping by for meals or takeout from the local diners, but now it was after eleven. Silence surrounded her and her footsteps echoed as she passed by each alleyway. Nerves on edge, she slowed to check each one before moving forward. The sensation of being watched had started last week and continued—first, a prickling of neck hairs and the sense that someone was right behind her, followed by turning to find nobody there—but the week before Halloween always put her on edge. The town of Black Rock Falls went all out over the festival. It was total immersion, with displays in every storefront and spilling onto the sidewalk. Moving cautiously, she made it past Aunt Betty's Café and the giant spider making an archway of its legs over the entrance, and then as if on cue, the mist from the river bubbled over the riverbank and spread through town like the steam from a witch's cauldron. As she walked by, the gruesome displays lit up with red eyes flashing in cackling corpses or with grinning skulls, as if taunting her every step.

A noise from behind had her spinning around and her heart pounding. She searched the puddles of yellow from the streetlights for any signs of movement. Nothing stirred in the shadows, but above, an owl flew soundlessly from tree to tree with a mouse dangling lifeless in its beak. As the bird dived across Main, the streetlight illuminated its outstretched wings against the dark sky for a second. Freya wrapped her coat tighter across her chest and kept going. She passed the town hall and then the sheriff's office and turned left. She walked faster. Here the streetlights spread out, leaving dark spaces in between, but she reached Maple, and ahead, light streamed from the medical examiner's building. It now took up the entire block, incorporating two large old red-brick buildings. She hurried on, glad of the light splashing across the sidewalk and turned onto Elm. Ahead, two more empty buildings, with FOR SALE signs in the windows, and then she'd arrive at her building. It was an old fire station converted into six apartments. Beyond, a line of old red-brick buildings were currently being sold for renovation. This block of old industrial buildings had become a gold mine. As the population increased, the need for more local housing had exploded into small apartments.

Freya slowed her pace as she neared her building and swallowed hard. The light over the front entrance was out. The foyer was in darkness and yet she'd turned on the lights when she'd left earlier. Fear gripped her as she looked around, fumbling in her purse for her keys. Sighing with relief as her fingers closed around the cold metal, she ran up the steps and pressed in the code for the main door. Her footsteps sounded deafening as she dashed through the foyer and down the passageway to her apartment. Glad she'd chosen one on the ground floor, she fumbled getting the key into the lock. At last, the door flew open and she fell inside panting. One hand went to turn on the lights, the other to lock the door behind her. She leaned against the door, looking around the room. Seeing it was just as she'd left it, she took a deep breath and kicked off her shoes. She dropped her purse and phone on the counter and headed for the bedroom. She bent to look under the bed and, feeling stupid, straightened, shaking her head. "You're getting the Halloween spooks again."

She removed her coat, undressed, and went into the bathroom. A long hot shower and a glass of milk and she'd sleep like a baby. Tomorrow she had a few job interviews. Anything would be better than walking home in the dark each night. She didn't own a weapon for protection and had planned to buy one before her truck died. Right now, the repairs had become a priority. Ten minutes later, she stepped out of the shower and reached for a towel. Drying swiftly, she went to the mirror to brush her hair and froze. A message written in the condensation chilled her to the bone:

I'm going to kill you.

As the letters dripped down the glass, and her reflection cleared, a scream caught in Freya's throat. Behind her, a man in a grotesque Halloween mask was holding a knife and twisting it as if showing her. Terrified, she gaped at him, frozen with fear. Her head jerked back, and the cold blade sliced across her throat. Brilliant red blood splashed across the mirror and the bright bathroom light faded.

"Happy Halloween, Freya."

ONE

MONDAY

Cold seeped through every seam of Sheriff Jenna Alton's clothes as she scanned the partially exposed gravesites. It was a typical late October morning in Black Rock Falls, Montana. Deep in the forest, the constant spill of water vapor rising from the river crept through the trees, making all around her damp and cold. The watery sun and the stiff breeze from the mountains would eventually blow away the mist, but right now, it just added to the level of creepy she'd come to expect for the week or so before Halloween. Any plans she'd made for the festival might as well be tossed into the wind, because as sure as the sun would rise in the morning, something would happen to spoil them. It was her first Halloween with her adopted son, Tauri, an inquisitive four-year-old with the eye color of an eagle. Her ex-special forces husband and deputy, Dave Kane, had wanted to make it a special family occasion.

In the five years or so since she fought her way to sheriff, life had been a little crazy. The sleepy town that witness protection had settled her in was far from it. In fact, her past life as DEA Agent Avril Parker had been tame in comparison, but there was no going back. With a new name and face, like her off-the-grid husband, this reality had become their new lives and she liked it just fine. She'd gathered a first-rate team around her. Dr. Shane Wolfe, the medical examiner and Kane's handler, had become like a brother. Same with Deputy Jake Rowley, who'd come to her as a rookie, and former gold shield detective Zac Rio, who was an asset with his retentive memory, especially at crime scenes. She glanced around the small clearing at the faces she knew so well. The newest addition, Dr. Norrell Larson, had joined Wolfe's team. A forensic anthropologist, she and her team were currently examining graves found throughout Stanton Forest by good friend and Native American tracker Atohi Blackhawk.

This was the second gravesite they'd visited, but only this one at the top of Bear Peak had been excavated. It was a slow process, Norrell and her team on their knees all day brushing away soil and sieving it, looking for evidence. Blackhawk had insisted these graves were not known as ancient Native American burial sites. Someone had disposed of bodies and Norell needed to know when this occurred. Who they were would come later. The idea of digging up dead bodies this close to Halloween sent chills down Jenna's spine. She turned to Kane. "Both burial sites are in threes." She pulled up the hood of her jacket and shivered. "That's strange, don't you think? All within fifty yards of each other and buried in sets of three, and then there's that partially dug grave in another direction, but the same fifty yards away as if he'd planned another three and something happened to stop him." She pushed a hand through her hair. "At least this means he stopped killing. I wonder what happened to him?"

"With luck a grizzly got him." Rio grinned.

"I have an idea." Kane pulled out his satellite phone and looked at the maps. "Ah well, this will probably freak you out as it's Halloween." His mouth twitched at the corners. "All the graves' coordinates form a perfect triangle."

Frowning Jenna stared at him. "What does that have to do with anything?"

"Folklore." Rio was standing on the other side of her. "You know, they have so many weird beliefs about the number three and triangles. For instance, some say bad things happen in threes. Others say it's a perfect number. Greek mythology says one thing, Chinese folklore says another. Christians have the Holy Trinity." He shrugged. "I'm guessing Dave is thinking outside the box, as in these graves might be connected to a cult or a person with certain beliefs."

Jenna turned to Kane. "Is that what you think?"

"I'm looking at all angles." Kane's attention was fixed on the gravesite. "We don't know if there are human remains in the graves." He frowned. "Ah, Norrell has uncovered something."

The pink blanket was in remarkably good shape and Jenna held her breath as Norrell gently uncovered it. A tuft of blonde hair poked out from a rounded skull. As Norrell and her team lifted it into a body bag, she took a step closer. "What do we have, Norrell?"

"Give me a minute." With almost reverence, Norrell unwrapped the blanket. "It's female, from the teeth and size, I'd say around fourteen to eighteen. There are no remnants of clothing." She peered closer and shook her head. "There's something here, wrapped in plastic." She took a small package from the blanket and dropped it into an evidence bag. She held it out to Wolfe. "Shane, this is more in your line of expertise. I'll check out the grave again for any evidence, but in my opinion, this young woman was just wrapped in a blanket and buried. There was no sign of any ritual or marker on the grave. This is just a means of disposal."

"I know y'all are anxious to get to uncovering the graves." Wolfe turned to look at them. "We need to allow Norrell time to give each one her complete attention. It's a long process and she can only examine one body at a time."

"It's better to leave the others undisturbed until I can give them my full attention." Norrell smiled. "One small piece of lost evidence could be the missing part of the puzzle you'll need to solve the case."

Jenna nodded. "Yeah, that makes a lot of sense." She stared at the grave. "Any idea how long they've been here?"

"As the graves are in relatively close proximity and we don't know how old they are right now, you might need to consider they died during an epidemic." Norrell frowned. "Long ago, it would be considered normal for people living in the mountains to bury their loved ones close to home." She sighed. "Murder, of course, is always a consideration, but there will be signs."

Jenna understood the long process of exhumation, especially when it might be a murder. "Okay, if you are able to give me some idea of when this person was buried, we'll start hunting down what information is available."

"As soon as I've made that determination, I'll call you." Norrell smiled. "I am aware that winter is fast approaching and the ground will be frozen anytime soon. I can assure you I want to have these people in my lab as soon as possible." She glanced at Wolfe. "The cause of death might take time if it's by illness or poison, so if it's not obvious, I'll leave that part of the investigation to a later date and keep on exhuming the bodies."

Nodding, Jenna smiled at her. "Thanks. Please call my office when you intend to come back again. It's really not safe to be here without backup. I'd like at least two of my deputies with you at any time." As a cool breeze whispered through the pines, she scanned the forest. "It's not just the bears. We don't know if this girl was murdered, and if she was, the killer could drop by to visit the graves. They often do and I wouldn't want you and your team at risk."

"I'll be sure to call." Norrell indicated to her team to move out with the body bag and evidence bags filled with soil samples from the grave.

Relieved to be heading back to the office and the warm, Jenna spun around to her deputies. "Take a break and then head back to the office. We're done here for now." She ducked under the crime scene tape and followed Kane and their bloodhound, Duke, back through the forest. "I sure hope we get all those bodies to the surface before the first snow or it's going to be April before we know what's happened here."

TWO

Although no smell of death lingered at the gravesite, Jenna had worn a mask. She peeled it off and inhaled the fresh pine-scented air with a hint of snow. The mountaintops already had a generous coating of white powder and hinted at a hard winter —or a good winter for the ski resort. She could hear her deputies coming up behind her on the trail.

"What do you figure is going on?" Rowley caught up to her. "I scouted around in a wide area with Blackhawk when he reported the graves and we only found traces of one burned-out cabin. All that remained were a few blackened stumps. The rest had been reclaimed by the forest."

In a somber mood, Jenna looked at him. "That's interesting. Not that we'd find any evidence after so long, but maybe we should take a look next time we're here. I actually hope they did die of illness. There are too many murders in my county and knowing they've been happening for years before I arrived in town is chilling."

"It doesn't help that the filing system was nonexistent before you took office." Kane whistled to Duke, who had wandered off in the opposite direction. "It was like pulling teeth searching through death notices in old newspapers and the like trying to discover what went on here before we arrived."

"Tell her everything you know about this area." Rio wound his way between the trees, making his own path back to the fire road where they'd left their vehicles. "Everything is significant in cold cases."

"You know the old cabins up at the top of Bear Peak?" Rowley's shoulders sagged and the tips of his ears pinked. "They were a hangout for me and some of the kids from school. There's a road that goes from the highway to the cabins."

Wondering where this was leading, Jenna stopped walking to look at him. "Yeah, I've been there. It's some ways from here. Too far to carry a body."

"At Halloween, the kids would dare each other to go down the path and into the forest." Rowley cleared his throat. "There's a cabin about five hundred yards from the foot of the mountain. Local legend says a crazy old man haunts it and he comes out each Halloween to hack people to death with an ax."

"Seems to me there's a truckload of haunted places in Black Rock Falls." Kane rubbed the back of his neck. "Those of you who believe in ghosts and put yourself in danger as kids due to peer pressure are lucky to be alive. Those stories often have a grain of truth. There may well have been an ax murderer there in the past, or a bear tore someone to pieces. Either way, kids are just offering themselves up to potential psychopaths by engaging in a myth. Who knows when a real crazy person might be waiting for the next batch of innocents to slaughter?" He grinned and wiggled his fingers at them. "*Woo woo.*"

"I don't believe in ghosts." Rio grinned at Rowley. "You do, right?" He chuckled. "There's nothing wrong with that. It's a common thing and what would the world be without horror movies?"

"I was a kid then but now I'm a father, so I don't get scared easy." Rowley straightened. "Seems to me, being raised here has benefits. I know all the inside information."

The image of the blonde hair on the skeleton had stuck in Jenna's mind. "That poor girl in that grave isn't a ghost and we need to know what happened to her and the others. The one thing I noticed is the grave is deep. It's taken Norrell forever to uncover the body. It's as if the grave was dug before the murder or whatever."

"Yeah, but where did she die? Carrying a body from the fire road wouldn't be easy for most people." Kane straightened. "They'd be on an adrenaline high for the murder, but that usually wears off, leaving a person exhausted. Unless they killed them on scene, but then getting someone to walk into a forest to be killed wouldn't be easy either. This is a hunting area, people, and forest wardens could be around from dawn until dusk, and no woman would walk in here after dark. Not willingly."

Running possible scenarios through her mind, Jenna shrugged. "Oh, I don't know. We've had killers who hunt their prey. He might have driven her here on a date, let her out of the vehicle, and chased her down. There are endless possibilities, but I still believe after seeing the unfinished grave, he dug the graves first. Usually, killers wouldn't be so careful. Digging a grave that deep wouldn't be easy alone. Shallow graves are what we usually see, although most just dump the bodies and run."

"In LA the murder cases I handled were mostly in situ." Rio walked along a wider path beside Jenna. "People murdered in their homes or on the streets, in parking lots, shot in stores. We had a few who dumped the bodies, but then I wasn't dealing with a serial killer. It seems many of them hide their kills."

Trying to keep all the horrific crime scenes out of her mind, Jenna glanced at him. "It's impossible to rationalize a psychopathic killer. They all have their own little eccentricities, all have so many different psychoses, it's impossible to really know what's going on inside their heads. Trying to figure out their next move is practically impossible. Although with the help of Jo Wells, we've gotten close."

Special Agent Jo Wells, a behavioral analyst working out of the Snakeskin Gully field office with her partner, Agent Ty Carter, an ex-SEAL, had become close friends and having them close by, along with computer whiz kid Bobby Kalo, a teenage hacker who worked for the FBI, had been priceless.

As they stepped out onto the fire road and headed for Kane's tricked-out bombproof truck affectionately known as the Beast, Jenna smiled at Rowley as Kane slid behind the wheel. Kane liked speed, and from the way his stomach was rumbling, he wouldn't be waiting around before heading to the diner. "We'll meet you in Aunt Betty's Café. I'll save you a seat."

THREE

As he ducked through the legs of a giant spider and stepped inside Aunt Betty's Café, Kane inhaled the aroma of freshly brewed coffee and pumpkin pie. His dog, Duke, wiggled his backside at the sight of Susie Hartwig, the diner's manager, and was greeted by a smile. Duke, being a patrol dog and carrying his own deputy's shield attached to his collar, was allowed anywhere when accompanied by a law enforcement officer. Kane waited for Jenna to order and wanted to add his own, when Wendy, the assistant manager, pulled him to one side. He glanced at Jenna. "Order me the pie. Wendy needs a word."

"Okay." Jenna glanced at her watch. "It's lunchtime. Do you want a burger and fries as well?"

Nodding, Kane grinned at her. It had taken him some time to get Jenna to come to terms with his voracious appetite. "Sure, thanks."

He walked a short distance away, wondering why Wendy would want to speak to him alone. He looked into her troubled eyes and frowned. "Is there a problem?"

"There might be, but I feel stupid if there isn't." Wendy's

eyes slid to the line of customers and back to him, but her head didn't move.

Sensing the agitation, Kane nodded. "Whatever is worrying you, you know you can come to me anytime. I won't think you're stupid. What's wrong?"

"You know those phone extension sticks or whatever they're called?" Wendy moved her eyes to the line of customers and back to him and then lowered her voice to just above a whisper. "That guy in the line, the one in the green jacket, has been using his phone to... I believe... take pictures up women's skirts, particularly the schoolgirls." She looked stricken. "I was buying groceries and he was in the store doing the same thing yesterday. I think he's a creep." She took a sharp intake of breath. "He's doing it now, right in front of the sheriff."

Kane turned around and scanned the line of people waiting to order. Lunchtime was always busy in Aunt Betty's, but Susie always moved anyone from the sheriff's department to the front of the line. Time usually being of the essence, deputies dropped by for a quick snack before heading back to work. They also had a couple of reserved tables at the back of the diner and Jenna was heading in that direction. He watched the guy with the phone, holding it down beside one leg on an extension and then moving it toward a young woman and aiming it under her long coat. As they moved forward in the line, he slid it under a teenager's skirt. Kane turned to Wendy. "Go and tell Jenna I'll be delayed. Mind if I use your office?"

"Go right ahead." Wendy nodded. "I'll tell Susie as well and she'll hold your burger."

Kane thought for a beat. "Send Rowley back when he arrives. He's right behind me."

"You got it." Wendy hurried away.

In three strides, Kane had gripped the man's arm and gave him a tight smile. "Deputy Kane, would you mind coming with me? I think we need a little chat."

"What?" The man in green glared at him. "I'll miss my place in the line."

Kane tightened his grip. "That's the least of your problems." He pulled him from the line and escorted him behind the counter and then pushed him into Susie's office. "Hand me the phone."

"Why?" The man slid up the extension and was about to turn off the phone when Kane grabbed it.

The phone was recording and Kane turned it to face them. "I have just taken this phone from... Your name, sir?"

"Jacob Seemly." The man glared into the camera. "I haven't done anything wrong. This is police brutality."

Shaking his head, Kane turned to him. "Ah, well, we'll let the courts decide, as you have it all on file." He stopped the recording and went into the video files and then played back the last recording. He held it up to Seemly. "You know, I figure it takes a new form of low to record up a kid's skirt. Apart from that, it's against the law to record a visual image of the intimate parts of a person in a public place without their knowledge. This girl and the other woman you recorded have a reasonable expectation of privacy." He ran through the settings on the phone and removed the password. "You'll be held in custody until we peruse the footage on your phone." He turned him around and cuffed him with zip ties.

"You can't arrest me." Seemly glared at him. "I haven't had lunch."

Biting back the need to teach him a lesson about respecting women, old-school, Kane stared at him. "Well, seems to me you'll just have to wait until I've had mine. If I remember, I'll bring you back something when I'm done."

The next moment, Rowley stuck his head around the door. Kane nodded to him. "Sorry to add another burden to your day. Can you grab Rio and take Jacob Seemly back to the office? Lock him in a cell and bag the phone as evidence. That's all and then come back here for a meal and I'll explain everything."

"Sure." Rowley grabbed Seemly and hauled him out the door.

Shaking his head in disbelief, he made his way back to the sheriff's table. He removed his jacket and gloves and sat down. "You know, Jenna, we get some strange people in this town, but this one beats all."

He gave her a rundown of the situation. "We'll deal with him back at the office."

"This has been happening all over for years, men with mirrors on their shoes, planting cameras in changing rooms. It's just a new version of a Peeping Tom, I guess." Jenna sipped coffee and stared at him. "There are some very weird people on this earth. I don't think there's a fetish that hasn't been covered by someone. Seems to me the laws aren't keeping up with all the gadgets. The more innovative and amazing devices that come onto the market the harder our job becomes—AI, for example— how long will it take people to twist that software into criminal behavior? I'm waiting for one of those robot vacuum cleaners to become pest exterminators as well." She giggled. "Next, people will be dragged from their beds and sucked into oblivion."

Rubbing a hand down his face, Kane sighed. "At least we'll have the killer. No trial, just straight down to the auto crusher. Life will be a breeze." He smiled at her. "We might even get a vacation."

"I live in hope." Jenna squeezed his hand. "From now on, we must take vacations. We have a son to consider. He's never seen the beach, and we have so much to show him. I want him to have everything he wants in life."

Kane shook his head. "If you do that, he'll end up a spoiled brat." He took her hand. "Yes of course, we raise him with vacations and all the trimmings, but I want him to appreciate the value of things too. Helping out with chores is part of being a family." He sighed. "He likes helping with the horses and it's something I want to encourage. If he wants to help out in the kitchen or help around the house, we should encourage that too. It's all part of his education, so he knows how to do things to survive when he grows."

"I'm guessing you'll want to teach him how to fight." Jenna bit her bottom lip. "How to shoot and kill?"

Incredulous that Jenna should be concerned about this subject when Tauri was only four years old, he smiled at her. "That's a long ways away, Jenna, and we can decide at the time. For now, riding and swimming are priorities. It's obvious he's going to be big like me. Have you seen the size of his hands and feet? They're the same as mine when I was a kid at his age and he's so much bigger than any of his own age already. Sometimes being big can be a problem. People pick fights just to prove a point, like they need to prove they're stronger than you are. It happened to me many a time and still does, so yeah, when the time comes, I'll teach him how to defend himself. How far he goes depends on him. It takes dedication to become an expert in hand-to-hand combat. It also takes self-control to know when to use it... All this is part of any training I'd want to give him." He sighed. "He'll discover I was in the military and may want to join. I don't want him to become a sniper because it's not a life I'd recommend to anyone, but again, that would be his choice."

"You're not answering my question, Dave." Jenna looked at him. "He wants to be just like you, and I never want to see him in combat mode, not ever."

Leaning back in his chair, Kane stared at her for long seconds. "That's not something my father taught me, Jenna, and not something I'll teach him. I will teach him how to shoot when the time comes, and from now on, he'll understand the danger of firearms. You know darn well having knowledge and respect of firearms in Montana is common sense." He paused as Susie delivered their meal and gave a plate of leftovers to Duke.

"Thanks, Susie." He looked back at Jenna. "If he follows us into law enforcement, yeah, we'll teach him everything he needs to know. We'll want him to be able to deal with any situation, and you can be sure Blackhawk will be teaching him how to survive in the forest as well." He squeezed her hand. "You'll teach him compassion, Jenna. One thing is for sure: he'll never be short on love." He bit into his burger, chewed, and swallowed. "I know being a parent is a big responsibility, but can't we just enjoy raising him before we get into worrying about the future?"

"One day at a time, right?" Jenna smiled at him. "Well, it seems to have worked out just fine so far." She sighed. "With us and with him. It's like waking up to sunshine even on a rainy day. I still can't believe he's ours."

Kane chuckled. "You're worrying about years ahead and I'm concerned about how we're going to explain Halloween. The stories are a little different behind the festival for us and Blackhawk's people."

"I wouldn't worry too much just yet." Jenna laughed. "Once we take him trick-or-treating, all he'll be thinking about is the candy."

FOUR

Jenna had just eaten the last forkful of pumpkin pie when her phone buzzed. It was their receptionist, Maggie. "I'm at Aunt Betty's, with everyone. What's the problem?"

"I just had a call from a young woman, Clara Finch, she lives in an apartment on Elm. Her friend, Freya Richardson, has been missing all weekend and she's worried about her. She asked the landlord to open the door to see if her friend was okay and says the bathroom is covered in blood. No sign of her friend."

Staring at Kane, she sucked in a deep breath. Here it was, the Halloween she'd hoped wouldn't occur this year. *Only in Black Rock Falls.* "Okay, send me the details and we'll head out there now." She disconnected and explained the call to her deputies.

She now had three cases to worry about. The cold case was in Norrell's hands for now. She turned her attention to Rio and Rowley. "Okay, when you're done here, head back to the office and go through the files on Jacob Seemly's phone. Make a copy of the files and then see what he has been recording and how long he's been doing it. Find out if he's been sending files to anyone else and then write it up." She glanced at Kane. "Dave witnessed him in the act and that's on tape. So, you'll be handling Jacob Seemly."

"I'll write up a statement as soon as I get back to the office." Kane stood and pulled on his coat and gloves. "Seemly will need a meal, if you can grab something before you leave? Maybe give the DA a call, tell him what you've got, and see if he wants to issue an arrest warrant. I guess it depends on what you find in the video files. If so, you know the drill: read him his rights and ask him if he wants a lawyer before you question him."

Standing, Jenna pulled on her jacket and gloves. "I hope this won't take long. I'll call the hospital on the way to Elm and make sure the missing girl isn't there. I'll keep you in the loop." She followed Kane and Duke out of the diner with a wave to Susie.

"What is it with Elm Street and Halloween?" Kane deposited Duke on the back seat and clipped in his harness before swinging behind the wheel. "Last year, or was it the year before, something happened on Elm?" He glanced at the map on the GPS and shrugged. "An apartment building. That's a risk for a killer. I guess we'll see more problems with them soon enough. They seem to be going up all over of late." He headed down Main.

As they moved through the traffic, Jenna made the call to the hospital and received no information. Chills slid down her spine at the possibility of finding a homicide victim at the apartment building or, worse still, an empty bloody crime scene. Not knowing where someone had taken the victim was always a problem. Most times, she'd receive a call with details of a body someone else had found and had the chance to prepare herself for a horrific sight, but going in alone, without any idea of what might be waiting for her was nerve-racking and not at all like the cop shows on TV. Her legs always trembled, even with her deputies close behind her, and as sheriff, she must always appear strong and confident, even if she'd rather cut and run.

With effort, she pushed the thoughts of mayhem and murder from her mind for a few minutes. Reality would be hitting her in the face soon enough and Jenna moved her attention to the activity happening around town. The banners had been hung across the road with grinning jack-o'-lanterns and HALLOWEEN FESTIVAL in bright orange and yellow letters. The townsfolk had already started to decorate the street, and outside Aunt Betty's Café the giant black hairy spider covering the front door had grown a gossamer web complete with a multitude of red-eyed babies blowing in the breeze. Every year, people tried to outdo each other with the macabre and she loved it.

She wanted to go to the ball dressed as a vampire and had already arranged with Nanny Raya, Tauri's nanny, to care for him for the few hours they'd be away. Those were special times. Although she spent all day with Kane, the work environment wasn't romantic, but at a ball, Kane seemed to change into her very own handsome hero. She glanced at him. "I know you like to keep your Halloween costume a surprise, but can you give me a hint?"

"I haven't given it much thought." Kane turned onto Elm. "Something that's not annoying. Costumes seem too bulky, or I freeze wearing them. What about a secret agent? Then I get to wear my shoulder holster and sunglasses." He grinned at her. "You've never seen me like that have you?" He chuckled.

Turning in her seat to look at him, she grinned. "No, I bet you looked amazing in the secret service. Okay, but then I'll go as a vampire with a baseball bat. I'll need it to keep the women away from you."

"Oh, I'll never stray, Jenna, and I also have my ring of protection." He waved his left hand. "A wedding band works wonders and, anyway, I won't be leaving your side. I've seen that slinky dress you intend to wear. I'm the one who needs to be worried about your admirers." He glanced out of the window. "This looks like the place."

Dropping back into professional mode, Jenna stepped from the truck and shivered as a bitterly cold wind wrapped around her, bringing with it a spiral of dancing fall leaves. "It must have been converted into apartments. I don't recall seeing it last year. Most of these old places are for sale."

"They would make a good investment." Kane scanned the street. "Apartment buildings on this side of town would be perfect for college students." He opened the back door of the Beast. "Stay, Duke. We won't be long." He grabbed a forensic kit and headed to the front door.

Jenna checked her phone and pressed the number of Clara Finch's apartment, when a scratchy voice came over the intercom, she leaned closer. "It's Sheriff Alton."

"I'll come down."

The door clicked open and Jenna waited for Kane to examine the lock. "Anything?"

"No forced entry." Kane bent closer. "No scratches to indicate someone picked the lock." He followed her inside.

The elevator chimed and a young woman walked out wearing a sweatshirt and pants with bright blue sneakers Jenna nodded to her. "Clara Finch?"

"Yeah, I'm worried about my friend." Clara pushed her hands inside her pants pockets and appeared to be anxious. "I didn't search the apartment. I went inside with the complex manager and could see the blood in the bathroom. We came out without touching anything and called 911."

"Was the manager wearing gloves?" Kane was taking notes.

"No, but he only touched the door handle, and I only went along the hallway. I called out but she didn't answer." Clara moved from one foot to the other. "The bathroom door was open and when I saw the blood I ran out."

"When did you last see her?" Kane lifted his gaze to look at her with his pen poised over his notepad.

"Friday afternoon." Clara chewed on her bottom lip and her eyes brushed the floor. "We cross paths every day at the same time. I mentioned catching a movie on Saturday night, but she said she'd be too tired after work. She works all over, taking cleaning jobs until she can find a sales position. I went by on Sunday and knocked but she wasn't there. I was worried this morning when she still wasn't answering the door. I took a personal day and wanted to go to Aunt Betty's Café with her. When the building manager opened the door and I saw blood, I called you guys." She frowned. "Before you ask, I didn't see anyone hanging around the building when I came home on Friday after work. Since then, I've been in my apartment."

Jenna glanced at Kane. "Go find the manager. We need to get inside."

"Oh, he left it unlocked." Clara wrapped her arms around her middle. "I can't go back in there."

"Unlocked?" Kane frowned at her.

"The units have deadbolts, so inside you need to turn the key twice to lock it." Clara looked at him with large unblinking brown eyes. "If I don't lock it, it stays unlocked, so anyone can walk inside. It's not very safe. It's easy to forget to turn the key every time. Most doors shut and lock at the same time."

Perturbed by the possibility a killer knew this fact about the apartment building, Jenna nodded. "Okay, wait here. We'll go and take a look." She led the way to the apartment.

"They didn't see anyone inside and if she'd been missing since Friday, we'd be smelling her by now." Kane walked beside Jenna, removing his gloves and pushing them into his pocket before replacing them with examination gloves. "I do smell something bad." He wrinkled his nose and slowly turned the handle to Freya's apartment, swinging the door wide. "Sheriff's department. Anyone home?"

Nothing.

The door opened with a creak and the smell of blood and excrement oozed from the apartment. It was open plan, with a kitchen at one end and a small living room with a single light blazing. Jenna pulled a mask from her pocket. She stared at Kane. "We'll wear booties. Someone died here."

FIVE

Kane pushed the door wide open using the flat of his hand and scanned the room. It was a reasonably neat apartment. A purse had been dropped onto the kitchen counter, and shoes kicked off just inside the door. The living room was comfortable, with cushions and a colorful throw on the sofa. Figurines of ballerinas lined the mantel above an electric fire resembling burning logs. A TV sat in one corner. He pulled his weapon and, as usual, he went into the room high and Jenna went low, clearing each space as they moved along the hallway. The bedroom door was shut, and after Jenna gave him a nod, he backed against the wall and turned the knob. Inside, the bed linen was missing and a streak of blood ran from the bathroom door, across the carpet, and to the bed. It was silent all around and Kane turned to Jenna. "We'll go back along the hallway and clear the bathroom from the other side. It's got two entrances."

"Okay. Close this door." Jenna's face was grim. "I don't want anyone sneaking out behind us."

Kane led the way along the hallway. "It feels empty to me. I figure they're long gone." He stopped at the bathroom door and gaped at the wall of blood spatter across the mirror. "No one is walking out alive after that."

"Arterial spatter." Jenna moved beside him. "Murdered here and then dragged through the adjoining door to the bedroom." She turned and backtracked down the hallway and, holstering her weapon, opened the bedroom door and peered at the bed. "The killer wrapped her in blankets. The pillowcases are gone too."

Surveying the scene, Kane bent to the pool of blood on the bathroom floor. "This isn't fresh, and by the smell, it's at least a few days old." He followed the long smear across the tile and onto the bedroom carpet. "Dragged by her feet in here, and then rolled into the blankets. He had the blankets on the floor before he moved her." He flicked open the closet and peered inside. "Hmm. How did he get her out of the building without anyone seeing him?"

"There's a fire exit at the end of the hallway. We'll search for blood spatter. He might have left a trail." Jenna stared around the room. "He must have parked out back. So, he planned to kill her and take her body with him. How did he get in?"

Walking back to the patio doors, Kane slid open the screen door and then the glass slider. "These doors aren't locked."

"Oh, that's too easy." Jenna's eyes widened. "What about a blood trail?"

Kane took out his flashlight and ran it over the carpet. "Nothing evident. What gets me is there are no footprints and it's a bloodbath in there." He glanced at Jenna. "I'm assuming this killer is a man, taller than the victim. When a throat is cut, it isn't easy. It takes strength and skill. The victim is fighting, throwing their head around, and their heart is pumping quick-time. This makes the arterial spray violent, and although it usually sprays in one direction, it would be difficult to avoid some degree of splash back and stepping in the pool of blood.

Possible, but difficult." He waved the flashlight back and forth. "Wolfe will spray the area with luminol and pick up any spatter. I can't see anything on a brown carpet." He looked at her. "The thing is, people don't bleed once they're dead, so if he wrapped her once she'd stopped bleeding, it would have avoided seepage from her clothes." He held up one finger and went back into the bathroom. "Come and look at this, Jenna."

"What have you found?" Jenna met Kane in the hallway as he stepped from the bathroom, and she followed him back into the living room.

He indicated behind him. "Clothes in the laundry basket. She took a shower but that's not all."

"What are you seeing?" Jenna stared at him.

Placing himself in the role as the victim, Kane went to the front door. "The timeline. I can map out what happened by the evidence. Freya comes home from work, kicks off her shoes, dumps her purse on the counter, and heads for the bedroom." He led the way along the passageway. "There's a winter coat in the closet, so she removed her coat and decided to take a shower." He stepped around the pool of blood and went into the bathroom. "We'll bag these clothes and ask Clara if she can recall what Freya was wearing the last time she saw her." He indicated the towels. "The towels are bunched up on the rail, like she planned to pick them up later or straighten them to dry."

"So she came out of the shower, went to the mirror, and someone attacked her from behind?" Jenna frowned. "She'd have seen him coming."

Kane shook his head. "Not if the mirror was steamed over." He walked into the living room. "Look here." He went to the sliding patio door. "It's unlocked, right? This is his point of entry. It's ground level, with concrete all around so no footprints. If he'd parked his vehicle outside in the alleyway, he could have entered and exited from this door. I'll examine the lock, but these are a breeze to open. He could easily have sneaked up here, unlocked the door, and waited in the alleyway for her to come home. From out there, he'd have seen the bathroom light go on, even heard the shower. Then all he had to do was wait for her to get into the shower before going inside. He murdered her when she stepped from the shower. I've watched you. You shower, dry, and then go to the mirror. I'm guessing most women do. Once she turned her back on him, he was on her."

"Just a minute." Jenna went to the kitchen counter and peered inside Freya's purse. "No phone." She went back into the bedroom and opened drawers and peered under the bed. "She was looking for work and would have a phone." She stared at Kane. "Oh, my goodness. We'll be able to trace her and her killer if he's taken her phone."

Kane rubbed his chin. "Even after seeing all this blood, we can't assume she's dead. We can't track her phone unless we can prove it. We'll need a warrant. I'll get the paperwork over to the judge when we get back to the office."

"Okay, get Wolfe and his team out here to do a forensic sweep." She indicated toward the door. "I'll ask Clara about what Freya was wearing. If it's the same as the clothes we found, it will give us a closer time of death." She headed for the door. "I'll ask her for Freya's phone number as well. I'll call and see if the killer picks up."

Shaking his head, Kane pulled out his phone and called Wolfe. "Morning."

"Don't tell me. I've already figured out why you've called." Wolfe cleared his throat. *"It's Halloween and y'all have discovered a homicide."*

SIX

Standing in the middle of Freya's apartment, Wolfe turned a full circle. He'd examined the crime scene and prepared for a luminol examination for blood spatter. Luminol being a known carcinogenic, he preferred to mask up in hazard gear and get everyone to step outside before coating the carpet. He'd darkened the room and set up his camera, ready to document the images. As Jenna shut the door behind her, he got to work and sprayed the chemical. The killer had taken every precaution, but a few drops of blood had formed a trail from the bedroom to the sliding glass door, just as Kane had suggested to him on arrival. The blood spatter fluoresced nicely, and he aimed his camera and recorded the scene. He moved around the apartment checking other places and found a smudge on the doorframe, not a fingerprint but likely a very small trace of blood from a glove. Content he had covered every angle, he opened the door and stepped outside. He dragged off his face mask and handed the camera to Colt Webber, his assistant and badge-holding deputy. "That camera needs to be cleaned before handling it without gloves." He turned to Kane. "You were correct. He left by the sliding glass door. I found a blood spatter trail from the bedroom and a small imprint of, I think, a glove on the doorframe."

"That's good." Jenna nodded slowly. "We searched around outside and found a few tiny dark drops on the edge of the alleyway but nothing significant."

Wolfe looked at her. "I'll need swabs. It likely proves the theory that the body was carried to a vehicle in the alleyway." He removed his gloves. "Webber, go and grab samples of the blood spatter in the alleyway."

As Webber hurried away, camera in one gloved hand, Wolfe turned to Jenna and Kane. "You recall the package Norrell discovered in the grave out at Bear Peak?"

"Yeah, was it anything interesting?" Jenna removed her gloves and rolled them into a ball.

Holding out a bag for her, he shrugged. "Maybe." He waited for Kane to add mask and gloves to the garbage bag. "It's a phone. I've checked it out and it looks undamaged. I have it sitting on a charger. It seems very strange to me that someone would be buried with a phone wrapped in plastic. As if the killer made sure it would survive. It is only seven years old, so we now have a date of burial at least." He noticed Jenna's color drain from her face and frowned at her. "You feeling okay there, Jenna?"

"Yeah, it's just that Freya's phone is missing too." She rubbed her temples and looked at him. "I called and got voicemail. Is this a strange coincidence or am I missing something here?"

"We need to track her phone. I'll head to the courthouse the moment we get back to the office to see if I can twist the judge's arm to obtain a warrant." Kane took the bag from Wolfe and tossed it down the garbage shoot. "The problem is, without a body, we can only assume she's dead. That being the case, it will be difficult to get the warrant. Blood in a bathroom isn't probable cause. There's no proof she left the house, dead or alive."

Wolfe bent to his forensic kit and pulled out a notebook. It was a pad of death certificates. He issued them on the spot when necessary for relatives of the deceased. "I can't issue a death certificate without a body, but I'll write a note to the judge saying that, in my opinion, no one could have possibly survived the blood loss I've witnessed in the bathroom. Take this, it might be enough to sway him until we find the body as proof of death. The judge is tough, but he might issue a warrant. If he does, ask Bobby Kalo to trace the phone. What's the use of having an FBI computer whiz kid at our disposal if we don't use him?"

"I have Freya's phone number. We can go from there." Jenna smiled. "I'll call Kalo now." She headed out into the foyer.

"A phone in the grave and one missing here." Kane rubbed his chin. "Murders seven years apart. I'm starting to get that gut feeling that they might be connected, but why the break in kills?"

Shaking his head, Wolfe looked at him in disbelief. "One coincidence doesn't make a link, Dave." He sighed. "On the other hand, there could be plenty of reasons for the gap. He might have been killing in other counties or even states. He might have been in jail or have moved away due to his work. Or it could be just a coincidence." He slapped Kane on the back. "Bring me a body and I'll find answers."

"Has Norrell made any progress of the cause of death of the body in the grave?" Kane leaned against the wall.

Wolfe shrugged. "I'm not aware of any progress. As she works in a different building, we don't stop for lunch as much and discuss things like before. I'm sure when she has information, she'll call you. I'm guessing we'll find more information on the phone. I'll head on back to my office and see if the phone battery has taken the charge. If not, there are other ways of making it work." He smiled at Kane. "I'll know within the hour.

Has anyone hunted down Freya's next of kin? If she's missing, or presumed dead, they should be informed."

"I'll give it priority." Kane turned as Jenna walked down the corridor toward them. "How did it go?"

"Kalo has the details, but without a warrant, his hands are tied, although, he doesn't always stick to the rules." Jenna smiled. "If he can track the phone, maybe for once we'll crack the case in one day." She glanced at her watch. "It's getting late and we need to go collect Tauri. I'll follow up at home."

Wolfe looked from one to the other and bent to pick up the forensic kit. "The one thing I admire about you is that y'all are optimistic." He chuckled. "Unfortunately, it will take me at least forty-eight hours to process the material we collected from the scene... and I'll need a body. There is no obvious trace evidence here to arrest anyone."

"Trust me." Jenna turned and headed for the door, shaking her head. "I'll find her. It's Halloween. With my luck, I'll just need to give it a few days and her corpse will come knocking on my door."

SEVEN

Wendy, the assistant manager of Aunt Betty's Café arrived home late. She lived in a beautiful cabin down near the river that ran behind Maple. The neighbors were good people and had been there for her when someone tried to poison her little dog, Lola. Seeing the dog lying in her backyard, they'd rushed her to the vet in time to save her life. Wendy had been by the vets twice today to check on Lola, and she was doing just fine but would be there for a couple of days. Lola was the perfect companion for someone who worked odd hours. She was self-sufficient and could go in and out of the doggy door, had her feeder inside and a warm basket. Wendy missed hearing her cheerful bark as she climbed from her Jeep and headed for the front door. An owl hooted and a shadow passed over her. Suddenly afraid, she glanced around, peering into the darkness between the pools of orange streetlights. Her neighbors, an old couple, had left today to visit their grandchildren for the festival, and chills slid down her spine at seeing their house cold and empty. She stared at the deserted road and shivered as wisps of curling mist drifted along the blacktop like ghosts out for their nightly promenade.

Owning the end house before the river was a mixed blessing: beautiful in daytime, but at night around Halloween, not so. The fast-flowing river resembled a tar pit, crawling its way past maples and cottonwood trees, their branches hanging down and casting black witches-cloak-like shadows across the riverbank. Cold air brushed Wendy's cheeks as the wind disturbed the trees, and all around them became animated. A silent movie flickered into action and sticklike creatures held their outstretched arms as if reaching for her. She backed away, heading for the door, when something moved in the shadows. Swallowing hard, she sprinted for the front door, slid her key into the lock, and fell inside, slamming the door behind her. She reached for the switch and leaned against the door, breathing heavily as the room flooded with light.

Unnerved, she turned the deadbolt, dumped her keys in a bowl by the front door, and headed for the bedroom. Had she imagined someone was out there, watching her? She shook her head, trying to dislodge the illogical ideas filling her mind just because it was Halloween. A shower and a hot drink before falling into bed would calm her nerves. She removed her coat and boots and slid on her slippers before heading to the kitchen. A scraping sound came from the front door and she stood paralyzed in the passageway following the sound as it moved around the house. Without a second thought, Wendy ran to the back door to check it was secure. Breathing a sigh of relief, she walked back into the kitchen to put on the kettle. Her imagination was getting the best of her. The scratching came again, as if someone was dragging a stick along the outside walls of the house. Eyes fixed to the window, she gasped in horror as a Halloween mask loomed out of the dark and then vanished.

Someone was out there and she'd left her Glock in the Jeep.

EIGHT

TUESDAY

After playing with Tauri before he went to bed, Jenna and Kane worked in the office at the ranch, spending the entire evening hunting down relatives of Freya Richardson. Jenna had come up empty and moved her investigation to the young woman's friends. The few she had spoken to hadn't given her any useful information. Freya was a workaholic, taking any odd jobs she could find, and saved every penny. This morning, she'd focused on the places Freya had worked. A very hard worker was the conclusion, but no one had seen her since Friday. She didn't have a boyfriend and between jobs kept to herself. With absolutely no leads to follow, when Jenna arrived at the office, she'd issued a missing person report to the media, using the photograph from Freya's ID. She'd also asked for anyone who'd been on Elm anytime on Friday evening to come forward. So far, the hotline had remained silent.

When Rio stepped into her office, she expected an update on Jacob Seemly, the man using his phone to record up women's skirts. "How is the Seemly case going?"

"Oh, the DA charged him on the evidence on his phone. His office had Seemly in front of a judge by three, and now he's out on bail awaiting a court hearing." Rio frowned. "It all moved along really fast and we had him out of our hands before I left the office last night." He shrugged. "That's not why I'm here. Last night Wendy from Aunt Betty's called about a possible prowler or prankster. Late last night, after eleven, someone was outside her house wearing a Halloween mask. Wendy said it sounded like nails being dragged along the outside of her house and then someone looked through her window."

Raising both eyebrows, Jenna looked at him. "Wendy isn't the hysterical type and she owns a weapon. What was the outcome?"

"I went to see her." Rio shrugged. "I did a drive-by first and I didn't see anyone lurking about, but if they were wearing a costume, they'd blend into anyone's display. She has a walkway around her house and I didn't see any footprints. I walked through her house to make sure everything was secure. She came with me to get her Glock from her Jeep and I waited until she was inside safe and sound. I called again this morning and she hadn't been disturbed."

Jenna nodded. "Okay, make a note about it for the records, just in case we have some idiot frightening people." She sighed. "It's Halloween and people behave strangely." She stood. We're heading down to the library to look at old newspapers. Hold the fort until we're back."

"Okay." Rio headed for the door.

Grunt work was always boring, and Jenna wished Bobby Kalo worked in her office. Having someone who had the resources to hunt down people in seconds would save so much time and energy. She sat in the local library going through copies of old newspapers, each one scanned to file as far back as fifteen years ago. If people had gone missing, it should have been reported in the newspapers. What she found disturbed her. Seven to ten years previously, Montana had been terrorized by the Halloween Slasher. For two consecutive years, young women had been presumed murdered in their homes. No bodies had ever been discovered, but each scene was a bloodbath. She turned to Kane, seated at the next desk. "I figure I've found something."

"Yeah, me too. Three young women vanished from here seven years ago, before those three went missing from Louan." Kane blew out a sigh. "Apart from a bloody crime scene, they never found a trace of them."

Jenna leaned back in her seat, wetting dry lips. "Yeah, and the crime scene sounds much the same as what we found in Freya's apartment." She blew out a long sigh. "I've made a note of their names. We'll need case files from Louan's sheriff's department, and crime scene photos to use as a comparison."

"If this is the Halloween Slasher, he killed in threes." Kane's mouth formed a flat line and a nerve in his cheek twitched. "If he's decided to start up again here, it's one down, two to go."

Jenna's phone chimed. It was Wolfe. "I'm in the library. We're just leaving."

"Okay, I'll hang on until you're in a better location. Kane will want to hear this too."

They hurried outside and climbed into the Beast to the accompaniment of Duke's thumping tail. As Kane turned to rub Duke's ears and gave him a doggy treat, Jenna put the phone on speaker. "Okay, we're in the truck." She explained about the Halloween Slasher. "That's all we have for now. What do you have for me?"

"The killing in threes is pertinent information as we seem to have two sets of three victims. The other interesting discovery is the phone Norrell discovered with the body. It belongs to Josephine Wade. I found information on her. She went missing from here some years back. I have her dental records and the girl in the grave isn't her. The thing is, there's a voice recording on

the phone and it's confronting. The killer has recorded the actual murder, but he refers to her as Lydia. The voice is distorted, so I'm only assuming it's male."

Disturbed, Jenna stared at Kane and swallowed the bile creeping up the back of her throat. "Am I to understand he recorded himself killing?"

"*Yeah, in brutal detail.*" Wolfe took a deep breath. "*Like I said, it's confronting, but from what I can hear, the echo from the screams, it could easily have been in a bathroom. I haven't listened to all of it, but I believe he took a shower after the murder. He wasn't in a hurry. I'll need to go back to the current crime scene and examine the shower. I need to know if there's any blood residue or hairs we can use. If there is something, and this killer makes a habit of showering after the murder, he is well organized and knows the victims' movements.*"

"We have a Lydia Ellis missing from Louan." Kane frowned. "Can you hunt down her dental records? I'll send you her details."

"*Not a problem. There's only one dentist in Louan. You mentioned in the current case that Freya Richardson has a phone missing? I believe, even considering the cases are wide apart in time, they might be connected. If we find another phone in any of the graves, I figure this guy is playing a sick form of paying it forward. I mean, maybe he took the phone from the first girl he killed, and he's using it to record the next murder and so on.*" Wolfe let out a long sigh. "*We'll need to open the other graves ASAP. I want to know if this is the case because it would link all the murders.*"

Trying to get her head around the incredulity of what Wolfe had just told her, Jenna sucked in a deep breath. "Okay, ask if Norrell can identify the victim she has in her examination room from the dental records. I'm chasing up crime scene images from Louan. We have nothing in our old files, but I'll recheck."

"*Okay.*" Jenna could hear Wolfe's office chair squeak as he stood, followed by footsteps on tile. "*I'll send Webber to pull the shower apart at the crime scene and I'll head over to speak to Norrell. I'll see if we can move ahead with the exhumations. I'll have the dental records for confirmation before the end of the day.*" He disconnected.

NINE

Mulling over the case similarities, Kane headed for Aunt Betty's Café. The soothing comfort of the diner took the edge off when it came to disturbing crimes. Just going there was like walking into a different world, a place protected from the horrors all around it, like the memories he had of his grandma's kitchen. He could almost feel her hugging him every time he walked inside and inhaled the aromas of baking. Jenna had said nothing since leaving the library. Her head bent over her tablet, she was making formal requests for viewing the case files on the missing Louan women. As he pulled up outside Aunt Betty's, he smiled at the giant spider, legs spread to form an archway into the diner. The display was growing daily and now an old witch sat at a table outside before a crystal ball, red eyes flashing and cackling when people walked by. Behind him, Duke was on his feet, mouth open and stretched into a doggy smile as if he found the display amusing. His thick tail banged against the seat. The one place he liked above home was Aunt Betty's Café.

"Okay, I'm done here. Let's go eat. I'm starving." Jenna pulled her cap over her ears, pulled up her hood, and slid from the truck.

A cold wind buffeted Kane as he stood on the sidewalk. It came in gusts, determined to slam the door on Duke before he had his harness unhitched from the back seat. The rush of mountain air made the skeletons and other decorations rattle and howl. Sometimes a strange eerie whistling sound would reach his ears. It was as if the wind was getting involved in the Halloween spirit by adding its own twist on the spookiness. He followed Jenna inside and went to one side of the counter, Susie had erected a small sign that said SHERIFF'S DEPARTMENT. It saved arguments from the people lining up to order or pick up. As usual, the diner was busy, more so this week because, being a notorious town, tourists flocked here over Halloween to join the murder scene or haunted house bus tours that had become popular and attracted people from all over the US just to be frightened. Kane shook his head. Just watching the news was frightening enough these days, and what he and Jenna experienced dealing with psychopathic murderers was nothing he planned to share with anyone, but terrifyingly came close.

After waiting for Jenna to order, Kane smiled at Susie. "What do you recommend? I'm cold and hungry."

"Well, we had a special order for barbecue ribs that went out just before. We made extra because they're always popular. I have some great sides to go with the ribs: smoked corn on the cob, baked potatoes, coleslaw, baked beans with ground beef and bacon. Oh, and the pie today is cherry."

Kane's stomach gave an undignified rumble that sounded like the thunder rolling through the mountains, and he rubbed it and gave Susie an apologetic stare. "Yeah, that sounds wonderful."

"All of it?" Susie stared back at him, her eyes wide.

Nodding, Kane indicated Duke. "Yeah, and the usual for Duke. Add it to our tab. We're up to date with paying you, I hope?"

"Sure, Maggie fixes us up every Friday." Susie scratched

away on her order book and ripped off the top page and handed it to the chef behind the partition. She smiled at Kane. "Take a seat. I'll send someone over with a pot of coffee. It won't be long."

As he shucked his coat and removed his gloves, he could see Jenna smiling at him. "I'm guessing you went with the ribs? Now you can have them twice this week. I'm having them too."

He sat down. "I get hungry just walking inside the door. I don't get time to cook ribs on the weekend. Maybe I could, but it takes time and we never know when we're going to be called out for something. Good ribs take dedication."

"Changing the subject." Jenna's expression turned serious. "We'll need to drop by Wolfe's office and listen to the recording."

Kane nodded. It wasn't something he'd enjoy. "Yeah, Wolfe's great at anything technical but I figure we should speak to Carter about it." He sighed. "The FBI has so many resources we can use. There may be things our ears might miss. They can enhance the track and bring out background sounds. We should make a copy and send the original to whoever deals with old recordings."

"Do you figure Bobby Kalo is capable or is it a specialist thing?" Jenna smiled when the coffee arrived.

Kane leaned back in his chair. "I'll ask him."

"Hi, Wendy." Jenna smiled at the woman delivering their coffee. "I hear you had a prowler."

"Oh, maybe just a kid playing tricks on me." Wendy shrugged. "It was so dark and misty when I arrived home. With the neighbors away and my dog at the vet, it was spooky being all alone. I felt much better after Deputy Rio arrived. He made sure everything was safe."

"That's good to know." Jenna met her gaze. "You did the right thing, calling it in. Keeping everyone safe is our priority."

"Thanks. I'll go and get your meals." Wendy headed back to the kitchen.

Kane poured cream into his cup and added sugar. "She seems fine. I'm sure if she were concerned, she'd have told us." He pulled out his phone and called Kalo to explain the situation.

"So, it's an old phone, right? You should still be able to plug it into your laptop, access the sound file, and send it to me. I don't need the phone. The files will be identical." Bobby sounded confident. *"I have access to all types of equipment. The magic of living in an age of technology is we don't have to rely on being anywhere in particular. We just send a file to a program and get a result. Too easy."*

Relieved, Kane nodded to Jenna. "Okay, we're heading over to listen to it after lunch. I'll send you a copy as soon as I've downloaded it from the phone. Thanks for doing this for us."

"That's what we're here for." Kalo cleared his throat. *"My ears only, or do you want Jo's and Carter's slant on the murder?"*

Having the top FBI behavioral analyst in their local field office was a bonus. He glanced at Jenna, who nodded enthusiastically. "Sure, we'd value their input. Just mention this is a cold case—we think six to ten years old—but it might have a link to a case we're working now."

"Gotcha. Chat soon." Bobby disconnected.

The meal arrived and Kane surveyed the plates all around him and sighed in delight. "Now that's what I call a meal."

TEN

Apprehension slowed Jenna's steps into the ME's office. The inquisitive cop side of her wanted to know exactly what had happened to the victim tossed into a grave in Stanton Forest; the other side would rather not listen to someone being brutally murdered. As her stomach went into freefall, she came to the realization the latter was winning. The fact that fear, along with nightmares from the recent cases, still lingered after witnessing a murder troubled her. The terrifying ordeal of coming so close to death hadn't left her and she'd discussed her problems with Kane. Not wanting anything to impact her new role as a mom to Tauri or her job as sheriff, she'd taken therapy sessions to work through her problems. She'd seen so many gruesome crimes and mangled bodies over the last few years that she believed she'd become titanium, but in truth, being human and having deep sorrow for the victims and fear of the perpetrator was perfectly normal.

"Are you sure you want to go through with this, Jenna?" Kane took her hand and ran his thumb over the back. "I can listen and give you an outline. You don't need to put yourself through this, it's not essential."

Tension thrummed through Jenna with every step closer to Wolfe's office, but she lifted her head and smiled at him. "I need to, Dave. The victims need me to listen and it's my duty to be here for them, but I'll try and not attach myself emotionally to them. I'll listen to the facts, rather than get afraid."

"No, Jenna. We can never cut ourselves off from the fact this is a person being murdered. What I want you to do is listen around the actual crime. You know, this woman was terrified and murdered, but it's over now and it should be just like watching a movie. It's not you this is happening to." Kane squeezed her hand. "We know what happened to the woman, right? What we need to be listening for is what happened before, and clues to what the killer was doing. Was he already in the house? What happened just before he murdered her? What did he do afterward? Did he say anything? We need a timeline of the crime. Try and disassociate from the actual murder. Wolfe is the one who will be concentrating on that part of things. We need to do the investigating."

Jenna looked at him. "You've done this before, haven't you?"

"Yeah, I've listened to communications of troops KIA to determine what actually happened." Kane shook his head. "I knew many of them and it was difficult, but knowing exactly what went wrong was crucial. That's what I concentrated on, rather than the cries of the dying."

Nodding, Jenna straightened her spine, suddenly realizing she had been so wound up she hadn't noticed the awful smell of the morgue. "Okay, let's do this."

They sat around Wolfe's desk as he played a downloaded file from the phone. Jenna listened closely. The first thing she heard was a shower running, followed by a slight rustling sound and a few sharp intakes of breath. "Stop it there." She looked at Wolfe. "He's inside the house, but from the rustling sounds and heavy breathing, I figure he's undressing."

"Could be. That's interesting." Wolfe rewound the

recording and they listened again. "Hmm, hear that slight tapping sound, the tips of shoelaces hitting tile. I've heard that exact noise when I've been to the gym and changed out of my sneakers. So, we can assume he's in a tiled area, maybe the kitchen?"

The recording progressed: a soft brush of feet on carpet as he entered what Jenna assumed was the bedroom, followed by a grunt as blankets and sheets were pulled from the bed and presumably laid out on the floor. The sound of water running came in the background as if from another room and then the sound increased as if the bathroom door had been opened. Heavy breathing and then a slight tapping sound. Jenna leaned closer to the laptop. "I know that sound. I hear it each time I place my phone on the vanity. He's in the bathroom."

Nothing happened for a minute or so and then the unmistakable sound of someone opening the shower door. A soft sliding noise as a towel was pulled from a rack and then a woman's voice.

"*What?*" Her voice came out in a bubbly moan as a struggle ensued. Grunts and the squeak of feet on tiles, soft thuds and groans. "*Stop, please stop.*" The woman was fighting for her life.

"*Maybe I don't want to.*" A man's muffled voice. "*Maybe I like cutting you.*"

The slicing sound, as a knife tore through flesh followed by the bubbling last breaths from the victim sickened her. Heart pounding, Jenna could almost see a gush of blood hitting a tiled wall in spurts. It could only mean one thing: he'd cut her throat and then gone into a frenzy. The thuds as a sharp blade hit deep into soft tissue were unmistakable. Nauseous, Jenna dug her fingernails into the palms of her hands as the poor woman gurgled her last breath. As the sound of a body slipping to the floor in a splash of blood came through the speakers, she heard a sigh of contentment and then a male voice.

"Happy Halloween, Lydia."

He'd killed her in seconds.

"Keep listening." Wolfe paused the recording and stared at Jenna. "The worst part is over, but the next part is crucial. I want you to think on the Freya Richardson crime scene we've just processed as you listen. Consider what we've seen and listen as it plays out. It could be the same scene. It's the same MO. I'd bet on it."

The next sound they heard was the shower running again and a man singing. When he turned off the water, his wet foot-steps could be heard across the tile. He slid a towel from the rail and then opened a closet, muttering to himself. The closet door closed and his footsteps vanished before the snap of examination gloves are clearly heard.

"I don't figure he's dressed at this stage." Wolfe looked at Jenna again. "He likely has taken towels from the closet, and maybe has one wrapped around him."

The man grunts and then a slithering sound as if a body is being dragged across the floor. Jenna can see it in her mind's eye as she recalls the gruesome crime scene on Elm.

"It sounds like he has her feet and is dragging her into the bedroom." Wolfe looked at her across the desk. "It's as if we're listening to Freya's murder. The crime scene y'all witnessed, I could walk through it using this recording. It's how I see her murder went down in my head."

The voice on the recording startled Jenna. It was soft, almost a whisper.

"Sit up, Lydia, or you'll drip blood all over the sheets. There's a good girl." Another grunt as the man hauls the body onto the blankets. *"Curl up nice and tight and I'll wrap you up. I need to fit you into the bag."*

Holding up one hand to stop the playback, Jenna stared at Kane. "This is new. Since when do killers care about women after they've killed them?" She pushed a hand through her hair. "Why is he removing the body from the scene? He knows what he's doing. Cleaning up means logical thought."

"The frenzied attack makes it personal." Kane rubbed the back of his neck. "We haven't found this woman, but from what we heard, he hurt her before cutting her throat and then went into overkill. He knew her and her movements."

Unconvinced, Jenna ran the scenario back through her mind. "Maybe in his mind, but I don't figure she knows him, otherwise when he snuck up on her in the bathroom, she'd have said something like, 'What are you doing here, Bob?' and she'd have used his name when he attacked her. 'Stop it, Bob.' Or 'What have I ever done to you?'" She thought for a beat. "She was terrified, speechless with fear, and I don't think she knew him."

"Yeah, but it's Halloween and this is likely the Halloween Slasher. The timeline fits and, if it is, thinking on what Wendy said about seeing someone wearing a mask and peering through her window made me think the Halloween Slasher could be wearing a mask when he kills." Kane sighed. "If it was around Halloween, just like here, there are idiots running around trying to frighten people at night. If someone saw him hanging around in a mask, they wouldn't take much notice, would they?"

The mask idea made sense and Jenna nodded. "And she'd be terrified if a naked masked man crept up behind her with a knife." She indicated to Wolfe to proceed. "Let's hear the rest."

More grunts and the sound of something being dragged across the carpet and then a chuckle before the recording stopped. Looking from one to the other, Jenna sucked in a deep breath and leaned back in the chair. "He went back to the bathroom to get the phone."

"I figure he made sure he had no blood on him, dressed, and took the soiled towels with him." Wolfe rubbed a fist under his nose. "I did notice the lack of towels in Freya Richardson's bathroom. Most people have more than two. Her closet was empty. It's the same MO as the cold case. Seems to me the Halloween Slasher is right here in Black Rock Falls."

ELEVEN

My year is divided into sections of good, bad, and better. Winter is a problem. The snow leaves tracks, the ground is hard, and as the years go by, I'm finding it more difficult to drag bodies around. Last winter, I started working out at the gym, rebuilding my body back to the shape it was when I was in my early twenties. I'm looking good, and although women come and go, most of them find me attractive, but the divorced and spinster types don't really interest me. I yearn for younger women and befriend any I can find. I take an entire year to make my selection. I first moved to Montana over ten years ago and became known as the Halloween Slasher. I have to admit that boosted my ego. Watching the cops run around hunting down bodies long buried and forgotten had amused me. I had a grand plan that last year in Black Rock Falls. All my offerings had been lined up in a row and one grave partially dug. It was going so well and then disaster had struck. Floods and mudslides had prevented me finishing. In desperation, I'd packed up and headed for another suitable location, but during all those years away, I'd been limited to offerings and in between Halloweens. I turned to killing sex workers, but I'd been stupid and, instead of burying them, had dumped them anywhere. The cops had almost caught me numerous times, and I'd moved on just in time before the net closed. Now, I understood the way of things. I'd listened to the voices. The forest was calling to me to return and now I'm able to continue where I'd left off.

I use my charm to make friends. You see, I live on a higher plane than other men, but acting like a regular guy out with his friends makes it easy to get closer to women. A man alone is always suspicious. Especially as I deliberate on each choice for my Halloween offerings. I prefer a slightly built woman, only because she's easier to carry. A body being a dead weight and all. She must live alone, preferably without a dog, but I can deal with dogs if necessary. A remote area is a plus, but I have the skill to sneak into most places without being noticed, especially in Black Rock Falls. Here, shadows bathe the sidewalks. The town is filled with tall pines, cottonwood trees, and the occasional maple that spill leopard-spot or zebra-stripe shadows over the sidewalks and alleyways. Then there is the mist and with the practically nonexistent and widely spaced streetlights offering only a small orange or yellow glow, it's perfect. Not that lights bother me, or CCTV cameras. Carrying a laser pointer and other small gadgets all easily purchased online makes me invisible and breaking into a house or apartment easy. Watching women is as easy as installing a camera on a window ledge or across the way. The clarity and sound being so good these days, I set and forget and go through the video files at my leisure or watch on my phone. Yeah, technology is my friend.

I made the acquaintance of Daisy Lyon some months ago. She'd given me a coy smile at first and then, just like all the others, ignored me. I've seen her talking to her friends, flirting with younger men, and playing nice. They all started out being like that, or was it all a pretense? Was it a game women of that age played? Did they tease and then dismiss men as if they had no value? I've met so many women who act just the same. I've formed a list of possible women, but I never write anything down. I'm not stupid.

My leisurely walk through the forest has brought me out opposite Pine. As I cross Stanton, I keep to the thick shadows spilling from the rows of pine trees alongside the sidewalk and make my way to the log-built house Daisy Lyon shares with her friend, Tara. The one remarkable thing about Tara is that she works from three each afternoon until late at night. She has two jobs, moving from one to the other and arriving home around midnight each night. I've watched her driving her battered old truck down Stanton before heading through the trees to the house. Daisy arrives home around seven, she does chores, eats, and watches TV until ten and then takes a shower and goes to bed. I've been watching the pair of them for two long months.

I take a look around before going to the back door. Most back doors have a stoop and offer cover from prying eyes, but someone overlooked this yard and I'll be able to drive my truck right up to it the moment Daisy steps into the shower. It amazes me how I can move around a person's home when they're in the shower. It's as if showers were designed for people like me to break in without anyone ever hearing. Today I took a peek inside to get the layout. I need to know where Daisy sleeps and discover the easiest way to get her body into the truck. The killing part is easy. Most of them are way too scared to fight back. I pull on examination gloves and then use a lockpick to open the door. This is my make-or-break time and I hold my breath and wait a few minutes for any alarms to chime, but nothing is happening. Seems they don't own a dog.

I slip inside and familiarize myself with the layout of each room. The home isn't overly clean, but I guess busy people working two jobs don't have the time to clean. My nose wrinkles at the garbage spilling from the trash can. Pizza boxes litter the kitchen table. No time to cook either. I'd been surprised when

Daisy refused my invitation to dinner. Now more so. She believed she was something special, but I've seen her mean side. Her lip curled when she refused my invitation as if I had no value or feelings. I sighed. Maybe she sensed something hiding deep inside me? Not that knowing anything would save her now. My heart is racing with the anticipation of returning to find her alone. I can't wait to surprise her and see the expression on her face. The startled look in her eyes as she takes her last breath. Believing she was all that won't help when I slice deep into her tender flesh.

I've found Daisy's bedroom. It has the smell of her, and I can't resist lying on her bed and inhaling the fragrance of her pillows. From the moment she'd embarrassed me by laughing at my invitation, I've fantasized about killing her so many times. Being here now makes it all the more urgent. I craved the thrill of watching her die. Reluctantly, I roll from the sweet-smelling sheets, stand, and go to the bathroom. Perfect. She has her own and it's scattered with her belongings as I'd imagined. Like the rest of the house, her private space was untidy. She didn't pay too much attention to cleaning. Perhaps, working at the Triple Z Roadhouse, she had enough cleaning to do all day. I checked the closets for the location of towels and went back to the bedroom. No need to smooth the bed, it was just as she'd left it this morning. I stood for a time imagining her blood-soaked body wrapped in the soft pink woolen throw and grinned. "I'm going to make this Halloween special, just for you, Daisy. Real special."

TWELVE

On her way back to the office, Jenna's phone chimed. It was Wolfe. "Hi, Shane, I didn't expect to hear from you until later."

"The speed of technology surprises me sometimes too." Wolfe's office chair creaked in a familiar way. *"The body in the grave is Lydia Ellis out of Louan. Norrell has been working on the body and I have a verbal report. She's heading back to Bear Peak first thing to excavate the other graves. If they're both murders and with the same MO, she doesn't need to be sifting through dirt hunting down artifacts. She'd appreciate backup as there seems to be another crazy running around town. I'm going with her, we'll have Blackhawk as well as her team, but I'll be the only armed guard."*

Anxious to hear Norrell's findings, Jenna chewed on her bottom lip. "Yes, of course. I'll probably go there with Dave. What did Norrell say?"

"The body has been buried for about six to seven years. It's female, eighteen to twenty-two years old, slight build, five feet, two inches. There are distinct marks, likely from the serrated edge of a hunting knife in the cervical spine vertebrae, to indicate

she was almost decapitated. The sternum and ribs indicate sharp force trauma. She also found similar markings to the victim's forearms, which would indicate defense wounds. One of her fingers was almost cut through." Wolfe blew out a long sigh. *"Norrell has confirmed the wrappings around the body consist of bed linen and blankets. She has a copy of the recording of the murder and played it during the examination, and she figures, the injuries sustained match what she's hearing. I agree."*

"Did she mention a weapon?" Kane glanced at Jenna. "If we're tying these cases together, that evidence might be crucial."

"Yeah, examining the sternum under the microscope, we both concluded the damage is from a hunting knife. A typical design and length with a serrated edge." Wolfe paused for a beat. *"We know from the recording, the last thing he did was cut her throat. He wanted to make her suffer, but from the arterial spray in the Freya Richardson case, that amount of blood would indicate the opposite. If a victim has been losing blood throughout a vicious knife attack, the gush of blood from severing the carotid artery would be slightly less. What we saw at the apartment was a massive gush of blood. So, if you're making a comparison between murders, we can't prove at this time that Freya was stabbed as well."* He sighed. *"I did find a partial thumbprint on the phone that doesn't belong to the victim. It's not on any database either. If you get a suspect, we can run it against him."*

Jenna nodded mostly to herself as she considered what steps to take next. The case was seven years old. *Cold case* meant just that—by this time, all the leads had gone cold. People's memories faded or became convoluted over time. "I'll get Rio and Rowley to hunt down her next of kin and any friends she had before she died. I need to find Freya's body. If this is the same killer, we have to assume he's going to bury her in the forest. If it's not, we'll have to wait until someone stumbles over the body. It could be anywhere."

"When we're there in the morning, maybe someone should take a look at the partially dug grave we found?" Kane pulled the Beast into his parking slot outside the office. "Maybe he's already buried her there. It's a possibility we can't overlook."

"Okay. I'll leave y'all to get back to work." Wolfe cleared his throat. *"Webber is back with the swabs from Freya's shower. I'll see you in the morning. Are you good to meet us at the fire road turnoff at nine?"*

Jenna stared out at the mist already crawling from the river and shivered. It would be the same in the morning and could hide anyone or anything at Bear Peak. "Yeah, sure, that works for me. Thank Norrell for me."

"I will." Wolfe disconnected.

As Jenna followed Kane and Duke inside the office, a cold chill slithered down her spine. She turned to look over one shoulder along the sidewalk to a Halloween display. At this time of the year, it was difficult to tell what was real and what was a display. Something moved in the display outside the general store. She stared, fixated. The automatons were particularly inventive this year, but as she watched, she could have sworn one of the figures turned to look at her. "Dave. Wait for me."

"What's wrong? You look as if you've seen a ghost." Kane put one arm around her shoulder and scanned Main.

Jenna leaned into him. "We know about two missing women and they're much the same build as me. What if I'm on his list?"

"If he attacks at night, he'd never get through our security." Kane turned her to face him. "Say he does? Do you honestly believe he could immobilize me and kill you?" He shook his head slowly. "I'm staying by your side twenty-four/seven until we catch this guy. Once we do background checks on his victims, we'll know more about his targets. I doubt he'd be stupid enough to attempt an attack on a married sheriff with a dog. Everyone in town knows we are never apart, and trust me, I'm not planning on going anywhere without you right beside me."

A wave of comfort swept over her and she nodded. "It's just I thought I'd seen someone staring at me just before."

"You're the sheriff. They probably caught you looking at them and figured they'd done something wrong." Kane smiled at her and turned her toward the door. "You know, you're like this every Halloween."

Jenna looked at him. "That's because every darn year something bad happens. That's not an overactive imagination. It's a fact. It's like some crazy is putting up a challenge to see if we can catch them. If this really is the Halloween Slasher, where's he been for the past seven years?"

"I guess we'll find out soon enough." Kane pushed open the door and ushered her inside. "In the meantime, trust me to have your back."

She turned and held open the door for Duke. "I always do."

Heading toward the counter, she smiled at Maggie. "Any calls on the hotline?'

"I've had a few, not many." Maggie took a book from the desk behind the counter. "Two were from reporters wanting more on the missing persons case. I informed them we'd send out a media release when we had more information. We had an interesting call from Hank Maxwell. He lives out at Twisted Limbs Trail in a cabin. He was on his way home and spotted a white van moving fast around midnight on Friday. He'd been on his way home from Antlers after having dinner with a friend." She lifted her head and looked at Jenna. "I've added his details to your files."

Glad to have any snippet of information, Jenna thanked her and took the stairs to her office, pleased to see Rio and Rowley waiting for her.

Kane was at his desk scrolling through files and glanced up

as she arrived. "The judge refused the warrant to track Freya Richardson's phone. He quoted privacy laws and warned us, if she isn't dead, we're not to proceed."

Jenna pushed her hands through her hair. "Did you make it clear we believe she's dead, but this is a chance to track her killer, who we assume has her phone?"

"Yeah, I made a list of probable causes, including the slim chances of her being alive and that it was our duty of care to find her." Kane shook his head. "It's the proof of death that's the problem and Wolfe's note about the amount of blood on scene didn't cut it. Dead people don't have privacy rights and we wouldn't need a warrant. The fact we can't locate her is the problem. He stated that she could be somewhere alive, without the phone. This being the case, issuing a warrant would be an invasion of her privacy."

Rubbing her temples in dismay, Jenna stared at him. "Well, I hope Kalo bends the rules this time. We need to catch this guy." She turned to Rio and Rowley and gave them the details of the call from Hank Maxwell. She turned to Rio. "Hunt down what you can find out about Maxwell. Where he works would be a start, and if he has any priors."

"Why do we need to do a background check on him?" Rowley frowned. "He called in information. Seems to me like he's just trying to help out."

Jenna sat down and nodded. "Yeah, but there's always a maybe with people volunteering information. Agreed, most are honest and just trying to assist, but then we have the criminals who insert themselves into the investigation to discover what we know. You see, it's been a time since Freya went missing and we haven't found a body. It could be the killer. Some of them like to see their crimes on the news. If we get more hints from this guy, we'll need to look closer."

"So we add him to the potential suspect's list?" Rowley nodded slowly.

Standing, Jenna went to the whiteboard and added Hank Maxwell's name. She'd headed the first third of the board with Freya Richardson's name. "Okay, that's one possible. What else have you got for me?"

THIRTEEN

Jenna sat down and looked expectantly at her deputies. "Rio?"

"Yeah. I looked a little deeper into Freya's timeline." Rio stared at her across the desk. He never looked at a note, everything was in his head. "She left work at the beauty parlor around eleven, at the same time the owner of the pizzeria noticed one of his customers hanging back, maybe urinating in the alleyway opposite. He gave his name as Frank Stark. He watched him for a time. He'd been sitting in the window eating his pie and staring at Freya as she cleaned the beauty parlor. The beauty parlor had all the lights blazing and Freya was on display through the storefront for at least two hours."

Noting the man's name on her legal pad, Jenna lifted her head to look at him again. "Did he mention what type of vehicle he drove?"

"Yeah, well, I asked him the same question." Rio stretched his long legs. "Seems he drives a white van, but it wasn't in sight that night. He noticed that Freya usually parked her truck out front, but she'd dropped by before work for a slice and mentioned it was in the shop. She was on foot, and as she lived on Elm, it would have taken her half an hour, maybe a little more, to walk home." He scratched his chin. "The owner said that he didn't see Stark's vehicle, not until later, but he did see him heading off in her direction. He said his vehicle came by fast a little after twelve when he was locking up. This would match the hotline call we received from Maxwell. He reported seeing a white vehicle driving fast around the same time." He met her gaze. "The pizzeria stays open late on Friday and Saturday nights and stops baking at eleven unless there's a crowd, like over the festivals. They open at ten each morning. It's always busy."

"It's strange he knows this particular guy." Kane twirled a pen in his fingers. "Did you ask him?"

"Yeah, he said he was a regular, in most nights and sits for hours. The owner figured Stark has no one to go home to."

Considering the implications of Stark following Freya home, Jenna nodded. "It would tie in with the report about a speeding white truck on Saturday night, but is the speeding vehicle relevant to Stark? If he followed her home and then murdered her, he'd have a long walk back to his truck if he parked it somewhere along Main, especially if he planned on taking her body. Would he risk going back for his truck and then breaking back into the apartment to take her with him?"

"That's not logical." Kane shook his head. "This guy appears to plan everything. Maybe he parked his truck near Freya's apartment and then walked to the pizzeria. He followed her home, murdered her, and then drove away with the body." He shrugged. "Perhaps the following and terrifying is all part of his thrill?"

Jenna stood again and went to the whiteboard. "I'll add him to our list of suspects." She dropped the pen back in its holder and sat down before moving her attention to Rowley. "Have you contacted the Louan sheriff's office and informed them about the remains of Lydia Ellis?"

"Yes, ma'am. They are hunting down her next of kin and

will notify them." Rowley glanced at his notes. "I did find Freya's grandmother. She's in a care facility in Helena. I've spoken to the person in charge and explained that she's missing. They insisted that unless we can verify Freya is deceased, they're not going to concern her grandmother due to her failing health." He sighed. "No other family members at all."

"That's sad." Kane pushed a hand through his hair and then glanced at his watch. "I suggest we hunt down the two men we have, as in find out where they work and when they're likely to be at home."

Jenna nodded. "Yeah, work on that for now. I'm going with Dave to Bear Peak first thing. If you find any more details on these men, call it in and then go and interview them. If not, keep looking and I'll drop by in the morning before we head to the burial site to see what you've discovered. I figure Maxwell won't be expecting a visit but Stark will. Whenever you decide to interview them, watch their body language and attitude. You know the attributes of a serial killer. I'm sure I don't need to remind you to remain outside their houses or places of employment at all times and never turn your backs on them."

"Yes, ma'am." Rowley stood and led the way out of the office with Rio close behind.

"You know, we have a couple of hours free." Kane leaned back in his chair making it groan. "I'd like to find out more about Freya Richardson. I'm guessing her truck is in Miller's Garage. Maybe we should start there. Where else does she work? We'll need to speak to the people she came in contact with on Friday and Saturday."

Jenna stood and went to the coffeemaker and poured two cups. As she added the fixings, she looked over her shoulder at Kane. "I'd like to know why Lydia Ellis was in Black Rock Falls at the time of her death. Where was she living and how come we didn't find anything in the newspapers about a bloody crime scene here in town, or a missing young woman?"

"I guess it's possible the killer murdered her in Louan, dumped her body in his truck, and drove her to Stanton Forest." Kane took the cup from Jenna with a smile. "I'll call Kalo and ask him if he's traced Freya's phone and if he can do a background check on Lydia. I'll put it on speaker."

Sipping her coffee as Kane made the call, Jenna tried to discover any similarities between the crimes, or markers, to determine if the victims were murdered by the same killer. Did he prefer the same type of women or was it random?

She listened as Kane explained what he needed.

"It's all good. I can look into that the moment you get a warrant, but I can't legally trace Freya Richardson's phone due to the privacy laws." Kalo cleared his throat. *"Give me a moment."* The sound of fingers flying over a keyboard came through the speaker. *"Okay, I can tell you it last pinged in Black Rock Falls, but I don't have an exact location. It's been turned off from what I can see."*

"Okay, I understand." Kane glanced at Jenna and rolled his eyes. "As soon as we find a body, I'll call you." He disconnected.

Jenna chuckled. "I wonder if the FBI director is in the office? Since when has by-the-book been Kalo's creed?"

"You could be right, but he gave us a clue at least. The phone is here in town." Kane turned back to his screen. "Okay, do you want to make calls or finish your coffee and we'll go and speak to these people in person?"

Emptying her cup, Jenna stood. "We'll go and see them. Download their details to my phone."

"Okay." Kane emptied his cup and collected the details. "Okay, Duke, walkies." He stood and waved Jenna through the door. "First up, Miller's Garage."

FOURTEEN

I dropped by Aunt Betty's Café just to catch Wendy working her shift. She moves from table to table like a butterfly as she carries a coffee pot, always happy, with a smile on her face. I need to finalize my master plan. I want three offerings in the graves. I've made excellent choices and all deserve to die. I've taken care of the one small problem at Wendy's house and her dog will be at the vet for a long time. The slow-acting poison I use should have killed it outright, but for the intervention of the neighbors, who left a day late on their vacation. Although the poison would take a long time to leave the dog's system and would give me the time I need. In truth, I'm doing the dog a favor. If I leave it to starve when I take Wendy, it will be a worse death. Yeah, I do have a heart, go figure. Although, come to think about it, I have no thoughts either way about animals. I hunt for meat and find no thrill in the killing. Nope, the only excitement I feel comes from frightening women and making them jump at their own shadow. By instilling the fact they have a vivid imagination, they believe their fright is overreaction, and then what happens? They try to convince themselves they're overthinking small things and push concern out of their minds.

When they've arrived at that stage, I can walk straight into the house and kill them. They ignore any small sounds because they've already made an excuse in their minds for the creak of floorboards or the slide of a window.

I give her my best smile as she comes toward me carrying a thick wedge of cherry pie in one hand and a pot of coffee in the other. As she lays it down, the smell of her hair sends a jolt straight through me. My hand trembles as I take the plate from her. Maybe she deserves one last chance? "You're so good to me, Wendy. You sure you don't want to come with me to the Halloween Ball? I hear the live band is something special."

"Maybe next year." She gives me a coy smile. "I'm going with Chance. He asked me on the first day of October. If I see you there, I'll save you a dance."

You won't make it to the dance. I wait for her to fill my cup and my gaze drifts to the pool of cherry juice leaking from the pie and spilling over my plate in a familiar crimson rush. My heart pounds. I want to kill her now and see her hot sticky blood spill over white tile but I act nonchalant, and lean back in my chair. I can be anyone's best friend, the nice guy. I can just turn it on anytime. "I'd say you're worth waiting for and there are plenty of dances between now and next Halloween. You remind me of this fine pie. You smell good and inside you're a sweet delight."

"You say the nicest things." Wendy turns and hurries back to the kitchen.

While Wendy finishes her shift, I'll drop by her house and find a way inside. I need a place to park my truck where no one can see me or suspect me if they do. I slowly devour the delicious pie, savoring each mouthful. Digging graves makes me hungry.

FIFTEEN

Kane walked into the office at Miller's Garage and smiled at George Miller. "Hey, George, we have a young woman missing. Her name is Freya Richardson and I believe she dropped her truck by for repairs. Can you recall the day she came by?"

"I do. You see, I usually offer one of our customer vehicles for people with repairs, but she was upfront telling me she couldn't pay for the work. The customer vehicles are used for short-term, not weeks or months." George rubbed a hand over his mouth. "I told her she could pay me a little each week but replacing the engine in her old truck with a new one was false economy. It would be better to buy something else. She wouldn't hear of it, so I've been trying to source a decent replacement engine."

Kane frowned. "You couldn't patch it up?"

"Come see for yourself." George led the way to the garage and indicated an old truck with the hood up. "I don't figure anything is salvageable. There's been no oil put in it for a long time. When I asked her why she hadn't put oil in it when the light was flashing, she told me she didn't know trucks needed oil. It's never been serviced. When it blew, it's as if a wrecking ball went through it."

"Oh, that looks bad." Jenna peered under the hood.

Nodding, Kane turned to George. "Poor kid. She was practically all alone in the world. From what I hear, she worked every job possible just to survive. I wish we'd known. The Broken Wings Foundation has funds for people in need."

"She might not have taken a handout." George met his gaze with a look of troubled concern. "She had a pride about her. Told me she'd work real hard to get the money and could walk or take the bus. She came by last Saturday and gave me one hundred dollars toward the new engine. I wrote it up in my book. She wanted to have the full amount before I started work. She was that kind of woman. She didn't want to owe anyone anything." He sighed. "Between you and me, I'd have only charged her the cost and done the labor myself. I could see she was trying to get by."

Kane slapped him on the back. "I'm sure you did everything you could to help her. Did she mention anything about where she was heading when you last saw her?"

"Yeah, she mentioned working at the beauty parlor. She cleans it from top to bottom." He thought for a beat. "I've seen her packing shelves at the general store. I'm not sure where else she worked."

Looking along the line of mechanics working on vehicles, he nodded. "Did she talk to any of the other guys around here?"

"Not in my presence." George shook his head. "We don't allow customers back here."

"Okay, thanks." Jenna smiled at him. "Mind if we take a look inside her truck? We're trying to find clues to locate her."

"Go ahead. It's open." George grimaced. "I hope you find her. This time of the year isn't safe around these parts."

Kane pulled open the truck door in a grind of metal on metal. "You can say that again."

Inside smelled musty and the seats had seen better days. He found her insurance and registration in the glovebox but little else. No scraps of paper or signs she'd been anywhere in particular. He bent to peer under the seats, looked through the back and found nothing. He turned to Jenna. "Nothing of interest here." He looked at George. "Do you recall if she was carrying a purse and a phone?"

"Yeah, she called us to haul the truck back here and had a phone in her hand when I last saw her. She was carrying a purse because she stuffed a few things inside it from inside the truck before leaving."

"You haven't heard from her since she left, have you?" Jenna moved to his side.

"Nope." George's gaze narrowed. "I said I'd call if I could find a decent replacement engine. I have her details, but I've had no reason to call her."

"Okay, thanks, George." Jenna smiled at him. "We've held you up long enough." She headed for the Beast.

Kane slid behind the wheel. "Beauty parlor next?"

"I've already spoken to the proprietor. Freya had a key and went in to clean when they shut down for the night." Jenna clicked in her seatbelt. "It was closed before she arrived, so she didn't come into contact with anyone. The time she arrived is debatable too, because as Freya works all over, there's no telling what time she arrived or left the beauty parlor. The owner said as long as the place was cleaned, the hours she worked didn't matter." She glanced at Kane. "George mentioned the general store. We'll try there next." She glanced at her watch. "Time is getting away from us. I want to drop by Nanny Raya's and get Tauri before it gets too cold. I promised he could see the spider outside Aunt Betty's. I figured we'd walk him down Main so he could see some of the other Halloween displays."

Raising his eyebrows, Kane glanced at her. "Do you think seeing them might frighten him?"

"I don't think so because he knows they're not real and they've been making Halloween masks all week in kindergarten. They have ghosts and pumpkins all over the room."

Kane nodded. "Yeah, I guess we should carve a jack-o'-lantern from a pumpkin for him as well. I remember making them with my dad. We could do it together. What do you think?"

"It was the best time for me too." Jenna laughed "I'm really enjoying having Tauri, he brings back so many happy memories. Now all we need is a pumpkin."

Kane stared along the sidewalk. "I did see a pile for sale along here somewhere."

"We'll look for one after we've collected him." Jenna smiled. "It will all be part of the fun."

Pulling up in a space outside of the general store, he climbed out. "Wait there, Duke. We'll be walking along Main anytime soon." He shot a glance at Jenna. "Do you want to eat at Aunt Betty's tonight? I figure he'd like it and it would give us more time with him before he goes to bed. It won't take long to move the horses into clean stalls when we get home. I'll muck them out in the morning and turn them out into the corral."

"Okay, but we'll grab a pie to go." Jenna rolled her eyes. "If you eat at six, you'll be starving by eight."

Grinning, Kane followed her into the general store. "Sure. You twisted my arm."

After speaking to the manager, Kane listened with interest. "So, Freya worked alongside a few people. Any of them happen to be male?"

"Yeah, Elliot Cummings." The manager raised both eyebrows. "They seemed to get along just fine."

Nodding, Kane looked at him. "Would you describe Elliot Cummings as just a workmate or was there anything between him and Freya?"

"I'm not too sure." The manager's eyebrows joined in the

center in a frown as if he was trying to recall their interactions. "I did hear him ask her out at one time."

"What did she say?" Jenna was making notes.

"Oh, that she works twenty-four/seven and doesn't have the time for dating." The manager shrugged. "It was quiet between them after that."

Kane straightened. "And before that, had they become close?"

"Hmm, don't quote me, but I have seen them in the break room drinking coffee and chatting, but then Elliot seemed to ignore her or she did him." The manager looked at Jenna. "I never heard any harsh words between them."

"When was the last day she worked?" Jenna's pen raised from her notebook as she looked at him.

"Saturday, she took her break around five, finished her shift at eight, she goes from here to the beauty parlor." The manager shook his head. "She was a good worker. I heard on the news that she's missing. I hope she's okay."

As he nodded, Kane's mind flashed to the crime scene. There would be no way anyone survived that much blood loss. He cleared his throat. "We do too. We'll need the details of Elliot Cummings. We're interviewing everyone who knew Freya. Do I need a warrant?"

"I don't believe that's necessary." The manager plucked a card from a small display at the checkout and handed it to Kane. "Elliot is a photographer. This is his card. It doesn't pay the bills, so he works here." He opened his hands. "He'd normally be here around this time, but he changed his shift, said he needs to be around town at night over Halloween to catch all the displays. People apparently like professional photographs during festivals."

"Thanks." Jenna folded her notebook. "We'll give him a call." She headed out the door and turned to Kane. "What do you think?"

Kane pushed his hat down on his head firmly as a cold breeze brushed his cheeks. "Another possible. This one has a motive. She shunned his attention and it had an immediate effect. Yeah, he's on the list."

SIXTEEN

A cold mist swirled across the sidewalk and turned the blacktop into a walkway for ghostly figures, all of them marching into the unknown. Jenna pushed away the shudder of uncertainty and looked into Tauri's face. He shone as if lit from inside, his happiness coming out in giggles and little skips of joy as she led him past the sometimes horrific displays. It had taken a long discussion to persuade her to expose a four-year-old to all that Black Rock Falls offered over the Halloween week. She'd spoken to Blackhawk, who'd shrugged and said it was a fact of life and Tauri should understand it was all in fun. Kane had said much the same, pointing out the decorations in the kinder-garten and just how many of Tauri's friends were involved in decorating their own front yards. She'd giggled when Kane mentioned he'd never had a problem with Halloween, but Santa Claus had frightened him as a child. The idea of a huge man with claws coming down the chimney in the night had been a terrifying notion, carrying gifts or not. He'd explained that after being well-schooled in stranger danger and not taking candy from anyone he didn't know, Santa Claus sounded very dangerous to him.

Dark shadows loomed ahead and, wishing Kane was with her, she stared through the swirling mist hoping to see him. But Kane had driven to Aunt Betty's and parked outside, and, leaving them to enjoy the displays, he had gone to purchase a pumpkin. After leaving it in the Beast, he'd walk along Main to meet them. The sidewalk wasn't busy, most people had headed home for their dinner, but a few people lingered. Ahead, the Halloween spirit was in full force, with every store trying to outdo the next, but between them, the banks and offices sat in darkness and all around them shadows had filled with mist, adding to the creepiness. The fog was so thick in places that people seemed to emerge at first like ghostly figures before their features set in place. With a killer roaming the streets, once they entered the thick cloud of fog, no one would see if someone attacked them.

Nerves on edge but wanting to keep the atmosphere around Tauri as relaxed as possible, she laughed and pointed at the skeletons dressed like gunslingers playing cards, their red eyes flashing and heads turning whenever anyone walked by. "They're so funny." She squeezed Tauri's hand, keeping him close to her side.

"It's funny because we made jack-o'-lanterns today to keep the bad ghosts away, and Nanny Raya says only good spirits of the elders come through on that night and she welcomes them to bring in a new beginning. She told me never to be afraid of the good spirits. Most are there to guide us." He gave her a quizzical stare and wrinkled his nose. "Who is right?"

Enchanted by Tauri's knowledge of both cultures' interpretation of Halloween, she smiled at him. "You should believe what's in your heart. These displays are for fun and shouldn't be taken seriously, but years ago people had many different interpretations of what some called All Hallows' Eve. I happen to agree with Nanny Raya and believe there are spirits who guide us. I think they guide us every day, not just over Halloween."

"Uncle Atohi said the same thing." Tauri laughed. "He comes to see me at Nanny Raya's and tells me stories. I like listening to him. He teaches me new words, same as Daddy. I want to speak to the elders, same as the other kids." He looked up at her. "I can teach you. It's easy."

Heart blossoming with love every time she looked at her little boy, she nodded. "I'd like that."

As they strolled along Main, a few people wandered past, nodding to her, heads bent against the cruel breeze that seemed to creep up behind her and send chills down her neck. Ice covered the mountain peaks, turning the snowcaps blue. Snow would come early. The winters had become worse each year and seemed to last forever before the melt. As she stopped in front of a group of wild-haired witches stirring a bubbling caul-dron, she caught a movement in one of the displays. Within a group of ghostly figures with hideous masks, a head turned toward her, the black eyes deep pits of nothingness. The hairs stood erect on the back of her neck, as they'd walked by just before and nothing had happened. Most of the automatons had movement sensors, and right now they were the only people close by. She pulled Tauri closer as he poked a fat spider with twirling black-and-white eyes that reminded her of old movies about being hypnotized.

As they moved to the next display, a shiver slid down her spine and every muscle went on alert as she caught the reflec-tion in the storefront window of a ghostly figure detaching itself from the group. It appeared to float on the mist to join the next display. She hadn't imagined it, not twice in a row. Had she? Casually, she unclipped the leather strap securing her weapon and moved Tauri on to the next display, keeping one eye on the reflection behind her in the storefront windows. Ahead, the street was empty. Shadows bathed the sidewalk outside the closed office buildings that stood on each side of the dark alley-way. Concern gripped her. Was someone following her to cause her harm or try and snatch Tauri from her? He was such a beau-tiful little boy and attracted attention from everyone. Not wanting to alarm him, she bent, gathered him in her arms, and hurried across the entrance to the misty alleyway. Heart pound-ing, she burst out of the darkness and slowed as she reached the next display. To her horror, in her peripheral vision she caught sight of the ghostly figure sliding into the alleyway. There was no mistake. Somebody was following her.

Acting nonchalant, she placed Tauri on the ground and clasped his hand as they moved toward a dancing skeleton and a man with an ax through his head outside Guns and Ammo. She searched ahead for Kane but couldn't see him. Through the swirling mist, she made out a mass of people around the entrance to the pizzeria waiting for takeout. The ghostly figure hadn't emerged from the alleyway, so they walked on. Heart racing with every step, Jenna tried not to allow her Halloween over-imagination take hold of common sense, but as they moved along the sidewalk, she stared into the storefront window straight into the face the of the figure heading their way, and in one hand he swung a machete.

She needed to get some distance between her and the man following her, and squeezed Tauri's hand. "How fast can you run to the next one?"

"Like the wind." Tauri giggled and dragged her forward.

Laughing, they ran toward the next exhibition of gruesome Halloween fun. Not wanting to frighten Tauri, she stopped, took out her phone, and took a photograph of him, making sure to capture the reflection of the figure now blending into the previous display. She allowed the little boy to explore the attrac-tions and called Kane in a whisper. "Someone dressed as a ghost and carrying a machete has been following us since we started to walk along Main. He waits, and then as we move on, he follows and blends in with the displays. I don't want to create a bad experience for Tauri, but if he comes any closer, I'll take him down."

"*I'm heading your way.*" She could hear Kane's footsteps running on the sidewalk. "*I'm across the road. I took Duke to the park. Leave him to me. I'll come around behind him. Make sure you keep Tauri busy. What's your exact position?*"

Jenna kept her voice low. "Just went past Guns and Ammo. Not far from the pizzeria."

"*Okay. If anything goes down, pick Tauri up and run to the pizzeria or Aunt Betty's.*" Kane disconnected.

Holding out her hand, Jenna smiled at Tauri. "Come on, the giant spider isn't far."

"Can we see the man with the funny teeth?" Tauri make a face. "He says, 'Hahaha, I want to bite your neck.' My friends told me."

Keeping a close eye to any movements, Jenna allowed Tauri to drag her to the Dracula attraction. The coffin opened as they walked by, and the dummy's arms stretched toward them. The voice was almost melodic and she couldn't help laughing, and then froze as she caught sight of the ghostly figure detaching itself from the previous display and heading straight for them. She picked up Tauri, ready to run for her life and then sighed with relief.

As if like magic, Kane appeared from between parked trucks and in two strides had slammed the ghost against a red-brick wall with his forearm across his throat. She didn't turn but kept Tauri's attention on the display, watching everything unfold in the reflection of the storefront window. The ghost's mask was dragged off the culprit to show a young man, his face white and eyes bulging at Kane. Words were exchanged and Kane took a photograph of the man's ID. He shoved the mask at him and gave him a push in the opposite direction. The next moment Duke came bounding toward them, tail wagging like a windmill and his backside in a happy dance to see Tauri. That dog sure loved the little boy. As they headed toward Aunt Betty's, Kane came to her side. Jenna looked at him. "You let him go?"

"He claimed to be an actor hired by the town council to scare people." Kane shrugged. "I have his details and will check tomorrow. I'll also be calling the mayor about the stupidity of doing such a thing in Serial Killer Central. I let the guy go with a warning."

Interested, Jenna looked at him. "What kind of warning?"

"Oh, I said messing with the sheriff is a big mistake, especially when she's out with our son. If he'd come close with that machete, which was plastic by the way, you'd have shot him dead." He cleared his throat. "I also reminded him that anyone who believes their life is in danger has the right to do the same thing and suggested he find another occupation."

"Daddy, come look at the spider." Tauri was jumping on the spot with excitement. "It has babies."

"Oh, I'm scared, maybe you should hold my hand." Kane grinned at him.

"Silly Daddy." Tauri laughed and took his hand. "You're big and scared of nothing. Uncle Atohi told me you are Eagle Eye the great warrior."

Jenna watched Kane's expression change to a softness she'd rarely seen. She took Tauri's other hand. "Come on, my eagle-eyed warriors. Let's walk through the spider's legs and eat. I'm starving."

SEVENTEEN

WEDNESDAY

After dropping by Aunt Betty's Café to collect a ton of takeout and coffee for lunch for the teams, Jenna went to the office to update Rio and Rowley. She sent them to interview two of the suspects in the Freya Richardson case and then headed out the door. She climbed back into the Beast. "Okay, we're good to go."

They'd planned to meet Wolfe, Norrell, and her team for the trek to Bear Peak. They'd handled many cases involving the area in the past and it had become familiar, but it represented a very small part of what was vast wilderness. With Blackhawk's assistance, they'd discovered the quickest ways to get to different locations. The fire roads offered the best choice and it was only a short walk to the current location of the graves. She'd considered the difficulty of carrying a body from the fire road to the burial site and decided the killer must be a strong man, unless he drove his truck and horse trailer to the fire road and transported the body on horseback.

Although, this is where old cases became cold cases. After six or seven years, the surrounding trails around the graves offered no clues nor any signs of what method he'd used. The thought still lingered in her mind as the convoy of vehicles pulled to a halt. She turned in her seat to Kane. "As we have a body missing, we should scout around and see if we can see any fresh tracks. If the killer is still using this location as his burial grounds, he could have driven here like us and maybe brought a horse with him."

"If he had, he'd have dug the grave before the murder." Kane pulled a black woolen cap over his head to cover his ears. "From the empty gravesite we found, that's what he does. So, we should look there and see if he's left a body in that grave. If he has buried her, Atohi is here. He'll be able to track him." He shrugged. "I doubt the killer is hanging around, but Wolfe is armed and so is Webber. Norrell will be safe while we go and poke around."

After greeting the teams, Jenna went to Atohi's side as they began their hike through the forest. "Would you mind coming with us to the partially dug gravesite? If the recent murder victim has been buried, that place would be logical. If he has buried her, could you track him for us?"

"I'll ask the boss." Blackhawk winked at her and turned to Wolfe. "Do you need me? Jenna wants to check out the other gravesite."

"Nope. If Norrell finds anything unusual that we need you to examine, I'll call you." Wolfe glanced at Jenna and smiled. "Atohi is officially a member of my team now, but as my team and your team are inseparable, if you need his help, there's no need to ask."

Recalling how Blackhawk had refused to become an employee of the sheriff's department, she turned to look at him. "Oh, that's good. What changed your mind?"

"Ah, the nature of the work, Jenna." Blackhawk raised both eyebrows. "Norrell explained the importance of having me around when necessary for excavating burial sites. I won't be here unless I'm needed. Most of her work will be in the forest, and although the majority of forest is outside the res, long ago it all belonged to us. There are sacred sites throughout Stanton Forest, and you need a good tracker from time to time. So as I'm employed by the medical examiner's office and not the sheriff's department, it's fine. On the res we have our own law enforcement. I wouldn't want to be accused of jumping the fence." He chuckled. "Although being part of your family now, Jenna, I believe I have one leg on either side."

Frowning, Jenna squeezed his arm. "I hope us adopting Tauri hasn't caused any problems with your elders. It wasn't our intention. We have the greatest respect for Native American traditions."

"If it had, they wouldn't have allowed it, Jenna." Blackhawk's expression was serious. "We can see what is inside your hearts. Tauri belongs with you. I had a dream about him soon after he arrived on the res—he was riding with Dave in the forest—and then another the following night. I saw him grown in a photograph with Dave and you standing beside him when he graduated. They were powerful dreams and we take notice of dreams. He has a bright future with you and Dave. We are very happy he has found his way home."

Stunned, Jenna hugged him. "Thank you."

"Is there something I need to know?" Kane walked up behind her, one eyebrow raised.

"No." Blackhawk grinned at him. "Don't allow those eagle eyes to turn green. We were discussing your son."

"Did she mention the fool following her and Tauri last night?" Kane shook his head. "Jenna is the last person I know to take out a serial killer. She always gives the order to bring them in alive, so she can question them, but last night, I swear she'd have shot that guy dead if he'd stepped a yard closer to Tauri."

"Mothers are like bears with their cubs." Blackhawk led the way in the direction of the other gravesite. "They'd die to protect them."

Shivering, recalling the previous night, Jenna nodded. "I

was focused on keeping Tauri safe at all costs. It's strange, I wasn't worried about me, as if I'd become a shield to protect him."

"Really?" Kane barked a laugh. "Now you know how I feel and have felt since the day I met you. It's not something I can turn on and off. It's just there."

Jenna looked at him. "Don't you know I'd give my life for you, Dave? It's not since Tauri came into our lives either. I've always felt that way."

"That's good to know." Kane smiled at her.

Ahead, a small clearing emerged from the tangle of trees and they all slowed and searched the immediate area before moving toward the partially dug grave. As Jenna walked, mist curled around her feet. It was cold and eerily quiet. The only sound came from the river. Birdsong was missing and she glanced over her shoulder before she bent and scanned the overgrown mound of dirt. "No one has been here. Dammit, I was hoping he'd have completed his triangle or whatever."

"If it's the Halloween Slasher." Kane rubbed the back of his neck. "Someone murdered Freya Richardson, but her body could be anywhere. Let's face it. Even if it was dumped anywhere in the forest away from the usual hiking trails, the wildlife would have eaten it. She went missing Friday. It's Wednesday and she could be spread all over the forest by now."

"Many hunt at this time and it's the law to field dress at the kill site and leave the entrails." Blackhawk pointed to a few crows sitting silently, high above in the trees. "Crows would usually tell us where the dead lie but not during hunting season." He turned and indicated toward the mountain. "The caves are the same distance away, if the killer wants to risk disturbing the bears." He looked at Jenna. "You know how these killers think. What would he do? Where would he go?"

Hands on hips, Jenna looked around and shrugged. "I'll think on it some more, but we've had bodies dumped down wells, mine shafts, under floorboards, in root cellars—you name it. He might have her in an acid bath for all we know." She shook her head. "I'm just glad we don't have gators. That would be my first choice." She sighed. "I guess we go and see if Norrell has found anything."

"I figure we need to know more about the Halloween Slasher." Kane shrugged. "I'll call Jo when we get back to the office."

Jenna nodded. "Yeah, she'll have something on him. He's one of the cold cases and they never found a trace of him, did they?"

"Nope." Kane waved Jenna ahead to follow Blackhawk through the trees. "The murders stopped. I'm guessing he likely died. It might have been an illness or a car wreck. No evidence was found to point to anyone, much like our current case. Our case could be a copycat."

Glad to have Kane at her back, Jenna negotiated the undergrowth and tangled roots along the trail. "It would have been good if they'd caught him and he was in jail somewhere." She ducked under a low branch and held it back for Kane. "I find it unnerving but interesting to interview serial killers. I believe it slams home the fact how dangerous they are and how easily they can deceive people. Watching them change from seemingly normal to a person intent on murdering you in an instant really shocked me. All I could think of at the time was that's the same expression their victims saw just before he took their lives."

"A sobering thought, but what they reveal can be helpful." Kane moved silently behind her. "The main thing for me was that they don't need a reason to murder. It's like saying to a young kid, 'Why did you eat that candy?' The kid would say, 'Because it was there' or 'Because I wanted to.' It's as if the part of them that decides what is right and what is wrong was never taught to them. Adults teach behavior, and for a time, I wondered if this was the foundation for a serial killer, but we know now it can be genetic or caused by extreme emotional distress as a child."

Thinking through what he said, Jenna kept moving, following Blackhawk through the zebra-stripe shadows across the trail. "Maybe it's a bit of both. They do have a genetic tendency, but we know not all psychopaths end up murdering people, but a bad childhood is a defining factor." She cleared her throat. "With luck, Freya may have been the victim of a jealous lover from her past. She remains a mystery as well. We know she worked plenty of jobs. She could have easily snubbed the wrong person."

"Whoever he is, he knows how to cover his tracks." Kane came to her side as they reached the other burial site. "He took the body with him. That's a risky move. The question running through my head is why he did that. He broke in and murdered her. Most killers would walk out and hope no one saw them, but not him. He's so confident. I mean, who takes a shower at a crime scene? It makes me believe he's done this before. It's well planned. There has to be more murders. I hope Kalo will be able to find similar MOs from different states. We might have another visitor hellbent on joining Serial Killer Central's hall of fame."

EIGHTEEN

On his knees between two open graves, Wolfe held up a hand to stop the excavation of the one he'd been supervising. "Hold up, I see something. Go slow now."

"It's a blanket." Matty from Norrell's team brushed soil away and moved along the bundled mass of filthy bed linen with Colt Webber beside him, gently extracting loose dirt, until the shape of a body was uncovered.

Taking great care, Wolfe lifted the edge of the blanket to find a bloodstained pillowcase, the blood long turned to a rusty orange but easily recognizable. He moved his fingers over the pillowcase and turned to Norrell. "We have a body here, same as before. I suggest getting this one out in situ. You can unwrap it in an examination room. It looks fragile, we'll need to get it onto a board for support."

"Yeah, same, but this one is out." Norrell was kneeling beside a body bag. "I also found a pillowcase over the head. The body is naked and wrapped in blankets. It looks like it was buried the same time as before, around six or seven years ago. I figure these are the three missing girls from the Halloween Slasher from seven years ago." She waved a hand at the body bag. "I'll leave uncovering the head until I'm back in the lab, but I can plainly see the same knife marks on the sternum and ribs as before." She looked at him. Her eyes showed her despair. "Another homicide as we suspected." She held up an evidence bag. "There's a phone tucked in with the body. This body was wrapped really tight and had binding string holding it together. The body isn't stretched out, but it's like the other one, in a fetal position."

Wolfe stood as Norrell's expert team slid the corpse onto a backboard and removed the victim from the grave and deposited it into a body bag. "When you're done, search the grave in case there's something else in there."

He walked to Norrell's side. "I'd normally see a body in the fetal position when someone is left to die and they curl up in pain, or from a fire, but from what we've seen so far, these women died in seconds. It's impossible to live with the injuries they sustained."

"So, he posed them for some reason, wrapped and bound them with string." Norrell looked at him. "Why? Wouldn't that make them harder to move?"

Nodding, Wolfe glanced up as Jenna, Kane, and Blackhawk came back on scene. He brought them up to date. "We were wondering why he bound them in a fetal position. It would make them difficult to transport. Any suggestions?"

"I've seen the guys who mow lawns and tend gardens hauling the clippings away in a big bag." Blackhawk shrugged. "Maybe this killer runs a gardening service. No one would notice him dragging bags around, would they?"

"Good thinking, but wouldn't he dump them at the land-fill?" Jenna rubbed her temples. "Why go to all the trouble of burying them in threes out here? It's a massive landfill. It would be easy to lose a body there, wrapped and mixed with lawn clippings. No one sorts through the garbage. It's just pushed from one place to another and then covered with dirt."

"I figure it's going to be interesting to discover if they all have a phone belonging to the girl who died before them." Kane stared into the grave Wolfe had excavated. "If she has one, we'll know who is in the other set of three graves."

Wolfe shook his head. "And if all three have them, it will be like the chicken and the egg. How many people has this guy murdered and where are the bodies?"

"Maybe we should start with the other three graves." Jenna stood hands on hips staring into the shadowed forest. "If they're the same, we've solved six cold cases by locating the bodies. If the Halloween Slasher made one mistake when he recorded the murders, our technology today will pick up more than he anticipated."

"Or, if we discover Freya Richardson's body with a phone belonging to Lydia Ellis, the first victim we uncovered from this gravesite, at least we'll know for sure it's the same killer." Kane stared at the body bags shaking his head. "If it is, then something stopped him from completing his three sets of three. I figure this is an element of this crime we need to explore." He moved his attention back to Jenna. "If he's back to complete his fantasy or mission in life, whatever, where has he been for the last seven years?"

"That's something we need to look into." Jenna blew out a long sigh. "Who was jailed for seven years, would be a start. Who died around the same time, is another consideration until we find Freya Richardson's remains."

"I know you need information ASAP from the other graves." Norrell pushed a strand of blonde hair from her face with her forearm. "If you assist with carrying the bodies back to Wolfe's van, we'll grab a twenty-minute break to rest our backs and then head to the other burial site. I want the information as much as you do. This case is intriguing, but I can't expect my team to dig graves all day."

Wolfe surveyed the team of young healthy males and

barked a laugh. "Maybe you need to suggest fitness training? They're going to be spending a good deal of their time hiking up mountain trails and digging in all weather, riding horses and working long hours." He cast an eye over the young men. "Y'all need to be fit. You never know when y'all have to run for your lives, from a grizzly or a serial killer."

"Maybe some firearms training as well." Kane shrugged. "It's Montana. Not knowing at least the basics about weapons is a big mistake. Three guys should be adequate protection for Norrell, if you were armed. Going unarmed out here in the wilderness is asking for trouble."

"They rarely left the lab before coming here with me." Norrell frowned at him. "It wasn't necessary, but I can see your point." She looked at her team. "I work out with Dr. Wolfe every morning to keep fit. If you like, I'll arrange for some fitness classes for you." She turned to Kane. "If I recall, Rowley attends a dojo in town to keep in peak condition. Maybe he can talk to my team and get them motivated to join."

"Yeah." Kane nodded. "Good choice. They start off slow and build up their skills in various martial arts. It takes time. It wouldn't hurt to hit the gym in town a few times a week as well."

"Okay, enough talk about fitness." Jenna looked from one to the other. "Let's get these bodies back to the van. We have Thermoses of coffee and enough food to feed an army in the truck."

Wolfe looked at Kane and Atohi and raised his eyebrows. "Can you lend a hand carrying the bodies to the van? I figure these guys need a break."

"No." Leo straightened and looked at the other members of Norrell's team. "Matty and Tara will help me. We only need one other to assist." His ear's pinked as he looked at Kane. "I'll take you up on the firearms training if you have the time, and who do we talk to about joining the dojo?"

"Sure, and I'll help you carry the bodies." Kane smiled at him. "I'll send Rowley over to have a chat with you. He's around your age. Not long ago he was on a rope bridge that broke. If he hadn't been fit, he'd have fallen into the ravine." He shrugged. "Exercise is tough to start but it gets easy soon enough and then it becomes second nature to want to keep fit. We're only mentioning this for your own good. It's not in the job description, and if you don't want to do anything, we won't hold it against you, okay?"

"Thanks." Leo nodded. "I'm in."

NINETEEN

The thrill of knowing Wendy is inside the house sends shivers through me. I prefer to wait until the house is empty and then slip inside to familiarize myself with the layout. By coincidence I was close by and noticed her collecting her mail as I drove past. It was almost one and she'd be getting ready for work. I'd overheard her asking Susie, the manager at Aunt Betty's, if she could come in early today and leave before nightfall because she'd been spooked the previous evening. I smiled to myself. So, she'd seen me. A shudder of excitement sparks through me. I so love to frighten them. It makes my need to kill peak and my hands tremble with anticipation. I turn my truck around and park outside her neighbor's house. No Halloween decorations fill the yard and the place looks cold and deserted. It's an advertisement for anyone wanting to burgle the home. Some people just make criminals' lives easy. A simple thing like having a timer to turn on the TV, radio, or the lights would deter most criminals. Very few people bothered with security systems. The monitoring systems were expensive and an ordinary alarm could be easily disarmed by just smashing it from the wall or short-circuiting it.

Moving casually alongside the neighbor's house, I watch and listen. Wendy never closes her blinds and I can clearly see her moving from room to room. I've often sat outside in the dark and watched her for hours. I know what she does before work, before bed, what snacks she enjoys, and how many cups of coffee she needs before leaving for work. My mouth curls into a smile as I see her heading for her bedroom. The sunlight burnishes her hair as she walks past the window and pulls her sweater over her head. She'll take a shower before dressing and leaving for work. She spends time in the bathroom, making herself look good. I've timed her and she is a creature of habit. These people are the best targets. Those who stick to a routine like walking the dog before the news each night, buying a pizza or going to the gym the same time every week. Someone like me can take advantage of a person who has a schedule. I love schedules.

As she disappears from sight, I slip from my ride and leap over the fence. In a few strides I'm at the back door slipping on examination gloves. I have the door open in seconds and pushed wide. I'm not wearing a disguise and just pulled my hat down low over my face. I'm careful and chose to wear a generic denim jacket and Levi's. I could be one of a hundred guys around town. Inhaling, I step inside, catching her perfume as I walk through the kitchen and run my fingers along the countertops. I pick up her coffee cup. It's still warm and I run my tongue around the rim wanting to inhale her breath. I will soon and it will be her last. I need to frighten her some more and collect the dirty dishes and slide them into the dishwasher. Smiling, I close the door and switch it on. A little jolt of pleasure goes through me as I imagine her face when she finds it running. She'll know I've been here.

I walk with care to the bedroom and, finding the door slightly ajar, peek inside. My heart pounds as I open the door and see her work uniform laid out on the bed. I spend a little time to rearrange it and then look around. She is just beyond the bathroom door, so close I can almost taste her. I drag my eyes away and lift one pillow to my face to inhale her scent. I know that fragrance so well. I want to be here when she discovers someone has been in her house but that treat must wait. For now, she can have the trick. I look at my reflection in her mirror and smile, knowing she'd never suspect me. Nice guys never kill people, or do they? The sound of running water fills the room and steam leaks from the partially open bathroom door. Wendy isn't one for closing doors and I like that about her. It will make my time with her so much easier. I peer inside the steamy bathroom and make out her shape in the shower. She's humming a tune and I watch her for a time before going to the mirror and writing in the condensation: *Soon*.

I move through the house, slowly rearranging items, but constantly checking my watch. I don't want her to find me here. If she did, I'd kill her and that would be no fun. The sound of the shower stops and I hurry for the back door. I've enjoyed spooking her, but my reward would come soon. The kill would be the icing on the cake. It's a long buildup of exciting tension, growing into unbearable pleasure. The look of horror, the plunge of the knife, and the blood. Oh, the smell of the blood is like the nectar from ripe fruit.

TWENTY

Exhausted, Jenna leaned back in the seat as Kane drove back to town. They'd exhumed three more bodies at the other site, and although Norrell couldn't guarantee her timing was correct without further analysis, she believed the bodies were all buried within a year of each other. This would make perfect sense if the Halloween Slasher killed three each Halloween. The thing worrying her was, what had he been doing before killing in Black Rock Falls and Louan and where did he go in the interim between the last murder and Freya Richardson's obvious murder? She looked at Kane. "Do you agree we need to assume Freya is dead and the Halloween Slasher has buried her somewhere?"

"Yeah, I do. I called Jo when we stopped for lunch and her office is hunting down all the information they can find on his cases." Kane drummed his fingers on the steering wheel. "Blackhawk walked Duke along the fire road after giving him Freya's scent from the clothes in the evidence bag I brought with us. He didn't react, so if the killer used the fire road to get to Bear Peak, he carried her wrapped up as we found the others or Duke would have smelled her."

Jenna frowned. "I hope Jo does better than Rio and Rowley." She chewed on her bottom lip. "They had no luck finding either of our suspects. Both were conveniently missing when they went to interview them. They hung around for an hour or so at each location and then changed tack and hunted down Elliot Cummings but he was a no-show for work. The manager told them Cummings called in to do a later shift because he wasn't feeling well, but he wasn't at home either. Next, they drove all over Twisted Limbs Trail looking for Hank Maxwell's cabin without luck. When I spoke to them, they were hunting down where he works. That's if he has a job. He might be off the grid."

"Why don't you call Jo and see if she has profiled our killer?" Kane headed along Stanton. "She has all the crime scene images and I sent her a copy of the recording we had of the cold case murder."

Jenna made the call and gave Jo as much new information as she had. "All the cold case victims had phones buried with them. Wolfe will download any files he can find and send them to Kalo. All the victims have the same basic injuries as far as Norrell can tell. The MO and disposal of each victim are the same. Three sets of three, and then there's the other grave half dug and abandoned. There's no sign of Freya Richardson's body. She's out there somewhere but *where* is the question."

"*And they form a triangle? Could the triangle be inside a circle?*" Jo's fingers flew over the keyboard, making a slight tapping sound. "*Triangles are everywhere and mean many things to many people, but if he is enclosing them in a circle, it could be a cleansing ritual for him. In other words, taking Halloween to the point of obsession. In his mind, the victims made him kill them or they deserved to die, and it's his way of setting things straight. You know they like to blame the victims.*" She stood and Jenna could hear footsteps on tile and the clink of a cup. "*I've been working on the files all day and* have a couple of conclusions. The recording is harrowing but exceptionally useful. At the end he says, 'Happy Halloween.' This is significant. Inside his mind, sending three souls across the opening between life and death at All Hallows' might hold a significant meaning to him. Maybe his initial trigger happened at Halloween. Maybe one of his psychoses is obsessive-compulsive disorder, and because he killed three that night he must murder three every year." She poured coffee and Jenna could hear her adding the fixings. "The time between means nothing. They can stop killing for a time because something else more important took their attention, the scene for the fantasy wasn't right, sickness, jail, marriage, lack of opportunity… or he was killing elsewhere. It's nothing we can nail down right now. It will take time. The evidence from the local law enforcement is practically nonexistent. Finding this guy before he strikes again is going to be difficult. There is one thing. Did you hear the heavy breathing and the pause before the victim reacted? I figure he likes to scare them. He could well be wearing a mask. The voice at the end is very muffled and yet the victim is clear enough. We'll keep working on it and keep you posted."

Glancing at Kane as they stopped outside the office, she raised an eyebrow at him. "Okay, Jo, thanks for your help. We'll call if we have any more info." She disconnected and turned to Kane. "That gives us an idea of who we're dealing with, someone obsessed with Halloween who has OCD." She sighed. "Oh, this is going to be a nightmare."

"We'll catch him." Kane smiled at her. "They always make a mistake. The first one was coming back to Black Rock Falls."

Jenna climbed from the Beast and collected her things. Kane had unclipped Duke and was carrying the box of Thermos flasks to the office. When Duke barked, Jenna turned to look down Main, scanning the sidewalk. Nothing seemed out of place, but when Duke barked again, Kane came back through the glass doors to the office and stood on the sidewalk until she joined him. "What's up with Duke?"

"Dunno." Kane rubbed the dog's ears. "Maybe he smells something. Duke, seek."

The dog headed down Main and stopped at the first alleyway, sitting and barking. Jenna hurried alongside Kane. "He's found something."

Searching her pockets for a spare pair of examination gloves, she pulled them on as Kane moved in front of her, weapon drawn.

He cleared the alleyway and turned to look at her. "Clear." He holstered his weapon and walked to Duke. "What is it, boy? What do you smell? Seek."

Duke moved to the first dumpster just inside the alleyway and sat down, his soft brown eyes alert and his tail wagging.

"I don't smell a corpse and after so long Freya would be well into decomposition." Kane pulled on gloves and pushed open the lid to the dumpster. "I see something." He turned around and picked up a crate left beside the dumpster and then dropped it. He stepped onto the crate and reached inside coming out with a blood-stained pillowcase.

When Duke barked and did his happy dance, Jenna patted him. "Good boy." She looked at Kane. "Would Duke still be able to recognize Freya Richardson's scent?"

"I have no idea, but he could track you or me by using our names, so I guess the answer is in the affirmative." He held the pillowcase between thumb and finger keeping it well away from his body. "There's an evidence bag inside my jacket pocket." Kane stepped down from the crate. "Grab it for me, will you?"

Sliding her hand inside Kane's jacket, Jenna found the evidence bag and opened it, holding it wide for Kane to push the pillowcase inside. "Anything else in there?"

"Nope and it was on the top. There's only the smell of garbage not a dead body and most of it is cardboard. It's a recycling bin." Kane lifted the evidence bag and examined the contents. "The bin is emptied in the morning. Does the killer know this? And why dump it here, why didn't he bury it with the body like the others? The bloodstains are dry and have been dry for a time. If he'd screwed the pillowcase up and thrown it inside the dumpster while wet, the blood pattern would be different, like a tie-dyed piece of material. The blood marks are all down one end, which would indicate a cut throat."

A cold wind whistled through the alleyway, raising goosebumps on Jenna's flesh and making the skeletons hanging from the streetlights dance. There could be only one other conclusion. Swallowing hard, she shuddered. "Unless he hasn't buried her yet."

TWENTY-ONE

Wendy stepped from the shower and went to wipe the mirror and froze, gaping in horror at the words written in the condensation: *I'm coming for you*. Each letter dripped tears, running down the glass as it melted away. With no weapon, nothing around her for protection, she snatched up the deodorant and held it out before her. Trembling with fear, she peeked around the bathroom door and into her bedroom. The closet door hung open and she could plainly see there was nobody inside. The bed was too low for anyone to crawl under. The door to her room was slightly ajar and the smell of freshly brewed coffee crept up the hallway. Her legs went to Jell-O and she couldn't breathe. Someone had turned on the coffee machine.

Naked and vulnerable, she needed to act now. Staring through the open crack in the door, she waited. Nothing moved in the hallway. Too scared to move, she waited a few more seconds and watched intently. She had one option to save herself and acted on instinct. Taking a deep breath, she dashed across the room, shut and locked the door as silently as possible. Breathing heavily, she leaned against it listening. All she could hear was the pulse pounding in her ears and the wind whistling through the trees outside her window.

Panting, she stared in disbelief at the clothes laid out on the bed. The order she'd placed them had been reversed. Shaking, she looked all around, making sure no one was in the room with her. Goosebumps rose on her flesh as the terrible feeling of being watched consumed her. Someone had been inside her room while she'd taken a shower. Heart pounding, she scanned the bedroom, noticing how her things had been rearranged. Her shoes had been neatly placed in the bottom of the closet. Her bottles of perfume in a line on her nightstand and the photograph of her and Susie Hartwig at the rodeo had been placed face down. The thought of someone touching her things made her skin crawl. She choked down a sob. Had they been watching her in the shower? What did they mean by *I'm coming to get you*? What kind of sick freak did something like that? Was it some type of creepy Halloween joke?

The floorboards creaked and panic gripped her by the throat. Someone was still inside the house. This time, her weapon was in her purse on the kitchen table ready to take with her when she left for work. That wouldn't help her now and there was no way she'd set foot outside her room. She grabbed her phone from the nightstand and called Rio. He'd insisted she call him direct if anything strange happened again. Stumbling over her words and gripping the phone like a life jacket, she explained what had happened. "I've locked myself in my bedroom. I heard the floorboards creak and I'm too scared to go and look who's out there."

"Okay, we're close by." Rio's voice was calm. *"Stay where you are. I'll be there with Deputy Rowley in a few minutes. Stay on the line."*

Heart pounding, Wendy put the phone on speaker and dragged on her clothes. She sat on the bed, phone in one hand and spray can of deodorant in the other. Her damp hair leaked water in rivulets down her cheeks but she ignored it, keeping her attention fixed on the door.

"We're outside your house now. We'll take a look around." She heard doors slamming and footsteps. *"There's no sign of forced entry, ah, but your back door is open. We're coming inside."*

Terrified, Wendy listened closely, hearing shouts of "Clear" coming through the speaker. Footsteps came closer and there was a knock on the door.

"It's Deputy Rio. You can unlock the door now." He disconnected.

Wendy swung open the door and, seeing Rio and Rowley in the hallway, tossed the deodorant onto the bed and jumped into Rio's arms. "Am I glad to see you." She clung to him and then looked from one puzzled face to the other. "Did you see anyone?"

"Nope, and you should really lock your doors when you take a shower." Rio raised one dark eyebrow, straightened, and stood her away from him. "After seeing a prowler the other night, you can't be too careful."

Blinking, Wendy stared at him. "I locked all the doors before I came upstairs. With my neighbors away, I'm being extra careful." From their expressions, she wondered if they believed her. "Come and see for yourselves. Someone wrote the words *I'm coming to get you* on my mirror."

Leading the way into the bathroom she gaped at the mirror as nothing remained. The reflection was clear. Shaking her head, Wendy turned to the deputies. "It *was* there and there are other things. My clothes had been rearranged, shoes placed in the closet, my perfume bottles all lined up."

"Okay." Rowley made notes and nodded. "Best you come take a look around the house and see if anything else is out of place."

Wendy followed them through the house. As the smell of

coffee reached her, she stopped midstride. "The coffee machine has been filled and switched on. I'm heading for work. I wouldn't make coffee. Someone else did that." She glanced around moving from one room to another. "And all the dishes are in the dishwasher. I didn't do that."

"So, you're saying, that someone came into your house, tidied the place, put on a pot of coffee, wrote 'I'm coming to get you' on your bathroom mirror, and then left?" Rio gave her a long skeptical stare. "Don't you figure that sounds a little sketchy, Wendy?" He sighed. "You sure you're not allowing all this Halloween hoo-ha to get under your skin?"

Astounded, Wendy glared at him. "No, I am not. I don't have an overactive imagination. Someone was here and I did see writing on my mirror. Explain that."

"There's no evidence." Rowley glanced at Rio. "Best you call in our position, the sheriff is expecting us back at the office." He waited for Rio to leave and turned to her. "We'll always come by if you're in trouble, but if this is a way of spending more time with Rio, he's already taken."

Outraged, Wendy's cheeks burned with embarrassment. She hadn't meant to jump into Rio's arms, but she'd been so glad to see them. "I know that, but someone was here. You have to believe me. Trust me, I don't have any designs on Rio. I have my own circle of admirers. You've known me for years, Jake. I'd never do such a thing."

"Okay." Rowley removed his hat and ran a hand through his thick hair, making it stick up in all directions. He pushed the hat back on his head and nodded. "If you have any more problems call 911. I figure someone is trying to spook you for a joke, is all. Usually when someone is out to do you harm, they don't drop by first to warn you and, trust me, they never drop by to clean the house first." He gave her a long look. "Does anyone have a set of keys? A close friend maybe just having some Halloween fun?"

Wendy folded her arms across her chest. "No. Everything I've told you is true. Someone was in my house."

"I believe you." Rowley nodded and his expression became serious. "Do you want me to report this to the sheriff? I can take a statement down at the office if you want to report it as a break-in."

Shaking her head, Wendy stared at him. He didn't believe her either. "No, what can you report? Wendy is imagining things? We found no evidence of a break-in? The stupid woman had left her back door open?" She sighed. "I'm sorry to have troubled you. I'll go and lock the back door, and then I need to get ready for work. I'm running late."

"I locked the door when we came inside." Rowley smiled at her. "No one is here, and I'll drive around the block to make sure no one is hanging around before we head back to the office. We'll drive by a few times to make sure you're safe as well. You'll be fine." He headed for the door.

Dismayed, Wendy stared after him. Why didn't they believe her? She went into the kitchen and switched off the coffee pot, collected her purse, and headed back to her room to fix her hair. From now on, her weapon would be in reach, and if someone broke into her home again, she'd take them down. The idea the deputies actually believed she'd made a false report to get attention from Rio riled her. As if she needed him, when Chance had asked her to the Halloween Ball. When she arrived with the buff, handsome rodeo cowboy, she'd show them. A shiver of concern slid over her. The problem was someone had been inside her house. Everything she'd said had been the truth. Suddenly very afraid, she swallowed hard. Now if someone broke into her house again and she called for help, would anyone come running?

TWENTY-TWO

Jenna waited for her deputies to file into her office and sit down. "Okay, what do you have for me. Any updates?"

"Not on the suspects, although as we were in the area, we did a drive by of Wendy's house." Rio straightened in his chair. "Nothing to report. We drove around the block and made sure the house was secure. It's all good."

"Good follow-up." Kane smiled at him. "Did you hunt down anything on any of the suspects? Priors?"

"Yeah, we did the usual checks but nothing of interest came up." Rio frowned. "Stark has a sealed juvie file, so something happened. He sounds a little creepy to me. We've been hunting him down all day and keep missing him."

Leaning on her desk, Jenna stared at him. "Did you discover anything else about him? Where he lives, his place of employment?"

"Yeah, he's a postal worker." Rowley looked at his notes. "He brings mail into our post office and takes mail out of town. This is why he's hard to pin down. Some days he handles the mailbags, takes them to the train in Blackwater, other days he does pickups of parcels. He works a few different jobs."

"He lives out near the Triple Z Bar in a cabin in the forest."
Rio sighed. "We searched all over but couldn't find a cabin.
Same with Hank Maxwell, the one who called in on the hotline.
He said he lives on Twisted Limbs Trail in a cabin." He threw
up his hands. "Rowley knows the forest and we found nothing.
There is a Twisted Limbs Trail and we walked two miles and
never found a cabin. I called the number from the hotline log
and it went to voicemail. I've been calling all day."

Jenna leaned back and sighed. "What about Elliot
Cummings? Did you make any headway at finding him?

"Nope, we went by his house on Pine three times during the
day and he's not there." Rio frowned. "He told his boss he was
sick but maybe it was an excuse to go fishing or something?"

"Maybe, but not being able to find any of them is unusual."
Kane stood and filled the coffee machine. "They'll hold until
the morning. We don't have a body and we only have circumstantial evidence at best. Cummings is only a vague witness to a
fast-moving truck, so hardly a suspect, although I'd like to speak
to him. Sometimes people see more than they think, and I have
ways of extracting information. In the meantime, we had the
unpleasant task of exhuming five bodies today. Jo believes Freya
Richardson could be a victim of the Halloween Slasher. She's
listened to the tape and studied all the crime scenes attributed
to him from seven years ago. If she's correct about it being the
same man, and I figure she is, he's going to murder two more
people over the next week or so before Halloween."

Nodding, Jenna looked from one to the other. "Get out the
map of Bear Peak and grid-search it using the drone. You'll be
hunting down anything that could be a gravesite. It will be
walking distance from a fire road, so that will narrow it down. If
you find anything at all, get the coordinates and we'll go look."
She thought for a beat. "If we find Freya Richardson, we'll need
to leave her undisturbed, horrible as it sounds, because if he has
another murder planned, he'll be back to dig the grave. When

he returns, we'll have him and hopefully prevent another murder."

"How do you plan to do that?" Rowley's brow wrinkled into a frown. "We can't camp out there twenty-four/seven. He'll see us for sure."

"We'll set up trail cams with motion sensors. Around the grave." Kane leaned against the counter with the coffee machine gurgling behind him. "I'll set them to alert me on my phone. We can position them in all directions and on the fire road as well. If we can get the plate on his vehicle, we'll have his name."

Knowing Kane would have a plan, Jenna smiled. "The beauty of it is that we don't have to charge in making a noise. It takes, what, four or five hours to dig a grave? We can sneak in and surround him." She pushed papers into a folder on her desk and dropped it into a drawer. "We'll be heading over shortly to see what Wolfe has found, so if you find anything interesting, call me. You've been out all day, like us, so don't forget to take your regular break. I need you both fresh in case we have a breakthrough."

Rio and Rowley nodded, stood, and left the room, closing the door behind them.

"The phone they found looks perfect. It hasn't been damaged by the damp. The killer obviously wanted it to remain intact, but why?" Kane poured coffee and then bent to take food out of the refrigerator. "We have cherry pie. Want me to warm it in the microwave?"

A chilling thought went through Jenna's mind and she stared at him. "Yeah sure, thanks." Her mind went straight back to what Kane had just mentioned. "He wanted to keep the phones intact." She swallowed hard. "You don't believe he wanted to call the graves, do you?"

"Nothing would surprise me anymore." Kane slid two wedges of pie into the microwave and then placed two cups of coffee on Jenna's desk. "When we get more phones analyzed we'll be able to check, but surely he'd know the batteries would die within a few days."

Sipping her coffee to quell her clenching stomach, she grimaced. "Unless he's calling the recently buried body to tell her that she has a friend coming? It's possible. You know how sick psychopaths can be. I'll never understand why they do what they do. It's all part of whatever delusion is playing through their heads. I guess it must be like being stuck inside a game. They have to keep replaying the same stage until they can finish... but they never finish."

"Until we finish them." Kane placed the pie and silverware onto the desk and sat down. "If their heads are like that, I'm not surprised how many choose death by cop. Dying would be a relief." He shrugged. "There are so many different species of the beast. Some like you described, I could pity. The ones who brag about their kills are in a nasty class of their own."

Jenna shook her head. "I don't feel sorry for any of them. Call me hard, but when I look at their victims all I want to do is remove their killers from society. They're the silent pestilence destroying lives and families. That's why I became sheriff, to stop them." She looked into Kane's eyes. "Underneath, we are much the same, Dave. We have a common goal and that's to protect people, no matter what the cost to our own peace of mind."

"Amen to that." Kane dug into his pie.

TWENTY-THREE

I slip into the forest, taking a well-used track and have no worries about being seen. Anyone passing would just see a regular guy hiking and enjoying his day. No one will take any notice. I could carry a gun or an ax without attracting a second glance. Many go in search of dead trees to collect firewood, and being armed is a given when bears are out hunting for food. I can drag things back and forth without anyone calling the sheriff because people carry their kills to their trucks and usually head for the meat-processing plant. It's nice to be regarded as normal, even if the carcass I carry is human. Who would know? Not in all my years of moving bodies has anyone questioned me or commented on the stink of blood. Why should they? The stink of death around the forest in hunting season is familiar, as is seeing hunters splashed with blood after field dressing a kill.

Never once have I been stopped by a game warden to ask to see my license or my sheet of tags. They are all too busy inspecting kills to bother about me. I'm following a trail that has become familiar now. I hunted down the perfect place to leave my offering, my blood sacrifice guaranteed to keep me safe. It has worked for a long time. I've never fallen sick, broken a bone, or had an argument with anyone. In fact, what had happened in Black Rock Falls seven years ago saved my life, and now I'll pay my debt. If I'd been in the forest over Halloween that year, someone would have noticed me, as at the time the place was crawling with people. Disasters bring people together, and I don't appreciate onlookers. What I do is private, sacred, and so I'd packed up and hightailed it out of town. Pushing back old memories, I move into the shady clearing and smile at the mound of dirt so carefully concealed with fall leaves and pine needles. "Hey, Freya, I'll have a new friend for you tonight. Do you know how lucky you are to be selected for my offering? Maybe I'll call you later and tell you all about it, but right now I have a grave to finish."

I move into the shadows to retrieve my shovel, hidden beneath a clump of bushes, and set to work. My mind dances ahead and adrenaline races my heart. Later tonight I'll watch, wait, and then slide into the house of my next offering. She'll be clean and fragrant just as all the others. That part of the ritual is crucial and it's so incredible that all the women comply. It's as if they know it's their turn and offer themselves willingly. Maybe they do? The fear is essential, the passing over in terror is a crucial part of the sacrifice that ensures my life will remain uncomplicated. My shoulders ache, but I keep digging as the hours pass by and I'm driven to work hard, heedless of the blisters on my hands. How many graves have I dug? The turning of the soil, the hardship is all part of it. I must toil and sweat to prove myself worthy, and each three I offer will give me nine more years. I chuckle. "I'm going to live forever."

TWENTY-FOUR

After dropping Duke by Wolfe's office, Jenna followed Kane to Wolfe's laboratory. When she flashed her card to gain entrance, she found him at a desk. On the desk he had a line of phones all attached to chargers. When he glanced up as they walked inside, she smiled at him. "Hey, Shane, found anything interesting?"

"*Disturbing* would be a better description. I haven't worked on all of the files yet, but I've been able to charge the phones—well, one of them. In the oldest grave is an MP3 player. None of the phones had passwords. Maybe they were removed by the killer." Wolfe raised both eyebrows. "Special care was taken to preserve them and I've not only been able to extract all the content on the first three, but I have the names of the owners, and although Norrell hasn't confirmed the identity of the bodies yet, we have the first four names. It seems the phone we found with each body belongs to the previous victim, so the MP3 player in the oldest grave must come from one of a group of victims we haven't discovered yet."

Trying to get her head around the implications, Jenna

frowned. "There's more than six? How far does this go back? The forest overgrows everything. It's only since the floods we've been discovering a ton of things buried in the past. This is why Blackhawk has been grid-searching the forest, but he is only one man. It will take him ten lifetimes to search everywhere." She stared at Wolfe, not really seeing him. The information was just too weird. "Let me get this right. The killer made recordings of each murder using the previous victim's phone? Why do you figure he did that?"

"I can only imagine when he began his murder spree, he had the idea to record the murders, but wouldn't risk using a phone or device he'd purchased." Wolfe cleared his throat. "There is another very disturbing aspect to this case as well. When we checked the phone logs from Lydia's missing phone, we discovered she'd made a call to the phone in her grave, which is owned by Josephine Wade. It obviously wasn't picked up and there was no message. Lydia's phone hasn't been used since. If this is the Halloween Slasher, there's a good chance we'll find Lydia's phone in Freya's grave."

"You're saying, the killer called the grave from the victim's missing phone? He called Josephine Wade's phone?" Kane frowned. "How could you know it was the killer? People would be calling a missing girl, right?"

"Once we identified the victim as Lydia Ellis, I called the sheriff in Louan to notify the next of kin. The second body is Josephine Wade, as we surmised as she's the owner of the phone in Lydia's grave. I called the sheriff's office again and asked them if the victim's parents knew a girl by the name of Josephine Wade out of Black Rock Falls. Luckily when Lydia went missing, they compiled a list of friends and acquaintances, anyone who might have seen her. They still had the list and Josephine wasn't on it. They lived in different counties."

"They were killed around the same time. How do you know

Lydia didn't call Josephine before she died?" Kane rubbed the back of his neck. "Maybe they met and she hadn't told anyone?"

"Well, this is where it gets creepy." Wolfe leaned forward in his chair. "The log puts the call hours after the time of the recording of the murder. Josephine Wade was already dead, and from the current evidence, so was Lydia."

Sickened, Jenna ran a hand down her face. "So, murder isn't enough for this guy. He has to call to make sure they're dead? Oh, what type of sick freak have we got in town this time?"

"I can only offer you the facts. I figure you need to use Jo's expertise on profiling this guy." Wolfe shrugged. "The third girl's phone was in Josephine's grave. It belonged to Sadie Bonner out of Blackwater. I'm still waiting for dental records to confirm, but we figure she's the third victim from the first gravesite."

Shaking her head in dismay, Jenna swallowed hard. "Have you listened to the recordings?"

"Yeah, but only two of them so far and they're the same MO. He names the women same as before. His voice is muffled." Wolfe's eyebrows met in a deep frown. "It's a frenzied attack to cause pain and fear, and then when they turn to run from him, he cuts their throats. It's like the same tape played over, apart from the victims. They are the only variation. It's like being there watching the attack. Like I said, it's very disturbing." He sighed. "I'm heading over to speak to Norrell to see if what I heard matches the injuries sustained by the victims, like the first one."

Jenna swallowed the bile creeping up her throat. "We want to be there too. I need to know more about the killer."

"Do any of the victims act like they know this guy?" Kane leaned back against a counter. "I'm trying to figure out his motive and it sounds ritualistic to me. We need to find out more about this type of thing. It's all through history. Maybe something this guy read or witnessed triggered something in his brain." He looked at Jenna. "It's unusual for a serial killer to only kill sets of three women at Halloween. There has to be more to this guy."

As usual, Kane was covering every angle and Jenna nodded. "Yeah, if we can discover that part of the puzzle, we might be able to prevent him killing girl number two." She looked from one to the other. "Don't stonewall me, either of you. I know this is the Halloween Slasher, the details of the crime scenes have never been leaked. When I listened to the recording of Lydia's death, I could have been there when Freya died. This maniac is following a pattern and I don't believe for one second, he stopped killing for seven years. If we dig deeper, we'll probably discover he's been murdering women all over."

"Maybe but he hasn't been burying them in threes where anyone can find them, although I do recall cases where three sex workers went missing, but they were found dumped in the same area alongside a river." Kane rubbed his chin. "Kalo could hunt down sets of three homicides around Halloween all over the US in the past seven years. I figure we should ask him."

Jenna nodded. "I agree. We'll call in the troops on this one. Six cold case files and one missing person is too much for us to handle. We'll organize a conference call when we get back to the office." She looked at Wolfe. "I'd appreciate your input, if you have time. Say, five-thirty?"

"Sure." Wolfe stood. "Y'all coming to see what Norrell has found?"

"Before we go, can you upload the recordings on the server so I can listen to them?" Kane folded his arms across his chest. "I'd like to use them as a reference when we're looking at the victims' remains."

"Already done." Wolfe smiled at him. "I'll upload everything I discover as I find it." He led them from the lab.

"Thanks." Kane glanced at Jenna. "I know you'll want to listen, but I can give you a report."

Knowing he was concerned the recordings would trigger her PTSD, she shook her head. "I'm fine, Dave. Listening only makes me more determined to catch this guy."

TWENTY-FIVE

Norrell glanced up from the remains on the gurney as Wolfe entered her examination room. She'd decided to keep all the bodies together in the one place. Comparing the injuries sustained by each victim was crucial. She nodded to Jenna and Kane. "When I came to Black Rock Falls, Shane mentioned we'd have months of nothing and weeks of long hours. He wasn't joking. I believe this is the first time I've had six sets of remains from the same case."

"I know it's early to be bothering you." Wolfe gave her an apologetic look. "After listening to the recordings of the last two victims from the first burial site, I wanted to see if what I heard on the phone in Josephine Wade's grave correlates to her injuries."

Having only opened the wrappings of the second three bodies to extract the devices, Norrell gave Wolfe a direct stare. "Forensic anthropology takes time. I do understand the need for expedience, but against my better judgment, I've rushed the recovery of the remains." She looked at Jenna and Kane. "You do understand I need to clean the bones so I can examine them to my satisfaction. Once that is done, I'll analyze the remains and establish a biological profile of each individual before I can begin to interpret what trauma occurred. When this is completed, I'll be able to establish the type and extent of the injuries." She sighed. "So far, I've skipped all of the above to match dental records and it seems we're using the phones in the graves to establish a time of death. It's like working backward."

"I understand completely." Jenna pulled on surgical gloves with a snap. "In normal circumstances, we'd leave you to complete the examination without interruption, but as these cases directly reflect on a current case, we need information yesterday." She glanced at Wolfe. "As Shane will explain, we believe the man who killed these six women is killing again. We found a bloody crime scene, no body, and the woman's phone is missing. We've tried to track the phone, but without proof of death or probable cause, we can't get a warrant." She sighed. "If it's the same killer, he plans to murder three women before Halloween."

A cold chill slid down Norrell's spine and she nodded. "I see." She indicated to Matty, one of her assistants, to pull out the remains. "It's normal after this time for the decomposition process to remove the flesh from the skeleton but as the bodies were wrapped and naked, the bones are relatively clean. I found remains of hair and jewelry, but apart from the phone, there was no other personal items." She went to the second gurney. "These are the remains of Josephine Wade. The phone we found with her is owned by Sadie Bonner but has a recording of Josephine's murder. We know this as the killer mentions her name. If we follow the pattern, we can presume Sadie Bonner is body number three. The phone we found with her belongs to Cora Griffin. Wolfe has yet to listen to that recording but it's likely to be the murder of Sadie Bonner."

"The first recording you heard before was Lydia Ellis's

murder." Wolfe stared at Jenna. "I know it's complicated, but as we go forward, the phones we've found appear to be owned by the previous victim."

"Oh, I understand." Jenna turned her attention to Norrell. "What I'd like to know is, when you examine the remains, do they fit with what you hear on the recordings?"

Wishing she could remove the recordings from her memory, Norrell nodded. "Yeah, it's morbidly intriguing, but if you keep a professional, detached attitude while listening and viewing the remains, it's easy to map out the injuries to the bones." She looked at Wolfe. "Do you want to play the recording for Josephine and I'll walk you through the damage to the bones?"

"That's what I'm here to do." Wolfe ran his gaze over Jenna and Kane. "Ready?"

"Yeah." Jenna nodded and stepped closer.

The recording started and Norrell moved closer to the gurney. She lifted one of the scapulars from the skeleton laid out on the gurney and turned it over in her hand. "You can hear her gasp of fear and then this would have been the first strike. She had her back to him and we can clearly see sharp force trauma consistent with the tip of a hunting blade." She replaced the bone and picked up a rib to display the nick in the bone. "Same here. He didn't intend on killing her outright or the cuts through the bone would be deeper and executed with more force."

"Why isn't she screaming?" Jenna glanced at Kane. "Someone is stabbing her."

"If she'd just stepped out of the shower and saw him behind her in the reflection in the mirror, the shock of being stabbed could have stopped her." Kane shrugged. "He could also have his hand over her mouth. Both injuries Norrell described would be extremely painful. From the thumps on the recording, he'd gained control in seconds."

Nodding, Norrell smiled at him. He was intelligent and from his comments had knowledge above and beyond that of a deputy. "Yes, so I'd say a powerful man who knows how to immobilize and cause pain. At this point, Josephine turned toward him, either he spins her to face him or she turns to fight back. We can hear her protests, no screams, but she wants him to stop. The defense marks on both the radius and ulna... ah, both of her forearms are considerable. Lacerations that cut deep into the bone I would say proves she's protecting her chest. This is when he gets angry. He doesn't like them fighting back. If you listen closely..." She glanced at Wolfe. "Rewind it one minute. He makes a growling sound, an impatient sound, like he's finished playing with her. Then comes a frenzied attack and finally he tells her to look into the mirror. She's still alive at this point. He attacks but knows how to keep them alive. He is aware of the lethal strike points on a body. Hear his voice now—satisfied, almost dreamlike. This must be the ultimate for him. He wants her to see him cutting her throat."

"Sadistic." Jenna had turned sheet-white. "I've heard enough." She stepped away and leaned against the counter. "If it's not bad enough finding bodies and discovering through autopsies the extent of the victim's suffering, this takes murder to a whole new level."

"These recordings were made to be found." Kane moved to her side. "He wants to shock. He wants to share his experience. He's saying, *Look what I did right under your noses, and you couldn't stop me.*"

Listening to the reasoning between Jenna and Kane intrigued Norrell. Her part was usually long reports, and it wasn't often she became involved in the why a person was murdered. She looked from one to the other. "I would imagine the other recordings are much the same."

"I figure he follows the same pattern." Wolfe looked from Jenna to Kane. "What I'm seeing here is a slight variation. I'd say, if they fought back, he killed them fast. If they screamed, he covered their mouths." He straightened. "Moving to the Freya case, I analyzed the swabs taken from the shower recess and found slight traces of her blood, no hair or anything else. So, we are correct to assume he took a shower. There were no imprints of bloody footprints, or indication he might have dropped bloody clothes to undress. I figure he murdered her naked and used the towels to step on during the attack. He likely bundled the bloody towels in with the body and took the wet towels he'd used with him. Then he wrapped the victim in the bed linen, dressed and left with the body."

"Yeah, we know he dragged the body from the bathroom into the bedroom." Jenna folded her arms over her chest. "The same drag marks are in all the cold case crime scene images as well. He knows his way around the house, which makes me believe he knows his victims or has been inside before. The entire thing is so slick. He breaks in, starts a recording, and is so confident he strips naked, sets up the bed linen for the body, and then murders his victim."

"He's cold and calculated." Kane stared into space. "He believes he can't be caught. If this is ritualistic, he could believe someone or something is watching over him. This is Jo's field of expertise, I'm only guessing. I've never read about anyone like this before."

Norrell exchanged a glance with Wolfe. They had so much work ahead of them, detailing each specific damage to the bones of six victims. The detective part of who and why was Jenna and Kane's job. She smiled at them. "Is there anything else you need? I'll keep working on the remains. Shane has the jewelry I discovered, and as soon as we can check out the other dental records, he'll be in touch."

"Okay, thanks." Jenna straightened and walked out of the door with Kane close behind.

Norrell smiled at Wolfe. "They are intense. So different on duty to off duty."

"Professional, yeah." Wolfe moved to her side. "Great people. I'd trust them with my life. Kane would take a bullet for all of us. He's that kind of guy. Right now, it's a rush against time. We know what's coming and, trust me, they'll do everything they can to stop it happening."

TWENTY-SIX

Finding it difficult to juggle so many cases, Jenna pushed both hands through her hair and sighed. "I've found Sadie Bonner. She went missing from Blackwater seven years ago. I've sent a request to the local sheriff to give us everything he has on the case. I've put him in contact with Norrell, so the moment she confirms ID he can inform the next of kin. I did get some useful information. She worked in a pharmacy at the counter, so was in contact with plenty of people from all walks of life. So, her job didn't help narrow down her recent contacts prior to her disappearance. She went missing from a blood-spattered house on her parent's regular Saturday date night. If it's the same guy, he must spend all his free time stalking his victims."

"People who are creatures of habit make the easiest targets for crime." Kane sighed. "Those who walk their dog at six each night or always buy groceries on a Wednesday or whatever." He ran a hand through his sleek black hair and shrugged. "It doesn't take too much time, to set up a camera. With the technology we have now, a criminal doesn't even need to leave home."

Jenna's phone chimed. It was Wolfe. "We've only been back at the office a few minutes. Do you have a breakthrough?"

"Yeah, of sorts." Wolfe paused a beat. *"The pillowcase you found has Freya's blood on it. It just came through as a match. I found nothing else of interest, apart from some saliva and a few hairs. The saliva is the victim's. The hair matches the color profile, but there are no roots to use as a match."*

"This guy is in town and close by." Kane shook his head slowly. "If Duke hadn't caught Freya's scent, we'd have never found the pillowcase before the garbage was collected." He glanced at Jenna. "I called the owner of the landfill and asked him to check the contents of all the dumpsters from along Main as they come in. He said he'll give it priority and get his crew on it when they arrive in the morning. So we'll see if the Halloween Slasher has changed his method of disposal."

Jenna held up a hand. "Jump on your laptop, Shane. The call from Jo and Carter is coming through."

As the conference call opened up on her screen, she smiled at the faces. Jo, Carter, and Bobby Kalo popped up, as did Wolfe and Kane. "Thanks for coming at such short notice." Jenna gave them a rundown on the evidence to date and handed it over to Wolfe to give his and Norrell's findings.

When Wolfe had finished, she looked at Bobby Kalo. "Bobby, did you discover any other sets of three murders during the seven years between the last body, Lydia Ellis from Louan, and the current bloodbath we found at Freya Richardson's apartment?"

"Too many, and they're spread all over the country." Kalo frowned. "Chicago had four sets of three; six went missing never to be found in Washington; there was nine over three years in Colorado. Same thing in most of them, a bloody crime scene and no body. He could be responsible for all of them or none of them." He shrugged. "Without a body, we have no proof. There have been sets of three bodies dumped all over, some on remote beaches in sand dunes. Bodies have been found in barrels in landfills but nothing specifically has been linked to the Halloween Slasher."

Amazed, Jenna turned to Jo. "After listening to the tapes, Dave is convinced these killings are ritualistic. The killer has a fixation on Halloween. Have you had any more thoughts on the case?"

"I haven't stopped running different possibilities through my mind." Jo tucked a lock of hair behind one ear. "I can see from the crime scenes and listening to the two recordings unearthed to date that he follows the same pattern." She glanced at her notes. "Shane, do you see familiarities between the injuries?"

"Yeah, I do." Wolfe cleared his throat. "Although we've only listened to two of the recordings, it's as if the killer is following a well-rehearsed pattern of strikes. I've examined the first three cold case victims and, apart from defensive wounds, they are the same. Yeah, he is reliving the same murder over and over."

"The showering prior to murder is a part of his ritual." Jo stared down the camera. "He needs them naked and clean. This is typical in ritualistic murders. Cleanliness has so many reasons, mainly to wash away sins. Often sacrificed people were bathed in milk to make them more pleasing to the gods."

"Breaking into a house while the victim is in the shower is genius. No one would hear him. He'd have the jump on them." Carter looked casual leaning back in his chair, twisting a pen in his fingers. "I did research on the three lots of three. So many rituals from past and present, not just religious but bad juju as well. They range from making it rain to extending life with all stops in between. We can't pin this down to one exact ritual. We figure he's taken parts from many, and used all the bits he considers meet his criteria." He scratched his cheek. "Over to Jo. She has an idea on his angle."

"Yeah, I do. Let me see." Jo's hair spilled over her face as she studied her notes and then she lifted her chin. "He's in control.

If this is ritualistic, he only kills three times each year. I'd say he spends the rest of the year finding suitable women to murder. I do believe he continued during the seven-year break."

"Seven years ago, you had a weather event." Kalo waved a red lollipop in one hand and smiled. "Mudslides all over, it rained for months. His killing spree would have been interrupted that Halloween. Maybe he moved away and got a job in another county or state?"

Impressed, Jenna nodded. "Thanks, Bobby. Jo, what else have you discovered?"

"Not discovered, I have reason to believe these murders at this time of year are self-serving." She twirled a coffee cup in her fingers. "As in he needs an excuse to kill, so in his mind he's used old rituals to validate his kills. Maybe he has a disease, but I doubt it. The sacrifice, if you like, of a woman just out of the shower tells me he's cleansing himself, making himself new again. The Halloween timing would validate that as well because we might look at Halloween as when the barrier between life and death opens and ghouls come through. We make jack-o'-lanterns to scare them away, while others believe it is a time for new beginnings and welcome the spirits as guides for the future."

"The thing is"—Carter leaned forward in his chair—"Halloween doesn't mean sacrifice, so this guy has his rituals screwed up, and although Kalo and I have been trying to match up what he's doing, we can't give you a positive answer."

Glad of the information, Jenna nodded. "That's okay."

"I figure threes are symbolic of a circle of life." Kane stared into the camera with intensity. "Rituals and cleansing. I see it this way: he needs to kill. Like Jo said, he needs an excuse, so maybe he's worried about how long he can go before killing again. Maybe he was out of control at one time and came close to being apprehended. We know by his MO he is smart and understands all about leaving behind evidence." He opened his hands wide. "I figure he thought things through, maybe he searched for something to help him. They don't think logically like we do. They validate things or events in their minds. We couldn't come close to understanding the way of it."

"I agree." Jo leaned forward her expression interested. "How do you see this behavior, Dave?"

"He might have only started the Halloween ritual seven years ago." Kane shrugged. "Previously he could have been killing randomly, because from what I'm seeing, the earliest victim we have wasn't his first kill. It's practiced, almost precision-like. No one can do that at first. Murderers usually panic, overkill, leave evidence behind, strike, and run. This guy is savoring his kills. I mean, how many are cool enough to take a darn shower after creating a bloodbath?" He took a sip of coffee and raised one shoulder in a half shrug. "Maybe he figures, by only killing three at Halloween, he becomes invincible. Since then, he's been killing and not been caught, which for him would validate his belief in the ritual."

"That works for me." Jo nodded.

"Maybe, but it doesn't help catch him, does it?" Carter shrugged and then held up four fingers. "This is what I've deduced. This person blends into society." He bent down one finger. "He's a regular guy and not a loner." He bent down the second finger. "His occupation means he's seen all over town, which makes him invisible. People only notice strangers." He bent down the third finger. "He drives a vehicle he can park where it's not noticed, a local delivery guy for instance." He popped a toothpick in his mouth and grinned around it. "He's a local, and probably moved away for a time, but not far. As Jo will tell you, he has a comfort zone, encompassing Black Rock Falls, Louan, and Blackwater, so those are his current hunting grounds. If there are bodies, they'll be in the other counties. I'd bet my bottom dollar he abandoned the rituals in Black Rock Falls the year you became sheriff and started again close by. He might not have taken his women from those towns, but I figure he brought them into his zone to bury them."

Amazed by the information Carter had collected, Jenna nodded. "We've been researching all deaths and missing people and we came up with no other local crime scenes. We did find women who went missing in waterways across the state. They went swimming or fishing and were never seen again. It's possible a shower wasn't his only way to cleanse his victims."

"I can dig deeper into those disappearances." Kalo smiled at Jenna. "Those around Halloween would be unusual, as its way too cold to swim in these parts."

"Maybe concentrate on boats or fishing. People fall into the rapids and are never seen again." Kane cleared his throat. "We need to consider everything. If this is the Halloween Slasher, he'll strike again soon." He looked directly at Kalo. "Notice any activity on Freya's phone?"

"Nope, I have been watching it." Kalo frowned. "I can't actually track it, but it hadn't moved the day you called. Since then, it's been dead. Someone has blocked the signal." He shrugged. "That's easily done. He only needs to turn it off."

"Wolfe described the attack as frenzied, but it seems the killer didn't want to kill outright." Carter's brow furrowed. "He knows where not to stab to keep someone alive. You've seen that, right, Dave?"

"Yeah." Kane stared at him. "The problem is, that knowledge isn't just military. Any branch of martial arts would teach the same techniques. On the tapes I hear a frenzied attack, but we don't hear the cursing that usually comes with it. The out-of-control maniacal breakdown. This guy is methodical and brutal."

"I can't wait to meet him." Carter grinned at the camera. "You calling us in on this case or not?"

Happy to spread the work, Jenna nodded. "Come on down.

The cottage is stocked and ready. Just remember we have a son now, so no talking shop in front of him."

"Cross my heart and hope to die. I'm looking forward to seeing him again. I promised him a ride in the chopper." Carter nodded. "We'll come in the morning. I'll leave the chopper at Wolfe's building if that's okay. We'll just need a ride for the duration."

"Fine by me." Wolfe smiled.

Jenna nodded. "I'll park my cruiser at the morgue and leave the keys with Wolfe." She blew out a long breath. "Thanks everyone. We'll pick this up tomorrow." She clicked off and turned to Kane. "That went well."

"Yeah, now if Rio and Rowley discovered any burial sites with the drone, we'll be making headway. I assume they found nothing so far as they haven't called in. The suspects seem to be eluding us." Kane smiled at her. "I figure if we can pry Black-hawk away from Wolfe for a time, he might know Twisted Limbs Trail and if there are any cabins hidden away."

Collecting her things into a pile, Jenna stood. "Yeah, we need to hunt down the suspects we have in the Freya Richardson case and hope they give us some information. Right now, without a body and no evidence, we're just chasing our tails. I'm ready to head home. We can work on the case later tonight." She sighed and pulled on her jacket. "*After* Tauri goes to bed. The few hours we have with him each night are so special. Time will go so fast and he'll be off to college before we blink."

"Yeah, I know what you mean." Kane smiled at her and pushed on his Stetson, running his fingers around the brim. "The time with him is very special, especially during our down-time. Those are diamond days that will stay with us forever."

TWENTY-SEVEN

Daisy Lyon had left the Triple Z Roadhouse after finishing work and instead of driving home had headed for Main to look at the Halloween displays. She purchased Halloween candy, knowing that the local kids would be by. They seemed to flock to Pine, although with most of the houses set back from the road and surrounded by trees, she could only imagine it was for the spooky factor more than the candy. She took a few selfies against a backdrop of some of the displays and then climbed back into her vehicle and headed for home. One hand reaching into the bag of candy, she popped some into her mouth before turning around and heading back along Main, taking Stanton, and heading for Pine.

Pine certainly had a different feel around Halloween. Most of the residences, including one house used for the local college, had a variety of terrifying, heartstopping Halloween dummies on their driveways. Some of the tree-shrouded entrances resembled the inside of a ghost train. They had long cobwebs hanging from the surrounding trees with spiders as big as dogs dangling down all over. She grinned but the idea of walking into her dark house sent a chill down her spine. She had installed a sensor light not three weeks previously but it had stopped working. With both her and Tara working long hours, neither had time or spare cash to call an electrician to fix it.

She pulled into her driveway and drove through the dark tunnel of trees, glad when her headlights picked out the house. As she turned, she drove slowly so the beams swept the house and surrounds. No one lurked in the shadows, but her heart raced and a prickling sensation ran over the back of her neck. Getting from her vehicle to the front door in the dark frightened her. She grabbed her purse and the candy. Taking a deep breath, she dashed to the front door, keys in hand. Fumbling with the lock, she fell inside breathing heavily and then turned to use the fob to lock her ride.

The house was silent, cold, and she slapped one hand on the switch, glad when light flooded the room. Breathing heavily, she turned the deadbolt and let out a long breath as she headed for the kitchen. She switched on the light and stared at the room. The place had been a mess when she'd left this morning. She grinned. Tara must have had one of her cleaning frenzies. It wasn't often, most times they were too tired to manage a house-clean more than once a week. The pizza boxes had vanished, the garbage can emptied, and the table and counters wiped down. She opened the refrigerator to find the extra pizza she'd purchased the previous night sitting in its box untouched. Grabbing a few slices, she slipped them onto a plate and popped them into the microwave. She blinked at the coffee machine, clean and filled. Shaking her head, she flicked the switch and pulled the phone out of her pocket to send a text to Tara:

Thanks for cleaning the house. I'll help next time, I promise. I've left you pizza.

She didn't expect a reply, Tara would be working until midnight. They rarely saw each other during the week and most times only on Sundays. She headed up to her bedroom, kicked off her shoes, undressed, and pulled on sweats. Turning around, she frowned. Tara never entered her room when she wasn't there. It was a kind of unwritten law. They always respected each other's privacy, but her bed had been tidied, towels she'd left in the dryer neatly piled on a shelf in the bathroom. She pulled open her closet door and blinked in astonishment. Her shoes were in neat rows, her clothes spread apart on hangers. She sent another text:

Wow! You went all out. You don't need to change the towels in my bathroom or make my bed, but thanks anyway. My turn next Sunday. No arguments.

Shrugging, she headed back to the kitchen. She'd eat first, watch a show on TV, and then shower and go to bed. The nights were cold and she liked her sleep. Work had become one long dragging second to the next. If she had to say, "Do you want fries with that?" or clean a table where kids had painted it with ketchup one more time, she'd go insane. She'd wanted to work at Aunt Betty's Café, but it had a waiting list. The hours at Antlers were too long and the Cattleman's Hotel had vacancies only for bartenders and she didn't have the qualifications. She needed to do something with her life. Marrying for money wasn't possible in her circle of friends. Maybe she'd drive to the ski resort and see if they were hiring for winter. Now *that* was a good place to meet men.

She finished her meal and watched TV. Feeling drowsy, she reluctantly dragged her weary body from the sofa, took her plate and cup to the kitchen, and placed them in the dishwasher. Feeling guilty for leaving a mess the previous day. She refilled the coffee machine and smiled. Maybe taking a few minutes to clean up would make their lives easier. After switching off the lights and dragging legs heavy from standing all day along the passageway, she headed for the bedroom. A sound came from outside. It sounded like a chuckle. A shiver of fear went through her and she turned to look down the passageway. Only the sliver of light from the crescent moon illuminated the glass panels on each side of the front door, and as the breeze moved the trees surrounding the house, strange patterns like goblins dancing moved across the floor and walls. She shook her head. Viewing the horrific Halloween displays had gotten into her mind and it was playing tricks with her.

Undressing, she went into her bathroom and slipped into the shower. The water was hot and soothed her aching muscles. Long hot showers were the only extravagance she allowed herself and with the solar panels on the roof, the cost wasn't more than she could afford. She washed her hair daily. The smell of cooking from the grill at the roadhouse seemed to cling to her. She wrung out her hair and stepped from the shower in a cloud of steam. There was something written on the mirror and she moved closer to read it.

Look behind you.

Heart in her mouth, she looked over one shoulder and gaped at a hideous Halloween mask. Before she could scream, something sharp slammed into her back, one side and then the other. Pushed hard against the vanity, a hand clamped down over her mouth and she couldn't move her arms. As the cold basin pressed into her stomach, pain shot through her. Her knees weak, she sagged when a husky voice came close to her ear.

"Oh, don't pass out on me yet, Daisy. I haven't started to have fun yet. Trick or treat?"

TWENTY-EIGHT

THURSDAY

Jenna and Kane spent a few extra minutes dropping Tauri at the kindergarten. He'd told them about the Halloween mask he'd been making and wanted to show them. It was a new experience for Jenna and seeing the little boy's excitement at having them there made her go misty. The way they taught the kids impressed her. It was a light and airy complex, where parents or grandparents could drop by to help out. The family unit was included and the children seemed to be enjoying themselves and eager to learn. In most cases, Tauri at four would have been too young to attend kindergarten, but when they approached the one in Black Rock Falls, seeing how big he was for his age and his ability to communicate so well, they had made an exception. Although he'd turn five on December first, he still towered over most of the kids in his class.

Impressed, Jenna examined the mask and smiled at Tauri. "Wow! This is beautiful."

Not a ghoulish face with fangs as she'd expected, the mask he'd made was adorned with feathers, white rings around each eye, and zigzag lines on each cheek. She handed the mask to Kane. "Isn't this wonderful?"

"Indeed." Kane turned it over in his hand. "You'll need wings on your costume. We'll go and look for something this afternoon. You are planning on trick-or-treating with Anna Wolfe? We did promise."

"Yes, I like Anna, and Nanny Raya is making my costume." Tauri beamed at them. "Will I look like an eagle, Mommy?"

Jenna laughed. "You will indeed." She wondered if they'd make the Halloween Ball this year, with a serial killer in town, but mentioning it now wouldn't hurt. "If we go to the Halloween Ball, would you mind staying with Nanny Raya?"

"Silly Mommy." Tauri giggled. "Nanny Raya already told me, as sheriff, you and Daddy need to be at the ball and we'd be busy sorting out candy." He looked around at the other kids. "See how they look at you, Daddy? One day you should come by and tell us a story about keeping us safe. I told them you were a great warrior."

"I will, soon as I can." Kane bent to give him a hug. "We need to go to work now. We'll see you soon."

Looking from one to the other, Jenna couldn't be prouder of both of them. She kissed Tauri on the cheek and waved to him as they left the classroom. She turned to Kane. "Come on, Great Warrior, get out your thinking cap. We need a breakthrough in these cases. There must be something we've overlooked."

"Rio and Rowley will be out with the drones again this morning." Kane glanced at his watch. "Carter and Jo should be arriving around ten. We'll rehash everything and take it from there." He pulled open the door of the Beast and slid behind the wheel.

Jenna's phone chimed and it was Maggie. "Hey Maggie, what's up?"

"*I'll patch a call through to you. It's a woman by the name of Tara Farrell. She's concerned something has happened to her friend.*"

Jenna waited for the call to come through. "Sheriff Alton. Am I speaking with Tara Farrell?"

"Yes, I live at 106 Pine. You need to come. Something has happened to my friend. I'm parked on the road, on the corner of Pine and Stanton. Can you come?"

Nodding to Kane as he spun the Beast around and headed for Pine, Jenna took a deep breath and hit record on her phone. "What is your friend's name and can you explain what happened?"

"Daisy Lyon." Tara gave a little sob and then appeared to gather herself. *"I work late, so I usually creep in, grab a shower, and go straight to bed. When I wake, Daisy has already left for work. We hardly ever see each other. This morning when I went into the kitchen, her purse and keys were on the counter. I went to her bedroom door and knocked. I figured she might have over-slept. The bed was stripped and I could see blood on the carpet. I called out but she didn't reply. The room smelled like blood. I was scared. I ran out of the house, got in my car, and drove here to call you."*

Exchanging a meaningful glance with Kane, Jenna cleared her throat. "Okay, we're coming up on you now. We're in the black truck." She disconnected and looked at Kane. "I hope this isn't victim number two."

"So do I." Kane turned to rub Duke's ears. "Stay, boy. We won't be long."

Leaning in the window of the passenger side of the woman's vehicle, Jenna took in the disheveled woman, wearing pj's and a sweater. "Can you drive back to your house? We'll be close behind, or I can ride with you if you're scared."

"I guess." Tara's hands trembled as she gripped the steering wheel.

Jenna pulled open the door and looked at Kane over the hood. "I'll ride with her. Stay close."

"Thanks." Tara turned the SUV and they headed along Pine.

As the vehicle slowed to drive through a dark tunnel made by a canopy of tree branches and overgrown shrubbery, Jenna turned to her. "Pull up outside the house but stay inside the vehicle. Lock the doors and we'll go inside and look around. Daisy wasn't suicidal or had threatened to take her own life at any time?"

"No, absolutely not." Tara looked horrified. "She was always planning for the future. A husband and a tribe of kids. She sent me messages last night and sounded just fine."

Nodding, Jenna pushed open the passenger-side door and waited for Tara to lock it. She nodded to Kane, and they pulled their weapons and stepped inside the open front door. The smell of blood had infused the house, and as they cleared the rooms one by one, it seemed to crawl toward them along the passageway. When they reached the open bedroom door, as usual Kane went high and she went low, scanning the room in silence, listening, and watching for movement. Nothing but the stench of blood and the usual release of bodily fluids that happened at death. The entire scene screamed death. Beside her, Kane held up one finger, holstered his weapon, and dragged booties and gloves from his pockets. Once covered, he drew his weapon and nodded to her. Teamwork practiced after years together needed no words. Jenna kept her weapon raised and Kane cleared the room, checking the closets and all around before moving cautiously to the bathroom.

"It's the same as before." Kane turned to look at her dark eyebrows raised. "Mirror image. It's the same guy. Do you want me to call Wolfe while you question the witness?"

Swallowing hard, Jenna nodded. She had no need to risk contaminating the crime scene, to see a pool of blood on a bathroom floor. "Yeah, she mentioned getting messages from Daisy last night. So, we should have a timeline." She glanced back along the passageway to the other bedroom. "Close the door on the crime scene. Ms. Farrell won't be able to stay here tonight. Once Wolfe has done a forensic sweep, I'll ask her to pack her bags and find out if she has a place to stay."

"Okay." Kane frowned. "I didn't see a phone. I'll check around in the bedroom and then take a look in her purse. I noticed it on the kitchen counter. I assume it's the one Ms. Farrell mentioned." He turned back inside the bedroom and paused to look at her. "Watch your back. This guy is an animal and there's a stack of places he could be hiding out there."

TWENTY-NINE

Aware of the danger, Jenna hurried outside, glad to be in the fresh air. After scanning the wooded area all around the house, she went to the Beast to collect a legal pad before making her way to the SUV parked in the driveway. Tara Farrell was sheet-white and trembling. "Daisy isn't there. So, we're treating her disappearance as a missing person. We'll need to call out the medical examiner to process the scene. He'll be able to determine what happened here. Do you have someone you can stay with for about a week?"

"I'm never living there again, that's for sure." Tara wiped her eyes on a tissue, rolled it into a ball, and pushed it up her sleeve. "My mom lives in Louan. I've already called her and she told me to go home. The problem is all my stuff is in there. I need clothes to go to work."

Nodding sympathetically, Jenna sat beside her. "You can collect the things from your room, soon. I'm happy to help you, but we have to wait until the forensic team has been through it."

"Okay." Tara's bottom lip trembled.

Needing to get as much information as possible, Jenna went down her missing persons checklist in her mind. "Okay, I'll need all the information about Daisy you can give me: her full name, date of birth, where she works, any relatives you know about."

She wrote as Tara gave her the information. "Okay, do you have a photograph of her?"

"Yes, we took a few last weekend." Tara picked up her phone and scrolled through the images. "This is Daisy."

Nodding, Jenna glanced at the image. "Can you forward them to my phone and those messages she sent you last night. What did they say?"

"The thing is, they didn't make any sense." Tara shrugged. "I didn't clean the house or make her bed. I figure it was some kind of a joke."

When Tara showed her the messages, the hairs on Jenna's neck stood to attention. The killer had visited the house to plan the murder and frighten Daisy by cleaning and moving things around. It was part of his game. She kept her expression emotionless, but inside, her heart pounded. "From what she said, she sounded surprised that you'd been inside her room."

"Well, unless we're invited inside, we give each other privacy." Tara shook her head. "We've known each other since grade school. It's an unspoken law. We didn't need to lock our doors. We trusted each other."

Thinking through her conclusions, Jenna frowned. "Did you notice anything out of place in your room? Was it just as you'd left it?"

"Yeah. My room isn't in a mess and I don't have clutter. I'd see if someone had been in there moving stuff. I did notice how clean the kitchen was this morning and it was in a mess when I left. Garbage piled up, pizza boxes everywhere. That's our staple diet. I didn't get the chance to turn on the coffee machine, but it was filled. When I saw her purse and keys, I figured she'd overslept." Tara sighed.

The information told Jenna the killer was already inside the house when Daisy arrived home. Hiding in Tara's room. He would have been way too smart to risk leaving any evidence behind, but she'd take Tara's prints to exclude them and make sure Wolfe checked the room. Not wanting to alarm Tara, she moved through her mental list. "So, what's your normal routine when you arrive home? Let's start with the time."

"Around midnight and I'm so exhausted I just shower and go straight to bed. I try to be as quiet as possible so I don't wake Daisy, but as our bedrooms are at opposite ends of the house, she doesn't disturb me in the morning when she leaves for work either." She blinked away tears. "She wouldn't go anywhere without telling me. Something has happened to her. I saw blood on the carpet, like she was dragged bleeding across it to the bed. She's not just missing; somebody hurt her bad and kidnapped her."

Keeping her voice calm and soothing, Jenna kept any conclusions from her expression. "We'll be able to find out what happened, but I need information. Do you know what time she usually gets home?"

"Around six, unless she stops for pizza." Tara made an effort to pull herself together. "There's one in the refrigerator, but that was from the day before."

Clearing her throat, Jenna pushed on. "Can you give me a family contact for her?" She made notes as Tara spoke. "Also, her phone number. Thanks." She glanced up. "Any boyfriends, anyone new she'd met recently?" She handed Tara her notebook and pen. "Can you give me a list of her friends?"

"We have friends but no one special." Tara bent over the notebook and made a short list. "Like I said, we really only have three friends, and we haven't seen them for months." She frowned. "It's the same every day: work, sleep, work, sleep. Sundays sometimes, we have a day where we go out, sometimes Saturday nights. The most excitement we have is waiting for pizza to cook in town. It's better than having it delivered. There are always people in the line ready to hang out. We often spend Saturday night there just chatting." She handed back the notebook.

Mind reeling, Jenna recalled another witness who mentioned seeing Frank Stark watching Freya Richardson and following her when she left the beauty parlor the night she died. The pizzeria might be the killer's hunting ground. "Okay, are there any other names you can recall? Casual people you might see at the pizzeria. It would be very helpful." She made the list and looked up as Kane walked from the house. "Wait here. The medical examiner will be here soon and we'll go inside and collect your things."

She headed toward Kane and brought him up to date. "Did you find a phone?"

"Nope." Kane stood hands on hips and feet apart. "It's the same MO. If you're going into Tara's room, I suggest you suit up. If the killer was hiding in there, Wolfe might find trace evidence. He'll be here in five."

Nodding, Jenna glanced back at Tara and then back to him. "Call Rio and Rowley. I want them to escort the witness back to her mom's house. Just to let anyone know who might be watching that we have her under our protection. Tell them to drop by the Louan sheriff's office and make them aware of the situation." She pushed a hand through her hair. "I'll wait for Wolfe to do his forensic sweep and then take her through to grab her stuff. She's a mess. I'll give her water and energy bars. I doubt she's eaten since last night." She headed for the Beast and then turned to look at him. "I'll let Duke out. He might be able to follow her scent. Did she leave dirty clothes in the bedroom?"

"Yeah." Kane turned on his heel and headed back into the house. He paused at the door and turned to look at her. "I'll grab something. Keep him with you for now. When I've found something for him to scent, I'll take him around the outside of the house and check the back door and windows for forced entry."

After letting Duke jump down from the back seat of the Beast, Jenna collected a bottle of water and energy bars from their stash and went back to Tara's SUV. She instructed Duke to guard her and climbed into the vehicle. "Here, you should try to eat something. It's been a terrible shock for you. You can rest assured that we'll do everything in our power to find Daisy."

"She's the second woman to go missing this week, isn't she?" Tara turned sad eyes toward her. "We have a radio on at work and I heard the news. Have you found her?"

Jenna shook her head. "Not yet. Did you or Daisy know Freya, the girl who's missing?"

"No, we don't know her. The thing is, I didn't clean the house, Sheriff." Tara slumped in the seat, staring at the energy bar as if just realizing it was in her hand. "Whoever hurt Daisy is a clean freak." She shuddered. "Oh, nooooo." She burst into tears. "He could have been in the house when I came home. If I'd known, Daisy would be okay. I have a gun in my nightstand. I know she's dead. I could see it in your face when you came out of the house." She dropped the water and energy bar and pressed her hands to her face. "I can't go back in there. Please don't make me."

Squeezing Tara's arm, Jenna pulled a packet of tissues from her pocket and handed them to her. "You don't need to go back. I'll collect your things." She watched the poor woman fall to pieces in front of her. She was in no state to be driving anywhere. "Is there anyone I can call?"

"No, I'll go to my parent's house." Tara wiped her eyes. "I'll be fine once I get there."

As Wolfe's white van appeared on the driveway, followed closely by Rio's truck, Jenna sucked in a breath of relief. "Just wait a little longer." She pulled the notebook out of her pocket and handed it with a pen to Tara. "Make a list of anything important you need me to pack for you. I'll leave Deputy Rowley with you while I grab your things. He'll drive you to your parents. Okay?"

"Yeah, thanks." Tara blew her nose. "Who is going to tell Daisy's mom?"

A dark cloud of sorrow dropped over Jenna's shoulders. Informing next of kin was her worst nightmare. She patted Tara on the arm. "I will."

THIRTY

Kane whistled Duke to his side and walked slowly around the house. The driveway extended along one side, curling around back to stop in front of an old shed. He pulled out his phone and took images of the disturbed grass in the backyard. The dirt was dry and hard-packed but some of the overgrown weeds had been bent over, suggesting a vehicle had used the area to turn around. He searched around but found no tire tracks, oil spills, or anything else and went to examine the back door. He used his phone light to illuminate the lock. Peering inside, he made out evidence to indicate the lock had been professionally picked. "This is how he got inside. No deadbolt on the back door, just a regular lock, maybe thirty years old." He patted Duke on the head. "I figure he carried the body out this way." He pulled an evidence bag from his pocket and opened it for Duke to smell the pair of socks he'd found in Daisy's room. "Seek."

Duke moved back and forth, from the door to the driveway, and stopped twice. Once, he returned to the back door and stood on his hind legs, barked, and sat down. Kane walked to the door and turned the handle. The door swung open and he could hear Wolfe giving orders from inside. "What do you smell, boy?" He scanned the floor and then inside the door found a small patch of discoloration on the paintwork of the doorframe. "Good boy." He took images and waved Duke away. "Seek."

Duke retraced his steps with his head moving back and forth, tail sticking out behind him like a rudder. When he reached the driveway, he barked and sat down again. Kane hurried over and dropped to his knees to examine the ground. Small brownish watery marks, as if something had been rested on the concrete driveway, stood out clearly. He took more photos and took a piece of chalk from his pocket and circled the mark. He glanced up as Jenna came around the side of the house and stood. "He carried her out the back door and had his vehicle parked here, out of sight. Duke found what could be blood on the doorframe and again here on the driveway."

"That sounds like he carried her out wrapped in the blankets, maybe rested her on the ground to open the back of a truck or a van?" Jenna chewed on her bottom lip. "That blows our theory that he carries the bodies around in bags."

Kane shook his head and waved a hand around. "Look at this place. There's no one close enough to see what he's doing. It could have floodlights, and no one would see. He could have dropped her into a bag here, and that's where he rested her to put her inside." He walked back and forth. "If he placed her in a fetal position before he wrapped her, like he's done before, that would account for the smear on the doorframe. It'd be difficult to carry her and open the door at the same time."

"Maybe he left the door open?" Jenna tapped her bottom lip with her finger. "We've already established when someone's in the shower they don't hear anything, and he'd be sneaking around. If he knew the movements of both women, he'd know how much time he had to kill and leave. He wouldn't know if Tara usually spoke to Daisy when she got home. Maybe the time for Tara to arrive home was getting close, so he bundled up Daisy and got out of the house. He dumped her into his truck and drove away before anyone noticed him. Maybe he took her straight to the burial site?"

Kane shook his head. "No one is that crazy. Digging a grave at night maybe, but carrying a blood-soaked body through the forest at night? He'd have every predator on him in seconds. They'd scent a fresh kill and he wouldn't survive, let alone have time to bury the body." He blew out a breath and then rubbed the back of his neck. "I figure he drives a big covered truck or a van. He would go home as usual and bag up the body. He probably soaks the van in something to hide the smell. Or maybe he carries bags of fertilizer, they stink. It has to be someone like that, who can move bodies around without people noticing."

"Yeah, that makes sense." Jenna looked toward the back door as Wolfe's voice called her name. "Ah, Shane's finished processing Tara's bedroom. I'll go and pack up her things." She smiled at him. "Jo and Carter are out front. Can you bring them up to date? Rio will help me. I'll tell Wolfe about the blood you found."

Nodding, Kane watched her go. As professional as always, they worked together like a well-oiled machine, and he'd been worried marriage and then adopting Tauri might have put a strain on their working relationship. Many had expected her to retire, and there'd been speculation around town his name would be on the ballot for the next sheriff's election. He'd never take Jenna's place as sheriff, but the idea had entered the mayor's mind. If Jenna decided to step down, they'd both leave and take Tauri and head for a safer place. As he headed back to the front of the house, he smiled to himself, and shook his head. Jenna step down as sheriff? Nah, she'd still be out there protecting people when she was pushing a walker.

"Hey, there you are." Ty Carter stood hands on hips, grinning around a toothpick, his Doberman, Zorro, by his side. "So, the Halloween Slasher, huh? What have you discovered?"

After nodding to Jo and bringing them up to date, Kane removed his examination gloves and rolled them into a ball. "So what do you think, Jo?"

"If what you say is true and it sounds logical, then this guy is single and lives alone. He'd need to move around without anyone noticing him coming and going. So somewhere like this place, not far from town but secluded." Jo paused a beat thinking. "He has a day job, likely shift work, or he works more than one job, odd hours and moves around in plain sight. Like you mentioned, a delivery driver, a gardener, an occupation that would normally carry things around, so people don't think it's unusual. Look at gardeners, they carry shovels, rakes, and bags of rubbish. No one would look twice at them and they work all hours."

"That takes in a list of contractors as long as my arm." Carter rubbed his chin. "You figure he carries the bodies out in bags during the day, but not this time. Is that because it was dark when he left and out here nobody is going to see him?"

Leaning against the Beast, Kane pushed his hands into his jacket pockets. "Yeah, we thought of that too. A gardener carries bags of leaves and grass, so that's a possible. Mail carrier, the ones that move letters between post offices, or a postal worker who delivers and picks up mail. They carry bags and they wouldn't be noticed."

"Someone who picks up kills from the hunters and takes them to the processing plant." Carter stared into space and then looked at Kane. "He'd have a reefer, even at this time of year to keep the game chilled. He'd be waiting for game to come to him and be back and forth from sunup until sunset. If anyone noticed his truck parked on a fire road, they wouldn't think twice about it."

Kane glanced over to see Jenna coming out of the house

carrying bags with Rio loaded up beside her. He hurried over to help. "She needs all this stuff?"

"Yeah." Jenna headed to Tara's SUV. "She's not planning on coming back anytime soon. This is personal belongings. I guess later she'll get a moving company to haul out the rest of their belongings and take it somewhere."

As they approached, Rowley climbed out and opened the hatch of the SUV. Kane looked at him. "You should drive and Rio will follow you. Tara is in shock, maybe advise her parents to call a doctor. Make sure you get all the details to the Louan sheriff. They'll keep an eye on the house, but I don't believe she was the target. Seems to me, the killer likes them small, probably so he can carry them a distance." He glanced over as Tara climbed from the driver's seat. "Tara is tall, maybe five-nine and heavy. From the images in the house of Daisy, she's tiny, five-three, and slim build. That's the same as Freya."

"Okay." Rowley glanced over his shoulder to the house. "Same MO?"

Kane nodded. "Yeah, I'm afraid so. Did you find anything in your drone search?"

"Nothing that looked like graves, a few piles of entrails are all so far." Rowley removed his hat and ran a hand through his hair. "I hope Wolfe finds something on this guy. He'll kill his third victim soon, won't he?"

Nodding, Kane cleared his throat. "I figure we have a couple of days to catch him. When you're done here, head back out and continue the drone search. If we can discover a gravesite, we'll catch him." He stared toward Jenna. "I know we haven't found evidence to point to any suspects, but we have a great team, and just need to trust our instincts."

THIRTY-ONE

It's fortunate morning frost coated the grass when I left for work this morning. The freezing temperatures will keep Daisy fresh, and once I'd packed other bags around her, I was able to carry on as usual. My job takes me over three counties and moving around made life easy, especially around Halloween. I've established a presence in Black Rock Falls, Louan, and Blackwater since returning. People have gotten used to seeing me around. In fact, I've become one of the invisible people working around the towns and there are so many. My occupation gives me the opportunity to sit in my vehicle and observe people. None of my offerings were chosen without deliberation and many make up my list by the end of each year. The only problem I've encountered is the need to kill. At first, when I read about all the people who went missing every year, I honestly believed that everyone was just like me. There is, after all, so many reasons to kill someone. I've seen terrorists mowing down people in their trucks, bombing buildings, but I don't understand why they do it. Most of them take their own lives, so where's the thrill in that? I've watched shows about crimes of passion, hate crimes, but I don't have passion or hate for anyone, so I figure I kill because I enjoy it. After reading the stories about serial killers being arrested for their murders, especially by Sheriff Alton, I'd laughed. *She'll never catch me.*

With everything possible to read about trace evidence and DNA on the internet and mentioned on every cop show, only a fool would get caught. I pull alongside the curb, climb from my truck, and go into Aunt Betty's Café. I've finished for the day and would grab a bite to eat and make sure Wendy was following her new schedule. I smile, a few little scares and she'd changed her shift. Now, with her home before dark, she followed a normal pattern. So far, she'd been a creature of habit, heading for a shower before bed at around ten. The dog is still at the vet. I had intended to kill it with the slow-acting poison because I couldn't allow anything to come between me and Wendy.

As I eat, my mind drifts to Daisy, waiting patiently in my vehicle, but she'll just have to bide her time. I need to make sure I follow a routine too. I want people to see me at certain times and in various places, on the off chance I make a mistake and set the cops on my tail. Alibis with witnesses mean I can keep doing what I enjoy for as long as possible. Although I have faith in my system, in Black Rock Falls, the sheriff will always be a problem, so when it all becomes too much for me, I'll head to any city, find a sex worker or maybe a homeless person, and take out my frustration. The fact they breathe my air is enough of an excuse to kill them and leave them without a decent burial. I've left them on beaches, tossed them into rivers and in ditches during snowfall. Snow was the universal cleanser, covering all my sins with white and hiding them for months at a time. The chances of anyone blaming me for the murders would be remote as I'm always long gone before the melt.

Earlier I drove past two of the deputies flying drones over

the forest. I'd laughed. They could well be looking for graves. By now everyone knew that Freya was missing and I'd seen the medical examiner's van and sheriff's vehicles parked along a fire road. They'd found the first three from so long ago I'd forgotten their names. A shiver of excitement curled in my belly at the thought of the sheriff listening to their last breaths. I must find the recordings and listen to them again. It had been years, but hearing them again would be just like being there. I could relive everything, smell the blood, and feel the knife in my hands. Hearing the funny little gasps as each one died would be wonderful.

Sighing, I turn onto a hard-packed entrance to another fire road. This one takes me away from the original gravesite to my new place. Watching the deputies with the drones, as one of many interested onlookers, it seemed from their current search area they've worked out I buried my offerings in a triangle. I suppose I should give them kudos for that, but after seven years if they really figure I'd go back to the old burial site and plant Freya in the unfinished grave, they didn't have a clue. I'm not that stupid. First of all, it didn't matter if they'd noticed the graves formed a triangle. I'd marked out a sacred circle on the map and inside I can fit many triangles. In fact, I can take any point from one of my original gravesites and create a new triangle. So many variants, such a massive forest. The possibilities are endless. I pull into a small offshoot between a clump of trees. The canopy above is so covered with vines my vehicle is invisible from prying eyes. I listen to the noise of the forest and smile. I've gotten stronger digging graves and carrying bodies. Maybe I'll start working out after Halloween. One more and the offering would be complete, and I'd have nine more years of protection. As I drag the bag containing Daisy's body from my vehicle, I glance up at the sky. Spring would have a deity, some old forgotten god who'd be grateful for an offering after so long. They'd welcome me with open arms. I can almost hear them making a bargain with me already and I didn't even know their name. I hoist the bag into my arms and move silently along a narrow animal trail. Perhaps, I'll research more of the old ones. Why wait until Halloween when there were three other seasons?

THIRTY-TWO

Once Wolfe's team had processed the scene, Jenna followed Kane inside with Jo and Carter close behind. Both dogs sat beside the Beast watching the goings-on with alert interest. Jenna surveyed Daisy's bedroom and bathroom. "It's like déjà vu or a recurring nightmare. This and all the crime scene photographs are the same, right down to the drag marks on the carpet or tile. This has to be the same guy. I figure he's a big guy to carry a body into the forest and bury it."

"The victims are all small women, light, so this doesn't necessarily mean this is a big strong man. If the perpetrator did heavy manual work, he might be small but as strong as a bear. How many guys do you see hauling their kills through the forest across their shoulders? It's not that unusual." Carter tipped back his Stetson and shrugged. "The thing I'm wondering is how old he is. Usually, these abductor type killers start in their late teens, early twenties, and Jo figured this guy has been doing this for a while. We could be looking at a man anywhere between thirty and fifty."

"Yeah, but if he's small, he'd need to be in good shape." Kane rubbed his chin. "Hauling one hundred to one-twenty pounds of dead weight a mile or so wouldn't be easy if the body was in a fetal position inside a bag." He looked at Carter. "If he's dragging it or carrying it in both arms, it would be difficult to negotiate through the forest."

"No way. You're overthinking what it's like to be a small guy. He could carry more than you imagine." Carter smiled at him. "How far could you carry me over one shoulder through the same terrain? I weigh approximately two hundred and twenty pounds."

"That's beside the point." Kane shrugged. "I'm six-five and two hundred and seventy. You couldn't make a valid comparison without knowing the guy's physique."

Interested by Carter's amused expression, Jenna looked from one to the other. "I'd like to know the answer."

"The answer is Dave would be able to carry me over his shoulder wearing his backpack, carrying weapons and ammo, which alone would weigh about one-twenty, for over five miles without breaking a sweat." Carter smiled. "Knowing Dave as I do, he'd carry me to safety if it meant walking twenty miles."

Understanding this was a shared military moment between the pair of them, Jenna looked at Jo. "Add the adrenaline spike and a smaller guy in good shape would have no trouble. Right?"

"I've seen killers do remarkable things and I wouldn't count anyone out." Jo sighed. "Have we found any suspects?"

Nodding, Jenna frowned. "A few possibles. Dave, what do you think?"

"I figure it's a guy around five-ten." Kane met her gaze. "Going on the blood smear on the back doorframe and if he was carrying her in his arms."

Taking in all the back-and-forth like a sponge, Jenna turned to Carter. "What do you make of it now?"

"In my humble opinion, yeah, Dave could be right, but don't discount a smaller guy." Carter shrugged. "You done here? The smell is seeping into my clothes."

Considering everything that was said, Jenna led the way back to the vehicles. Everyone had left, leaving the Beast and Jenna's cruiser parked alongside Daisy's vehicle. With the team all expecting her to pull a rabbit out of the hat, she explained the lack of possible witnesses. "We received a call on the hotline and we wanted to speak to Hank Maxwell, mainly because I had a hunch he might be trying to insert himself into the investigation. He might just be trying to help but no one can find his cabin. We'll go and search for him with Blackhawk later, but he's not a priority."

"I'm wondering if there's a link between the women?" Kane rubbed Duke's ears as the dog leaned against his leg. "From what Jenna got from Daisy's housemate, she didn't know Freya, but what do they have in common that could link them together? Daisy worked at the Triple Z Roadhouse, and Freya cleaned all over but regularly at the beauty parlor."

"Men visit both locations, and I'd say if both women buy pizza, there's a possibility they could run into people they see there every Saturday evening. Not friends but maybe people they all speak to." Jo shrugged. "This killer makes choices, very skilled choices. He must come into contact with the victims."

Thinking over the information, Jenna nodded. "Yeah, we're going about this all wrong. The workplace has to be the link. We need to discover who would visit and how often. I'm thinking delivery drivers more than customers. We need a list of all regular deliveries over the past two months and if the drivers come into contact with the victims."

"That leaves the guy from the pizzeria, Frank Stark." Kane's lips flattened. "He used the restaurant to watch Freya. We need to track him down. I figure he's a priority. The only loose end is Elliot Cummings, who knows Freya from her job stacking shelves at the general store. We haven't found him yet either. It's kinda convenient he's gone missing too."

Jenna looked at Carter. "He's a photographer as well, so

could be anywhere. We've spoken to the manager of the general store and he never saw Cummings harassing Freya." She blew out her breath in a sigh. "He is a person of interest, is all."

"Okay, give us the info and we'll find Cummings and then head to the Triple Z Roadhouse and speak to them about who Daisy came into contact with regularly." Carter smiled. "If we strike out, we'll call and help you with the other leads."

"Okay, well, find Frank Stark and drop by the beauty parlor." Kane straightened and opened the back door of his truck for Duke. "Maybe Freya was alone during a delivery. Some of them do deliver after hours."

Checking her watch, Jenna nodded. "We'll meet at Aunt Betty's at one and take it from there." She climbed into the Beast and looked at Kane. "I'm guessing you'll need to be refueled about then?"

"Yeah, thanks." Kane smiled at her. "There's coffee in the Thermos. I never leave home without it."

Shaking her head, Jenna stared at him. "Are you reading my mind now?"

"Nope." Kane headed through the dark driveway, bursting out into watery sunshine. "I just know you." He sighed. "The beauty parlor and the pizzeria are opposite. Do you want to split up and save time?"

"Yeah." Jenna poured half cups of coffee for each of them. "See what else you can discover about Stark. We need more info on him, that's for darn sure. He must be hanging around town somewhere if he's not at home." She sipped the strong aromatic brew, Kane's special blend, and sighed.

"Okay." Kane turned the truck onto Stanton and headed for Main. "If Stark isn't around today, it makes him a probable suspect and the only person we've got cause to chase down right now."

Jenna stared out of the window, and as they drove past Stanton Forest, the colors of fall sped by. Every shade of green interspersed with browns and golds, like a fine tapestry embroidered with the finest silks. Deep in its depths she made out the bright orange flash of a hunter's jacket and a murder of crows, sitting waiting for their next free meal. She finished her coffee as Kane pulled into a space on Main. "I'll come back to the pizzeria when I'm done. I doubt I'll be long."

"Okay." Kane drank his coffee. "I'll leave Duke here." He looked over at Duke and rubbed his head. "Stay." He slid from behind the wheel and strode toward the restaurant.

THIRTY-THREE

Inhaling the delicious aroma of pie, Kane scanned the restaurant, his attention lingering over two men sitting alone in window seats. The pizzeria was almost a replica of one he'd visited in Italy at one time. Wooden tables with red tablecloths, posters of Italy on the wall, wine bottles cradled in wicker baskets, and when he walked to the counter he could see strings of onions hanging up in the kitchen, bundles of fresh herbs in baskets on the counters, men dressed in white aprons tossing dough and making pizzas and pasta dishes. It was as if he'd just stepped back in time. Vacations had been few and far between, but he'd made the most of them and had his fair share of romances, but never found "the one" until Annie. After losing Annie, he'd given up, not knowing if he'd ever find or want love again. In his profession, nothing was certain. Threats came at him from all directions and involving a wife had been a mistake. He'd blamed himself for Annie's death for so long and then fate had thrown him and Jenna together. Now he realized, Jenna was his destiny.

He dragged his mind back to the present when he noticed a man with a pencil mustache behind the takeout order counter staring at him with one raised eyebrow. Pushing memories aside, he nodded to him. "I'm Deputy Kane. Are you the manager?"

"I am. Brian Rhoads is my name. What can I do for you, Deputy?" The manager sighed as if his time was precious. "I spoke to Deputy Rio and told him everything I know."

Kane pulled out his phone and scrolled through images to one of Daisy. "Do you recall ever seeing this woman in here. I figure she came by on Saturday nights."

"Well, yeah, she does look familiar. She comes by with another woman and they chat with the local crowd. Many of the young people buy takeout and eat in the waiting area." Rhoads sighed. "I don't mind. It's nice seeing them enjoying our food."

The man was observant and that would help. Kane pulled out his notebook and made a few notes. "Have you seen her chatting to Freya, the girl who went missing. The one who cleans the beauty parlor?"

"Can't say that I have." Rhoads frowned. "The other girl, Freya, sometimes drops by and buys a slice of what we have ready and then heads off. I figure she works a few jobs. She always looks exhausted and is in a hurry."

Looking at the notes Rio had entered into the file about his conversation with this man, Kane glanced up. "Don't look at him, but is Frank Stark here now?"

"Yeah, second window seat from the door." The manager hadn't shifted his eyes from Kane. "He knows the woman in the photo." He handed Kane a menu. "He's looking over. Ah... when she dropped by the other night he smiled and spoke to her."

Kane perused the menu and glanced up at him. "What did she do?"

"Not much, as I recall." Rhoads shook his head. "I had her

pie ready. She said something to him and then grabbed her pie and left."

Interested, Kane folded the menu and handed it back. "Did he follow her?"

"I can't say." The manager shrugged. "It was busy. When I looked up again, he'd left, but I did see her get into her vehicle. She was parked right outside."

Kane pushed his notebook inside his jacket pocket and turned around. Frank Stark's eyes bore into him, and his expression was anything but pleasant. The man was mid-thirties, broad shouldered, with large calloused hands. Kane walked to his table. "Mind if I sit down? I'd like to ask you a few questions."

"I can't stop you really, can I?" Stark leaned back in his chair. "I hear the sheriff's department has been making inquiries about me. Deputies dropped by where I work and I was hauled into the office by the boss. What's the deal? Why are you chasing me? I've not done anything wrong."

They all say the same thing. Kane nodded and dropped into a chair opposite him. "We've been trying to locate you because you know two of the women who went missing recently. We're trying to establish a timeline and we're speaking to everyone who came into contact with them. It's not just you."

Kane ran the man before him through the profile Jo had created. The age was right, he drove a van that carried bags of mail. He traveled all over. "So, when did you last see Freya Richardson and Daisy Lyon?"

"I don't *know* them as in like friends." Stark opened his hands wide. "Acquaintances, I guess you'd say. I spoke to Freya in passing when we were waiting for takeout. I didn't know her name until the pizza guy called it out for her order. The last time I saw her, she was cleaning the beauty parlor."

Nodding, Kane realized Stark was giving him what could

have been noticed by others. "You left just after she did. She was on foot that night and walked home. Did you follow her?"

"Nope." Stark's eyes flashed in anger. "Why would I follow her? My van was parked at the post office. I was waiting for the Louan mail to be loaded, is all. I deliver after hours as well."

"Okay." Kane gave him a long look. "So how do you know Daisy?"

"She works out at the Triple Z Roadhouse." Stark shrugged. "I work odd times and drop by there because its open all hours. She was there at the counter and took my order and then cleared the table next to mine. We chatted, is all. She's a nice girl. I dropped by there a few times to see if she was interested in me, but she wasn't. That was a couple of weeks ago."

This guy was a font of information. "You live in a cabin in the forest, right?"

"Yeah, heaps of people do. So what?" Stark sipped on a soda, staring at him.

Leaning back in his chair, Kane acted nonchalantly. He didn't particularly like this guy. "Do you take the postal truck home with you?"

"Yeah, I do some days because I work a fifteen-hour shift." Stark shrugged. "I often wait here for my truck to be loaded, grab a slice, and then leave. We have a schedule. I only get time to go home and sleep."

Kane smiled. "That's good you have a schedule. You'll know where you were last night between the hours of six and twelve."

"Last night, I arrived home about eight from a Blackwater delivery." Stark shrugged. "I had a few local deliveries this morning, is all. Now I'm eating and waiting for my truck to be loaded, and then I'm heading for Louan."

Writing notes, Kane nodded. "And what about last Saturday night?"

"I was here." Stark shrugged. "I like the Saturday night crowd. There's people to chat to."

Looking up from his notes, Kane glanced across the street and indicated the beauty parlor with his chin. "You recall seeing Freya Richardson working in the beauty parlor?"

"Yeah, I do. She works her butt off." Stark shrugged. "So?"

Seeing the man squirm in his seat, Kane wanted to slap the cuffs on him and drag him away for more questioning. His gut was screaming at him to do something. What could he do? Stark had cooperated, validated what the manager of the restaurant had told him. He twirled the pen in his fingers. "Oh, it's just that I have a witness who saw you leave just after Freya left the beauty parlor and walked home. Another witness mentioned a white vehicle went speeding by maybe an hour or so later. Heading in the direction of the forest. Why did you follow her?"

"I didn't follow her." Stark shrugged. "I walked to the depot to see if they'd finished unpacking my truck. They hadn't, so I hung around until it was ready and then I went home. My next shift wasn't until Monday. It wasn't me speeding along Main."

Noticing Jenna leaving the beauty parlor, Kane folded his notebook. "Just one more thing, what truck do you drive? A regular postal courier van with the writing on the side or something else?"

"Something else." Stark smiled. "I have a variety of jobs in the postal service because of the shortage of workers. I have a magnetized sign I place on the side when needs be, but it's a plain white van. Some days I carry mailbags, sometimes parcels that are home delivered, and I need a sign. On the road, between depots, it's not necessary."

Standing, Kane pushed back his Stetson and frowned. "Ah, before I go. Did you know Daisy drops by here with Tara on Saturday nights? They like to hang out here. Did you see them last Saturday night?"

"I've seen them around, maybe." Stark shrugged. "There's a steady stream of people through here on Saturday nights."

Pushing his notebook and pen back into his pocket, he pulled out a card and handed it to Stark. "If you think of anything else, like the names of anyone you know who spoke to these women, call me." He turned and headed for the door.

Meeting Jenna as she crossed the road, he gave her a rundown of the interview. "My gut tells me he is more than capable of murder. He was around town at the time both women went missing. He cooperated but he also has a truck and carries mailbags around. No one would question a mail worker or think twice about seeing one around town."

"The beauty parlor never gets deliveries outside of hours." Jenna pulled open the door to the Beast and climbed inside. "The only thing that gets collected near the beginning of Freya's shift is the towels. A laundry service drops by twice a week to drop off clean towels and pick up soiled ones, but the manager said she is always there when they arrive."

Kane slid behind the wheel. "So, Stark knew both women as acquaintances."

"I doubt, as you asked about both women, he'd deny speaking to them. He'd know someone would have seen him. He sounds confident because he's giving you the information he probably knows you already have on him. He has a truck that carries bulky bags around. He's shaping up as the prime suspect, but we haven't gotten anything to detain him for questioning. He'll be a watch and see." Jenna clicked in her seatbelt. "It's too early for lunch. I'll call Jo and see where they're at with finding Cummings." She made the call and listened. "We're done here. If you're still hunting down Cummings, we'll take the Triple Z Roadhouse." She paused a beat. "Okay, see you soon."

Wishing for a hot meal at Aunt Betty's Café, Kane drove past the big spider over the entrance with his window down and inhaled the aroma of everything that was Aunt Betty's. The diner had been tricking him lately by moving the specials around, but he could make out the delicious smell of apple pie baking and chili just as he liked it, red hot. His stomach growled and behind him Duke sniffed the air and whined. He smiled to himself. A man and his dog, huh? Now they were thinking the same thing. He glanced at Jenna. "The problem with working at the Triple Z Roadhouse is that people are in and out all the time. If she'd worked at the Triple Z Bar, it would have been easier to pin down someone chatting to her. There being two or three bartenders on busy nights, they'd notice if someone at the bar was chatting to her more than usual. At the roadhouse, there's women at the counter. They take orders—no time to chat —and clean tables when people have left."

"Well, I guess if we don't cast the net, we won't catch any fish." Jenna smiled at him. "I can hear your stomach demanding food again. I'll buy you a donut when we get there to help you make it through to lunch." She rolled her eyes. "On the proviso you eat it inside the truck. You know what they say about cops and donuts."

Kane grinned at her. "Yeah, but they don't have an Aunt Betty's in their lives." He turned the Beast around and headed for the Triple Z Roadhouse.

THIRTY-FOUR

Jenna grinned at the hideous smiling pumpkins hanging in garlands outside the Triple Z Roadhouse. In the window, a poster listed the upcoming attractions in town, and at the entrance, a witch on a broomstick sailed back and forth, cackling each time someone opened the door. Inside hummed with noise, and the smell of cooking and roadhouse coffee wafted toward her. Truckers and people passing by made up the majority of the customers sitting around the tables. Although dilapidated, the roadhouse was always busy, and maybe they didn't have time to replace the worn seats and cigarette-burned tabletops. There'd been no smoking inside establishments all over for years now. The old décor had remained the same for the last sixty years, from the pictures of staff hanging on the walls. Heavens above, they still had a jukebox in one corner banging out country music.

She went to the counter and selected a donut with powdered sugar and smiled at the young woman behind the counter with LINDA HOCUTT on a name badge pinned to her shirt. "Two large coffees to go, thanks."

As the woman filled the to-go cups and placed the donut

into a bag, Jenna placed bills on the counter. "Do you know Daisy Lyon? I'm told she works here."

"Yeah, she didn't show for work today and isn't answering her phone." Linda frowned. "She's never missed a day since starting. I'm working alone until the boss gets someone to come in and help out."

Jenna nodded. "Yeah, we're aware she's missing. What time does she usually finish for the night?"

"Seven." Linda served another customer and then went back to Jenna. "She left here right as rain last night. She mentioned stopping by to look at the Halloween displays in town and buy candy. The kids always drop by their house because it's so spooky along Pine."

Good, a timeline was forming. Jenna handed the donut and one coffee to Kane. She smiled as he headed out to the Beast, grinning. She turned back to Linda. "Ah... do you recall anyone chatting with her, or did she ever mention a guy asking her out or becoming a problem?"

"Sheriff, men do that all the time." Linda shook her head. "They figure because we work in this dump, we're easy. Yeah, she complained about one guy. I've seen him a few times in here. He sits for a time, like he's waiting for her to clean close by so he can talk to her. He's a postal worker—you know, a courier or driver. I saw him getting out of his vehicle after he filled up with gas."

Jenna's mind immediately went to Stark. "Did Daisy mention him at all?"

"Yeah, he asked her out like three times." Linda rolled her eyes. "She was with her friend at the pizzeria in line and he just started chatting with her. Then when he saw she worked here, he hung around." She shrugged. "I said I'd handle the tables when he came by, and she took over the counter after he ordered. I figure he'd gotten the message. I haven't seen him for a week or so."

Jenna nodded. "Okay, thanks." She handed the woman one of her cards. "If you think of anything else, let me know, and please ask anyone else who works here. We need to find Daisy." She smiled. "Do you mind giving the manager a card? What's their name so I know who it is if they call?"

"Sure, the manager is Karen Clifton. I'll go speak to her and the kitchen staff now." The woman walked away.

Outside, Kane and Duke had gone missing. Jenna scanned the area and then walked to the back of the roadhouse. She found Kane speaking to a driver of a white van. She moved to his side and listened to the conversation.

"Are you the same company that launders the towels from the beauty parlor?" Kane was standing with one hand rested on the butt of his weapon, slung low on one hip.

"That's us." The driver smiled.

Jenna stepped closer. "What areas do you cover and how many drivers are there?"

"We cover Black Rock Falls, Louan, and Blackwater." The driver turned to her. "There are four drivers. We collect the laundry from all over. The Cattleman's Hotel owns the company. They opened up when times were tough as a second enterprise a few years back. It made sense as they have their own laundry. They launder linen from motels, restaurants, hotels, beauty parlors, and now some locals use the service as well. Since the town became a tourist destination, the Cattleman's Laundry Service has expanded their building and staff."

Interested, Jenna nodded. "So how does it work? Do you collect the soiled laundry and deliver it back in a couple of days?"

"I deliver." The man rested his back against the side of the van. "Duane picks up on our route. We don't mix clean and dirty laundry in the same truck. Even though it's all in bags, some of the soiled linen stinks. We check the labels all the time to make sure nothing is mixed up when it gets to the depot."

"What's your route? Where do you go to regularly?" Kane inclined his head.

"Here at the roadhouse, the Black Rock Falls Motel, the ski resort, and the Blackwater Motel, beauty parlor here and in Louan and Blackwater. We handle the large orders. The other guys do pickups and deliveries for smaller venues or private homes."

Jenna pulled out her notebook. "I'll need your details and the name of your coworker. Do you know where he lives?"

"I'm Christopher Wills and the guy who does the deliveries is Duane Warner. He mentioned he lives on Stanton, on the other side of town, down near the river. He said he walks across the road to go fishing." He gave Jenna his details.

"Can you describe him?" Kane's gaze narrowed. "Height, weight, age?"

"Not your size, but taller than me. He's around my age, late thirties. I'm not good at judging a person's weight but he's not fat. The dirty laundry is heavier than the clean and he hauls those bags around without any trouble."

"Is he married?" Kane exchanged a glance with Jenna. "Or does he live alone?"

"He's never mentioned a wife and I talk about my wife and kids all the time." Wills scratched his beard. "Not that I see much of him. We sometimes see each other in passing, is all. Sometimes in the diner or Aunt Betty's between deliveries."

Running everything through her mind, Jenna chewed on her bottom lip. "So do you work regular hours?"

"Most times. We have the usual route, but sometimes we get called out to collect or deliver a rush job or pick up from a new client. The work is regular and we get overtime. We could be anywhere within the three counties in the same day." Wills looked from one to the other. "If that's all, I need to keep going."

"Not a problem." Kane handed him a card. "If anything else comes to mind, give me a call."

As Jenna led the way back to the Beast, Duke ran around her legs, sniffing her hands. "What's up with Duke?"

"Well, you went into a place that sells food, gave me something, and I guess he figures he deserved a snack too." Kane dropped one arm over her shoulder and pulled her to his side. "Don't worry, I have you covered." He pulled a doggy treat from his pocket and slipped it into hers. "Best you give it to him before he gets into my truck."

Laughing, Jenna pulled out the treat and unwrapped it. She looked at Duke. "What do you say?"

Duke sat down and barked, his mouth forming a doggy smile, his eyes fixed on the treat. Jenna tossed it to him. "There you go. Good boy." She looked at Kane. "We'll head to Aunt Betty's now and wait for Jo and Carter. We'll discuss the case then, it's pointless going over everything twice."

"Maybe check in with Rio and Rowley to see if they've found any gravesites?" Kane lifted Duke into the back seat and clipped in his harness. "We haven't heard anything from Wolfe either. That's not a good sign."

Jenna swung into the passenger seat. "I was hoping for an update from Norrell about the cold cases, but she said it takes time. All we can do right now with them is hope they can identify the victims. The crime scenes we've seen on file all point to the same killer."

"Yeah, they do." Kane headed along Main. "It will be interesting to know if Kalo can track down any similar crime scenes. I'd like to know where this guy has been killing over the last seven years."

Cold crawled over Jenna and she shivered with the implications. "Yeah, if he murders three women a year at Halloween, we're talking of a potential body count of twenty-one undiscovered bodies. If we add the current cold cases to the figures and the two new ones, he'll make it to thirty this Halloween, unless we stop him."

THIRTY-FIVE

Jenna found Jo and Carter laughing at a Halloween display not far from Aunt Betty's Café. She walked up to them and smiled. "There are some awesome displays this year. The townsfolk's imaginations are boundless. I love the witches cooking frogs in the bubbling cauldron."

"I figured the skeleton gunslinger smoking a cigar is my favorite." Carter followed Jenna into Aunt Betty's Café. "Although this spider takes some beating. It really feels like the babies are going to crawl over my back."

They ordered at the table and sat down. Once Susie had delivered two pots of coffee. Jenna leaned forward in her chair. "I called Rio and Rowley. They're still out with the drones. They've found nothing of interest but it's a huge forest. I figure the chances of finding anything would be slim but we must try."

"There's not too much for them to do right now." Kane added cream and sugar to his cup and stirred slowly. "We have at least some interesting information." He brought them up to date with the various deliveries linking both victims and the other information they'd collected.

"That's not conclusive proof though, is it?" Carter removed

his hat, ran a hand through his shaggy blond hair and dropped the hat onto a chair. "Seems to me, deliveries are happening all over town."

"Yeah, maybe." Jo sipped her coffee and sighed. "Knowing who is around town who hauls large bags and has been seen in the vicinity of the victims is something we can't ignore. Frank Stark ticks most of the boxes. The fact he answered your questions doesn't surprise me at all. Most serial killers come across as nice guys. He knows you have witnesses that saw him speaking to Freya and Daisy, so he can't deny it without causing suspicion. It's very typical of how a killer's mind would work."

"It won't stop him killing." Kane leaned back in his chair, with one hand wrapped around a cup. "I'm as convinced as you, Jo, that this is a ritual. He believes he can't get caught."

Looking from one to the other, Jenna nodded. "Yeah, anyone who has the guts to walk into a person's home and clean it before murdering the owner isn't our usual type of killer."

"I figure he breaks in well before he plans the murder." Carter's green eyes became intent. "It's all part of his game, like a stalker but he gets his kicks by walking around the house when no one is home. He likes to be in control of the situation so he familiarizes himself with the interior. He needs to know where to park his vehicle so he can remove the body." He leaned closer. "He checks out the location of where the victim keeps the clean towels so he can soak up the blood and take a shower. This guy is so cool he scares me."

Needing to keep everyone moving forward, Jenna glanced at Jo. "Did you have any luck finding Elliot Cummings?"

"Not at first as he's not answering his phone." Carter moved a toothpick across his lips. "I did discover he drives a Ram, so there's more than enough room inside the covered cargo bed to hide a body."

"We chased all over town hunting him down." Jo placed her cup on the table, still gripping it with both hands. "I had a light bulb moment. If he's a photographer, maybe the local newspaper knows him. We went there and discovered he is covering the Halloween festival and supplying the newspaper with shots of the local displays around town. We stopped every man we saw taking photographs and found him."

"I spoke to him at length." Carter smiled. "I flashed the badge to get his full attention and it worked. He didn't act like a serial killer, more like a quivering bowl of Jell-O. Stuttering and his eyes were looking this way and that, as if he didn't want to be seen with us."

"Not that anyone would know. We look like regular people today." Jo smiled. "He talked about Freya, said how lovely she is, and he'd wanted to pursue a relationship even as friends, but she cut him dead. He took the hint and asked for a different shift at work. He didn't mention it to his boss though... about Freya. He figured backing off was the right thing to do."

Jenna waited for the server to bring their meals and then looked at Jo. "Did you get any vibes from him at all?"

"Well, I figure the killer likes to dominate women. He is a control freak and plans every murder to the second." Jo nibbled on her french fries and then added salt. "This guy was scared of me, and Carter intimidated him from the moment he asked his name, and I might add, Carter was being really nice." She smiled. "I leaned on him, asked him his whereabouts on the nights of the crimes. He knew about Freya going missing Saturday night. He'd seen the media report on the news. He admitted to that, said he lived alone but was at home downloading his camera and sorting through shots both nights. He says he does that when he's not working. He gets shots of anything interesting around town and then sends the good ones to the newspapers. They pick what they want and pay him for what they use."

"He does wedding photography as well." Carter bit into his burger and sighed.

"I figure we need to find Duane Warner and the witness who saw the white truck." Kane dabbed at his lips with a napkin. "Hank Maxwell. He's like smoke but if we can find his cabin, we'll just wait for him to show."

Jenna nodded. "Yeah, I guess next step is to call the Cattleman's Laundry Service and find out where Duane Warner is heading this afternoon. Maybe we can meet him when he gets to his next stop."

"It would be easier if we took Warner." Carter took a long drink of coffee from his cup and set it down. "Dave mentioned needing Blackhawk to guide you, and if I take the cruiser into the forest, Maxwell will see it, and if he's involved, he'll head for the hills."

What he said was logical. Jenna nodded in agreement. "Okay, we have satellite phones. There are two in the glovebox of the cruiser as well. If you travel between here and Blackwater, there are some places along the way where the phone signal drops out. Call me when you talk to him."

"Any more info from Wolfe or Norrell?" Jo held a burger between both hands and eyed it closely. "I'm not sure I can get my mouth around this. It's so big."

"Here." Carter handed her a knife. "Cut it in half."

"Thanks." Jo smiled at him. "Although I'll probably wear more of this than I eat. It sounded so good when you ordered it, but it's a week's calories for me."

Looking from one to the other, Jenna raised one eyebrow at Kane in a silent communication. It had been a struggle for Carter at first working with Jo. He'd been off the grid for a couple of years and had lost his social skills but now they acted like close friends. "No, we haven't heard from Wolfe or Norrell. They'll call when they have something. They know we're up to our necks with the current caseload."

"I'll message Blackhawk and see if he can meet us in the forest." Kane pulled out his phone and tapped away. A reply came in a few seconds. "We're good to go. We'll meet him in half an hour on Stanton opposite Pine." He replaced his phone and pulled a large wedge of apple pie toward him with a sigh. "We'll need coffee and sandwiches to take with us." He glanced at Jenna. "We might be out there for a time."

Frowning, Jenna nodded. "If it looks like we're going past six, I'll call Nanny Raya and talk to Tauri." She pushed hair from her face. "He understands we need to work late sometimes, but it's better if I can tell him myself, especially as we both disappeared for a few days not long ago."

"He understands better than you think." Jo smiled at her. "We can always collect him and take him back to the cabin."

"Thanks for the offer, Jo. That's very kind of you, but we have a rule to keep him safe." Kane raised both eyebrows. "As Jenna is the sheriff and we deal with a ton of crazy people, Tauri must only go with us, Nanny Raya, or Blackhawk."

"I understand completely." Jo smiled. "I have the same arrangement with Jaime. It's the safest thing to do. Just keep it to a few people who are close to him."

Jenna's phone chimed. It was Rowley.

"We've found nothing. Maggie called. She's snowed under at the office. Do you mind if we call it a day and head back there now?" He cleared his throat. *"After we grab a bite to eat."*

Jenna brought him up to date. "Yeah, head back to the office. Clear the backlog and then take a closer look at the footage from the drones just in case you missed something." She sighed. "He's burying the bodies somewhere at Bear Peak. That place means something to him. Maybe it's because it's a serial killer's dumping ground. Who knows. Make a note of anyone you saw in the forest and any vehicles."

"Yes, ma'am." Rowley disconnected.

THIRTY-SIX

They reached the meeting point early and Kane took out their weapons, stripped them down, and checked them. He slid his M18 pistol into the holster on his hip. He liked to draw Old Western-style, although he could draw fast from just about any position. It was comfortable to have his gun at his fingertips. Rowley had taken to wearing his weapon the same, but his favorite weapon was a six-shooter and, of course, his crossbow. Kane stripped one of the rifles and reassembled it, checked the load, and handed it to Jenna. He wouldn't carry his sniper rifle into the forest unless he had a specific target in mind. He checked the backpacks. Although they all contained the same kit, he liked to make sure. Bear spray, extra ammo, water, and he added the sandwiches and coffee from Aunt Betty's. He glanced around at Duke, rolling legs up in the damp leaves, tongue lolling in bliss. He smiled to himself. Duke loved a romp through the forest and spent most of his time nose down and sniffing everything along the way.

"There's Atohi now. He's driving the horse trailer." Jenna looked at him surprised. "I figured we'd be hiking."

Kane straightened. "It would be faster on horseback, especially if he knows a few shortcuts. We can only go so deep along the trails in the Beast." He shut the back door and locked it. Not that anyone could steal the Beast. If they tried, they'd be trapped inside, and with bulletproof windows, there was no way out unless he opened the truck for them. He dropped the backpacks at Jenna's feet. "I'll go and help him unload the horses."

"Afternoon." Blackhawk jumped down from the truck, rifle in hand, and bent to rub Duke's ears as the dog did his happy dance at seeing him. "I hope you don't mind riding out to Twisted Limbs Trail. My horses needed the exercise. Working with Wolfe gives me no time to ride and they spend all day in the corral." He straightened and rested his rifle against the wheel and then pulled out a backpack. "This man we seek, is he a suspect?"

Kane took the backpack and his rifle and handed them to Jenna. "Not yet, we just have a gut feeling something isn't right about him, so we're checking him out. He might be a straight shooter, but we need to eliminate him if he is."

"That's good to know." Blackhawk frowned. "With all of us here, if something bad happened, there's no one to care for Tauri."

"Ah, but there is." Jenna smiled at him. "Your mom asked to be a contact in the event anything happened, and we added her to the list. She's family too, and you're cousins. Don't forget, Wolfe would step in in a second as well, as would Rowley. Don't worry, we've thought of everything. Tauri isn't alone in this world. He has a family."

"Okay." Blackhawk nodded slowly as if mulling over her words. "I'll unload the horses. They're a little frisky but not dangerous."

Amused, Kane followed him to the back of the trailer. Blackhawk gentled his horses and they'd never known mistreatment. It would be unusual to find one of his horses mean-spirited. He had plans with him for a pony for Tauri. As they unloaded the horses, he turned to Blackhawk. "Have you chosen a pony for Tauri?"

"He is little now but will grow fast. Each time I see him he gets taller." Blackhawk led a mare to Jenna and offered his cupped hands for her to mount. He turned back to Kane. "I was thinking a horse might be a better option. I have a gentle Appaloosa mare coming along. Has he ridden with you yet?"

Kane led Moon Dancer down the ramp and nodded. "Yeah, in front of my saddle. I gave him a few rides on Anna's pony, but when Wolfe comes by for a visit, his daughter is going to want to ride him. I have explained to Tauri that the pony doesn't belong to us."

"You should keep riding with him on Warrior so he is used to the height and the way a horse moves. Come spring, after the melt, he'll be ready and so will the mare." Blackhawk led his own horse from the trailer, slid the rifle into the saddle holster, and pulled on his backpack.

After handing Jenna the rifle, Kane shrugged into his backpack and mounted Moon Dancer. The horse sidestepped and threw up its head. "Easy, boy, easy." He turned the horse around in circles until he settled. "A nice amble through the forest will make you feel much better."

"Do you know where Twisted Limbs Trail is located? Rowley found what he believed was the correct path and found nothing." Jenna turned in her saddle as Blackhawk rode to her side.

"Yeah, it's broken by a dry riverbed, and at this time of the year it's fine, but heavy rain or the melt would make the trail unpassable." Blackhawk took the lead. "I know a shortcut through the trees. Follow me."

A cool breeze from the mountain forest brushed Kane's cheeks. He scanned ahead, peering into the shafts of sunlight and deep shadows. Fall had changed the vegetation from green to every shade of brown and yellow. The pines had lost their sprigs of bright green new needles and pinecones hung heavy from the branches and tumbled all through the forest. Inhaling the pine-scented air, Kane moved close behind Jenna and alongside him Duke trotted along having the time of his life. The easy going would be good for him and the horses. They traveled west, moving through the dense forest with no recognizable path. It was as if Blackhawk was using special skills to keep them in the right direction. When they emerged on a dirt track, Kane rode up beside him. "I'm pretty good navigating the forest but that was amazing."

"Ha." Blackhawk wiggled his satellite phone and grinned. "A good tracker never leaves home without GPS. I plotted the shortcut earlier. I did know the location of Twisted Limbs Trail, but there's always a shortcut through the forest."

"And there's a cabin." Jenna pointed farther along the trail. "There's smoke coming from the chimney. Someone must be home."

Scanning the trail, Kane searched for signboards. By law, they couldn't walk onto any property posted with KEEP OUT or TRESPASSERS WILL BE SHOT without the risk of being shot legally. In these cases, they'd call out or sound their horn if they were in his truck. He rode a short way in both directions and then returned to Jenna and Blackhawk, and shrugged. "It's not posted. Maybe it's an old hunter's cabin and he's just made himself at home?"

"I figure we call out anyhow." Jenna met his gaze. "It would be the sensible thing to do. No way I'm just marching up to the front door and hoping for the best."

Nodding in agreement, he looked at Blackhawk. "If we blend into the forest and Jenna calls out, if he believes she's alone, he might come out onto the porch." He looked at her. "Give me the rifle and I'll have it trained on the door, just in case." He smiled at her. "Trust me."

"Always." Jenna waited for them to hide and approached the house.

Kane dismounted and moved through the trees. He had a good view of the front door of the cabin and Jenna had placed her horse between two trees, making a direct shot from the occupant difficult. He held his breath as she called out. Moments later the door opened and a man stepped out onto the porch. Seeing he was unarmed, Kane relaxed and waited behind a tree.

"Afternoon." Jenna urged her horse closer. "I'm looking for Hank Maxwell. Would that be you by any chance?"

"Yeah, and who are you?" Maxwell's brow creased into a frown. "It's a ways away from the highway for a woman to be out alone."

"I'm Sheriff Alton and I'm not alone." Jenna dismounted. "We're following up on the report you called in on the hotline. I need a few more details if possible?"

"Okay." Maxwell folded his arms across his chest. "Although there's not much more I can tell you."

Kane handed the rifle to Blackhawk and strolled out of the trees to stand beside Jenna. Maxwell stood six feet, with a strong build and aged around thirty-five to forty, with a weathered complexion. Lived alone in a cabin and fit the profile. He gave him a quick disinterested once-over. "Deputy Kane. We've been trying to contact you. Do you live out here on your lonesome?"

"Yeah, I like the quiet." Maxwell shrugged. "I won a small lottery some years back and decided to live off the grid. I'm self-sufficient with enough saved and yearly payments to live comfortably. I turn on my phone only on Fridays. My friends know that and respect my privacy. What did I say in the call to drag you all the way out here?" He looked from one to the other. "I was reporting what I'd seen, is all. Doing my civic duty."

"We appreciate the call, but we need more information."

Jenna took out her notebook and pen. "You'd be surprised how many things we miss. Can we come inside?"

"I guess." Maxwell frowned. "I'll need to go out back for a spell. I left a fire burning and the wind has just changed. I don't want flying embers to cause a wildfire. My barn is out there and my horse." He stepped off the porch and walked around the house.

Kane leaned into Jenna. "The smoke isn't coming from the chimney." He pointed upward. "It's coming from the backyard. He could be burning evidence." He turned to peer toward Blackhawk and gave him a signal to follow them. He didn't trust Maxwell or what he might have stashed behind his house.

"You go first. If he's going to try something, you're a faster draw than I am." She chewed on her bottom lip. "I'm so glad you insisted we wear our liquid Kevlar vests when we hunt down suspects." She followed behind him.

Kane kept his eyes ahead. "Unless he aims for our heads, we'll be fine."

As he rounded the corner, Maxwell was poking at a firepit pushing ashes over what was burning and then kicking soil over the embers. From the smell, he'd been burning fabric, and Kane made out what could have been the sole of a sneaker just before it melted into the ashes. With the fire out, Maxwell waved them through the back door. Kane shook his head. "After you."

He stood back to allow him to pass and then followed. The door led into a small mudroom and then through to the kitchen. It was dark inside and as Maxwell opened another door, the smell of death hit him. Kane blocked the door preventing Jenna from following and drew his weapon. *It's a trap.*

THIRTY-SEVEN

Doing grunt work had never been something Carter enjoyed. It was called "grunt work" because boring jobs were usually given to privates in the military, in which he'd evolved. He'd done his fair share, but driving miles and just chasing his tail looking for Duane Warner was frustrating. He climbed back into the cruiser and looked at Jo. She always took everything in her stride. Nothing seemed to get under her skin. "They haven't seen him. The laundry is collected from a loading bay out back. They only see the other guy when he delivers the clean bags."

"The next one on the list takes us back to Black Rock Falls." Jo stared at the list on her phone of Warner's pickup route. "After he drops the bags back to the laundry he's done for the day. He's never at home it seems, so we need to catch him at the hotel laundry." She glanced at her watch. "We should head out now. We'll pass him on the highway if you use lights and sirens. Getting there ahead of time, we can't miss him."

Grinning, Carter looked at her. "Speeding along the highway sounds like my kind of fun." He started the engine and spun the cruiser around. "If he's running to time, and from what

I can make out he starts early. Not one of the places we visited say they see him pick up the bags. What does he do after work?"

"Maybe he has more than one occupation." Jo shrugged. "Many people work two jobs."

Carter moved swiftly through the town of Blackwater and took the on-ramp to the highway, and once they hit the open road, he hit the lights and sirens and pushed his foot down hard on the gas. The SUV lifted and they took off at high speed. He glanced at Jo. "Seems like Kane has been tinkering with the engine. It wasn't this good when we drove it last time."

"I figure that's his passion along with building Harleys." Jo laughed. "You'll have your own biker gang by the time he's finished."

They passed a few white delivery vans on the way to Black Rock Falls and any one of them could have been Warner. Carter enjoyed the rush of high speed, the countryside flashing by in a blur of fall tones. It was like flying, but in truth, he preferred to be high above the highways in his chopper. He flicked off lights and sirens as they took the exit for Stanton and headed straight for the Cattleman's Hotel. The laundry was around back, so they parked in the regular parking lot and walked around to the rear of the hotel. They strolled inside the office and Carter leaned on the front counter. When the same man they'd spoken to earlier came and gave them a weary look, Carter straightened. "We've been hightailing it all over three counties searching for Warner. Please tell me he hasn't finished for the day."

"Nope, he usually makes his last drop-off around this time." The man indicated with his thumb over one shoulder. "Soiled laundry is dropped out back. There's receiving and dispatch sections. Once he's done, he takes the truck home. It works fine for us as he starts early and needs to buy gas before he leaves in the morning."

Carter nodded and turned toward the door. He looked at Jo. "This time we'll catch him."

As they hurried around to the back of the building, a white van drove past them and turned around to back into the receiving bay. A man jumped out and moved around the back of the truck. He'd started to haul out large canvas bags and toss them to another man in the dock. Carter walked up to him. "Duane Warner?"

"Who's asking?" Warner wiped sweat from his brow with his sleeve and stood hands on hips staring at him. His gaze flicked over Jo and then back to Carter.

Holding up his badge, Carter took in the man's size, weight, and age. Maybe thirty-five, six feet, and he threw the heavy bags around as if they weighed nothing. "Agent Carter and Agent Wells. We'd like a word with you if you have time."

"What about?" Warner's lips twitched up at the corners and he straightened. "I pay my taxes, don't cook, grow, or sell drugs, so what would the FBI want with me?"

"We're not with the IRS or the DEA." Jo gave him a confident stare. "We're here as consultants to the Black Rock Falls sheriff's department. At this time, we're following leads concerning two missing persons."

Carter took a step closer. "Both missing women, work in places where this laundry service picks up and delivers. You are one person of many we'll be speaking to. We've already spoken to Christopher Wills, and he mentioned you pick up and he delivers to the Triple Z Roadhouse and the Black Rock Falls beauty parlor." He watched closely for a reaction and saw nothing. "Freya Richardson worked at the beauty parlor and Daisy Lyon at the roadhouse."

"I don't recall speaking to anyone at either venue." Warner shrugged. "I rarely see anyone. The bags are dumped out the back most times, and I just grab them and toss them into my truck. Most of them don't smell too good, so they don't hoard them inside and there's never been any gone missing. The clean ones are different. Chris has to haul them inside. If anyone gets to speak to the workers, it's him, not me."

"So the names Freya Richardson and Daisy Lyon don't ring a bell?" Jo eyed him speculatively. "You ever hang out at the pizzeria on Saturday nights?"

"I prefer Aunt Betty's Café, but yeah, I have been there, and yeah, I do recall the names. Hard not to as they've been all over the news this week. As it happens, I did speak to Daisy one night in the line for takeout at the pizzeria." Warner leaned casually against the back of the truck and folded his arms across his chest. "I didn't realize it was her until I watched the news."

Nodding, Carter made a few notes. He had no need to. It was just a ploy to make Warner believe it was a routine questioning, but he fit the profile, moved around, and carried heavy bags. "When was this and do you recall the conversation?"

"Let me see." Warner stared into space. "I did buy pizza last Saturday night. Maybe it was that week, maybe it was during the week. I'm not sure. We spoke about the weather, I think, and the crazy Halloween displays."

"Was she alone or with a friend?" Jo lifted her chin.

"Alone, I believe." Warner cleared his throat. "I was just being neighborly, is all. Making small talk in a lineup to pass the time. Everyone does it. It's a friendly town. I recalled seeing her only when her photograph came on the TV. I don't know her or the other woman."

Lifting his pen, Carter nodded. "You still live on Stanton?"

"Yeah." Warner rolled his eyes. "We nearly done here. I have a truck to unload."

"Just a few more questions." Jo smiled. "We won't keep you long."

Carter straightened. "Where were you between the hours of six and midnight Saturday night?"

"At home, relaxing." Warner rubbed his chin. "I get up at four most mornings, so I go to bed early."

"No wife or girlfriend to corroborate that?" Jo stared at him.

"Not yet." Warner laughed. "I date but the hours I work make it hard for romance." His gaze moved up and down Jo and he smiled. "I don't see a wedding band on you either. Maybe we should get together for a drink sometime? Two lonely people looking for companionship."

"That's very kind of you." Jo lowered her lashes. "But I prefer being single."

"Truthfully, so do I." Warner smiled at her. "Some women can be a pain in the ass."

Incredulous, Carter stared from one to the other, Jo was more of the "Do you know the consequences of hitting on a federal agent?" kind of gal. He cleared his throat. "Same question, where were you on Saturday night between the hours of six and midnight?"

"Like I said, I dropped by the pizzeria and took a pie home." Warner narrowed his gaze. "They have a CCTV camera there. You'll see me waiting. I didn't speak to anyone as far as I recall. The place was crowded."

"What about Saturday afternoon?" Jo was expressionless. "You don't work Saturday afternoon, do you?"

"Some days I do, but not last Saturday. It depends on what the clients need. Sometimes they want an extra pickup." Warner sighed. "Last Saturday afternoon, I went into the forest and collected firewood and pinecones. If you recall, there was a service announcement for everyone to help clear the dead branches over fall and winter to prevent wildfires next summer." He looked from one to the other. "As the forest is just across the road, I collect as much as I can and saw it into logs for winter. It sure beats buying fuel."

"Yeah, it would." Jo handed him her card. "If you remember

anything else, like if you saw anyone else speaking to either of the women, please call me."

"I will." Warner gave her a long look and pushed the card into his top pocket and patted it.

A man came out from the back of the bay and stood staring at them hands on hips.

"How much longer, Duane? We're waiting to process your load."

"Got to go." Warner nodded to Jo and climbed back inside the back of his van.

Carter folded his notebook and stared after him. He turned to Jo as they walked back to the cruiser. "He fits the profile."

"So does he." Jo indicated a gardener out front of the hotel, pushing twigs and branches into a large bag. "His truck is full of bags. He's six feet tall, strong, and drives a vehicle that is invisible to most people. We're pulling at straws trying to fit these crimes to the suspects. I looked at Warner's hands. If he'd been out digging graves, he'd likely have soil under his nails or rougher hands from using a shovel. I didn't see that. Strong, slightly calloused hands, but they're clean. Neat nails. Yeah, he hit on me, but sometimes that can be a way to deflect attention from themselves. Unless we find more evidence, I can't see Warner as a solid suspect. The evidence we have is circumstantial at best. Just how many people were in the pizzeria last Saturday night? How many people visit the beauty parlor or the general store? My main concern still lies with Frank Stark. He was seen speaking to Freya and was watching her. He followed her and then a white vehicle was seen driving fast along Stanton away from the scene of the crime."

Carter pulled open the door of the cruiser and slid inside. "Yeah, he'll be on the top of Jenna's list. We're done for now. I need to give Zorro a run in the park. Do you want me to drop you by the office?"

"No, thanks. I'll come with you." Jo smiled. "I need the

exercise, followed by a coffee and a slice of pie at Aunt Betty's Café."

Carter grinned. "Kane's bad habits are rubbing off on you." He snorted. "What happened back there? You usually bite off the heads of guys who ask you out."

"Not all the guys." Jo giggled. "Just those who might be serial killers." She raised both eyebrows. "With Warner, I was just testing his reaction. Often serial killers like to make friends with investigators, mainly to discover what they know about the case. The way I handled him, I left crumbs behind. He was expecting a rebuff and he was given a gentle refusal. He thinks he has me on his side."

Snorting, Carter pulled up opposite the park. "I figure he already has. You don't believe he's our man."

"I didn't say that." Jo turned in her seat to look at him. "I said, he is one of many who fit the profile, but we have no solid evidence against him. The thing is, if he tries to get closer, we'll know for sure."

THIRTY-EIGHT

Covering her face from the stench of death, Jenna almost bumped into Kane. The moment he drew his weapon, she did the same and took cover beside the refrigerator. Ahead of her Kane flattened against the wall, holding his M18 pistol out at arm's length.

"What's the holdup?" Maxwell walked toward the doorway and froze. "Don't shoot. I'm unarmed. What's this all about?" He held up his hands.

"What stinks?" Kane held his weapon steady.

"Oh, sorry about the smell. I should have said something." Maxwell smiled benevolently. "I do taxidermy, roadkill mostly. I'm used to the smell."

Gagging, Jenna holstered her weapon and pulled out a face mask. Kane wouldn't allow Maxwell to move a muscle. She pressed it to her face. "Is there anyone else in the house?" She slid her pistol from the holster. "Hands on your head and step away from the door. Walk backward. Kane, take a look around."

"Hey, what do you think I've done, murdered someone and brought them home?" Maxwell's eyes popped wide open in shock. "Stop waving that weapon at me. Is this what I get for calling in on the hotline? I'm never doing that again. That's for darn sure."

She moved closer to the doorway as Kane slid inside the room, his gun aimed at Maxwell. Her heart pounded as Kane cleared each room.

"I'm heading into the root cellar." Kane's voice came from deep inside the cabin.

"There's nothing down there." Maxwell's shoulders lifted. "The place gives me the creeps. At night, I often hear voices coming from down there as if it's haunted." He shuddered. "Maybe it's the wind but I keep the bolt across the door. Over Halloween it gets worse, as if evil spirits are trying to escape."

Swallowing hard but keeping her weapon pointed at him, Jenna glared at him. "If you're so scared about living in the forest, why live here all alone?"

"I prefer the solitude." Maxwell's gaze slid over her. "And I haven't been able to convince anyone to come and live here with me."

Wrinkling her nose, Jenna sighed with relief when Kane's footsteps came along the passageway. She hadn't taken her eyes from Maxwell's face. "Maybe the smell is the problem. I don't know many people who could live here in this putrid stench."

"Clear." Kane walked into the room wearing a face mask. "We'll talk outside. Take it nice and slow." Kane waved his pistol at the man. "Sheriff, we'll follow you."

Desperate to get away from the smell, Jenna hurried outside and walked some distance from the house, inhaling clean air. When Maxwell came out, Kane followed and holstered his weapon. She waited for them to come to her and turned to Maxwell. "Do you have a license for taxidermy?"

"Yeah, it just so happens I do." Maxwell nodded. "I'm guessing you won't want me going inside to fetch it, seeing as you somehow figure I'm a threat."

"Usually when we smell death it means someone has a dead

body inside their cabin." Kane stared him down. "Trust me, we've seen more than our fair share."

Still smelling death in her nose, Jenna looked at Maxwell. "The white vehicle you saw driving along Main, what else can you tell us about it? Make? Model? Did you see the driver?"

"It was a white van, like a delivery van." Maxwell stared into space and then back at Jenna. "I just caught a glimpse of it. It was moving fast, way over sixty miles an hour, and I only saw the taillights. I was just saying goodbye to my friends in the parking lot when it flew past."

"You own a vehicle?" Kane scanned the area. "Where is it?"

"I own a truck and a horse trailer. I leave it parked on the fire road, the one that runs from Stanton before it joins the one that goes to Bear Peak. You know that part that's covered in gravel? Everyone who goes hunting leaves their vehicles there. It's safe and my truck is old. No one would want to steal it." He waved a hand toward the trail. "I ride my horse here. This way I'm off the grid, and if I need to go to town, I take my horse with me. It's comfortable in the trailer."

Jenna nodded. "So, you went straight home after dinner at Antlers?"

"Yeah, I have a big old flashlight to find my way home in the dark." Maxwell grinned. "I carry a rifle and bear spray as well."

"What about Wednesday evening between six and midnight?" Kane straightened.

"Wednesday I went to the general store, picked up a few things around three, and came home." Maxwell shrugged. "I've been here since."

Jenna sighed. It was a waste of time. There would be CCTV cameras at both of the places he'd visited, and she'd check them out, but proving he was at home when he said he was would be impossible. Without solid evidence, they had zip. "Okay, thanks for your time, Mr. Maxwell."

Back at the horses, she went to her backpack and unzipped

it. Inside she carried a can of hand cleaner. She sprayed her hands and tossed it to Kane. "Spray me all over. I'm not taking that stink home with me."

"Sure, so do me as well." He aimed the can at her and shook his head. "You should have seen inside. The place was filled with animal remains, skins, drying skulls, it was like a Halloween nightmare. The cellar was empty and the only place in there that didn't stink." He sprayed his hands and then handed her the can.

Jenna liberally coated him and shook her head. "He was creepy. He said he hears voices at night and believes people are buried in the floor of the cellar. He never goes down there."

"It's probably wolves following the stink." Kane removed his face mask and looked at Blackhawk. "It was another off-the-grid weird person."

"How so?" Blackhawk handed him the reins to Moon Dancer.

"He has a house filled with animal body parts and taxidermy all over." Kane rubbed the end of his nose. "It smells like death in there."

"I thought as much, or there was sickness inside." Blackhawk smiled. "The spraying hasn't helped too much. Hopefully the fresh air will blow away the smell."

Jenna stepped into Kane's hand, and he boosted her into the saddle. "Can we get away from here and take ten? After that experience, I'd like a strong hot cup of coffee."

"There's that clearing we came through, we can stop there, it's five minutes ride from here." Blackhawk mounted and smiled at her. "We can at least enjoy the ride back. The forest is beautiful at this time of the year and Duke is enjoying the walk."

Jenna's satellite phone buzzed and she shot Kane a glance. "Oh, I wonder what's up? Maybe Carter has found a suspect?" She accepted the call and it was Wolfe. "What have you got for me, Shane?" She placed the call on speaker and Kane moved closer to listen.

"*I have a few things you need to know.*" Wolfe cleared his throat. "*With so many cases running alongside each other here, it's complicated. First, we'll talk about the missing woman, presumed dead at this point, Daisy Lyon. The blood smears and spatter Kane found belong to what we assume is the victim. It is a match to the blood in the bathroom. The MO is the same as the Freya Richardson case. We discovered blood-trace evidence in the shower but nothing else. In both cases, the drain in both showers was clean, as in the killer made sure they were clean. The residue we sucked from the pipes had no traces of blood, so the shower was cleaned and left running for a time. The blood traces we discovered came from the walls of the shower. To our advantage, the killer concentrated on the base of the shower and drain. He wouldn't have seen the blood traces on the tile. It was only because we swabbed the entire area they were discovered.*"

Jenna chewed on her bottom lip. "It's the same MO as all the crime scenes going way back, but the shower part is new. I'd say he did that all along and it was missed."

"*There's nothing in any of the forensic reports that mention the shower. I'm assuming they believed the victims stepped from the shower and were attacked, end of story. We know there was more happening because now we have the tapes of the murders.*" He sighed. "*The last one, cold case number six, had an old MP3 player in the grave. This is untraceable, so we have no idea who owned it. This means we have no clue to any other victims. If we'd been able to identify the owner, it would have given a clue to where the Halloween Slasher was operating before he came to Black Rock Falls.*"

"Have you identified any of the other victims?" Kane leaned closer and raised his voice.

"*Yeah, they all came from what Jo would call his comfort zone, so all we had to do was to put the names on the recordings*" *to the list of missing persons from seven and eight years ago. We then obtained dental records and medical records. We have a list of names. I'll send them to you with their last known locations. I've sent all the names to Kalo and he's hunting down the next of kin. I'll notify them, as after this long, I don't figure they'd appreciate a visit from the local sheriff. I'll be able to answer their questions."*

Impressed by how fast Wolfe and Norrell had worked to identify the victims, Jenna nodded. "That's amazing, thank you." She took a deep breath. "How long before we have the causes of death?"

"Norrell is working around the clock. She has done a preliminary examination on each victim looking for similarities, but it's early days. She did say they all have bone damage to indicate sharp forced trauma to the neck, as in cut from front to back with enough force to cut the vertebrae. This would indicate a strong powerful man. In the neck, it's not easy or necessary to cut through to the spine. A stab in the carotid artery alone would kill. This is overkill."

"It makes me wonder if he attacked someone at one time and they survived." Kane rubbed his chin.

"Maybe. That's why you're the investigators and I'm the medical examiner." Wolfe chuckled. *"I'll be interested to hear what you find. I'll call you when I get any more information."* He disconnected.

"So, now he makes sure they're dead each time." Kane looked at Jenna. "Killing as we've seen isn't easy. Most times, the first kill is messy and rushed. In strangulation victims, the killer renders them unconscious, but it takes four minutes of sustained pressure on the carotid artery to kill someone, and that takes a lot of strength with bare hands. It's easier with a cord, from behind and using a knee in the back to sustain the pressure. You'll notice as the stranglers go along, they usually adopt different methods to ensure death."

"I believe that is too much information, Dave." Blackhawk had paled and he rubbed one hand down his face. "My agreement with Wolfe is we not discuss the details unless it's tribal. Can we do the same?"

"Sure." Kane looked abashed. "I'm sorry, I shouldn't have been discussing methods of killing someone, when we're enjoying a ride in the forest."

"Thanks." Blackhawk gave him a nod. "I figure, after listening to ways to strangle someone, I need a strong cup of coffee too."

THIRTY-NINE

How interesting. I've never enjoyed being interviewed by law enforcement, not knowing if they plan to drag me away in handcuffs and take me to the sheriff's office for interrogation. All I could think of was, What had gone wrong? What had possibly led them to me? Circumstance, maybe but I was one of many people near Freya and Daisy before they became mine. Anyway, how could they possibly know my plans? They couldn't read my mind or see through my pupils and into the lenses at a reflection of what I'd done. Did a flash of red linger there in a beautiful memory of gushing blood? As they asked their questions, my mind kept moving from Freya to Daisy, reliving each step, hearing their last breaths, the feel of their blood on my bare skin. I wanted to bathe in the red warmth but then I'd have given the forensic department a part of me and that could never happen.

I can read them like books. They have nothing. I left nothing behind, I never do and my casual attitude would speak volumes to them. I could see their calculated glances, trying to read what I'd never reveal. I wanted to laugh at their feeble attempts to get inside my mind. If they knew what was in there, they'd be running away so fast all I'd see is dust in their wake. My mouth grows dry and my fingers itch to slide my knife silently into soft scented flesh. The night is coming, and I have one more to offer. The grave is dug, the preparation faultless. All I need to do is ramp up the fear factor. The final offering must be the best. The more fear and suffering I can inflict, the more bountiful will be my reward.

I wonder what will happen if they discover the graves? Will I need to abandon my Halloween offerings—again? Have they no idea how important it is for me to complete the ritual before the moon rises on the last night of the month? I shake my head in denial. It can't happen. I'm way too smart to leave evidence of graves behind. They'll find nothing—not now—not ever.

I grin at my reflection. You see, I'm just a normal guy. Everyone is safe for now because my next offering has been chosen, but Halloween comes every year and I'll be making my list. The things that go missing from your house and the feeling that someone has been inside your personal space isn't your imagination. It's usually me. I've already dug a grave especially for you. You see, no one ever knows when I'm coming, but the moment you step from the shower and see me, it's too late.

FORTY

After riding for a time, they stopped for a break. Blackhawk had taken them a different way through the forest and the trail had opened up to a small clearing opposite the river. The water flowed fast and wide and as the afternoon clung to the last rays of the sun, the mist already had started its journey through the forest and on its way to town. Watching the twirling ghostly shapes emerge from water and join the procession sent chills down Jenna's spine. This close to Halloween she wondered if they were witnessing the opening of the doors between life and death. Could the stories handed through time be true? How many myths had been proved to be true as archaeological digs uncovered artifacts from places once deemed to have been formed in someone's fanciful imagination?

"The rising mist resembles spirits leaving another world to visit." Blackhawk smiled at her as if he'd read her mind. "This time of year, we see this more often. The rising mist and strange figures traveling through the forest and along the sidewalks in town."

"Yeah, it sure adds to the creepiness everyone seems to revel in over Halloween." Kane emptied his cup of coffee and sighed.

"What it says to me is it's getting late and close to the time we collect Tauri, and we need to go. We try to keep to the same time schedule unless something comes up or he wonders where we are."

Staring at the misty swirls disappearing through the trees, Jenna's imagination could easily take hold of reality. Like looking at clouds as a child, she could see dragons, their wings spread wide, flying across the sky. They looked real as well. She dragged her attention back to Blackhawk. "You believe the spirits come to visit over Halloween, don't you?" She passed her empty cup to Kane to pack away. "Over the years many myths appear to be fact. I'm leaning toward your way of thinking."

"I find it strange that your version is about death and fear." Blackhawk mounted his horse and gathered his reins. "You should look back into the origins and see what the truth is behind Halloween. My thought is that it's been commercialized and lost its true meaning. Not that there's anything wrong with that because you all seem to enjoy the festival and the children gain special pleasure from trick or treating."

"I think Jenna likes the thrill of being scared at Halloween." Kane boosted her into the saddle and patted her on the thigh. "Although, we've had cause to be concerned over the last few years. For some reason, Halloween has become the World Series for serial killers. Just look at the reports coming in all over. It gets worse by the year." He handed Jenna her backpack.

Jenna dragged on her backpack and nodded. "Yeah, they're like werewolves on a full moon. All fighting to become the alpha."

"Well, I hope there's only one you need to catch this year." Blackhawk turned his horse into the trees. "For now, we follow the ghosts. They lead the way to town and go right past where we left our vehicles."

Within ten minutes inside the dark forest, the mist had reached her stirrups and all around had become a sea of rolling white waves, and yet ahead, Blackhawk moved forward as normal. His horse cutting a path through the white clouds and sending them rolling into another direction. Mesmerized by the strange and fascinating shapes moving along beside them, Jenna had the weird sensation she'd joined the procession. To each side of her the breeze whistling from the top of the mountain and through the trees, created different ghostly figures, from women in long gowns to men on horseback. She urged her horse forward. Her mind also made hideous shapes in the mist: faces with soulless eyes, beasts from nightmares that came so close she squeezed her eyes shut to push them away. She shook her head. As a mom and a responsible sheriff, she couldn't allow her imagination to take hold, but she recognized that the Halloween terrors came from her childhood. She had aways enjoyed reading spooky stories and watching scary movies, which remained fixed in her memory. She recalled a comic book she'd once read where a monster with long sharp claws had one hand clutching a bedroom door as if waiting to go inside. The jolt of fear she'd experienced from seeing that one story had imprinted on her to such a degree that she could never sleep with the door ajar, always expecting that clawed hand to creep around the door and a monster to appear. It had taken plenty of convincing from Kane to make her leave the door ajar so they could hear Tauri. Even now, with a special ops machine between her and the door, the image still haunted her and before she turned out the light she'd pull the door wide open, which Kane figured was hilarious.

After unsaddling and tending the horses, they assisted Blackhawk with loading them back into the trailer. Jenna waved him goodbye and they climbed into the Beast. In the back seat, Duke snuggled into his blanket and was asleep before Kane had started the engine. She blew out a long breath and they drove along the fire road, seeing the dust cloud from Blackhawk's trailer mix with the mist. In the last shafts of sunlight, it looked as if it had been sprinkled with gold. She turned to Kane. "We should have time to drop by the office before we collect Tauri." She checked her phone. "It seems strange we haven't heard from Jo and Carter. I hope they're okay."

"Call Maggie." Kane turned onto Stanton and accelerated. "They'd have called in. It's getting late. They probably went back to the cottage. I'm guessing they'll need to report in and keep Kalo up to date with their movements. They might be running the field office, but they still need to send reports to the director. When they're away, Kalo runs the office." He smiled. "I'm not exactly sure what would happen if something sinister went down in Snakeskin Gully while they were away. I can't see Kalo charging out to assist the local sheriff."

Smiling, Jenna shrugged. "They'd jump in the chopper and head home, I guess." She made the call. "Hi, Maggie. Have Jo and Carter checked in?"

"Yeah, and they're on their way back to the cottage." Maggie chuckled. *"It must have been a long day for Carter. He said to tell you he'd be buying some prime rib for dinner. Jo said she'd get all the fixings. I figure they're planning on cooking for you tonight."*

Jenna smiled. "Sounds good. What about Rio and Rowley?"

"They're here looking over the drone footage." Maggie sighed. *"I don't figure they've found anything yet. Nothing else has happened. It's been a very quiet day, well, apart from them darn witches in the Halloween display next door. Their cackling is driving me crazy."*

After checking her watch, Jenna took in the heavy mist on Stanton. It was so thick as they entered Main she could only see the Halloween displays by the flashes of light from the automatons. "It's very foggy tonight. Send the deputies home and shut up shop. We're not needed, so we'll go and collect Tauri and head home before it gets any worse."

"Okay, I'll tell them now." Maggie cleared her throat. *"The*

mist is pressing against the glass doors. Most sensible folks would be heading home. I'll see you in the morning."

As Jenna disconnected, Kane stopped outside the house close to her office to collect Tauri from Nanny Raya's home. The mist swirled around the truck, and as Jenna opened her door, across the road a white shape slid into the alleyway. It turned and a hideous face appeared for a second through the mist before it vanished into a cloud. Swallowing the rush of fear, Jenna hurried to Kane's side and gripped his arm.

"What?" Kane looked both ways and then down at her.

Ignoring the prickling of her skin, Jenna shook her head. She had a vivid imagination is all and would just have to deal with it. "Nothing, let's go."

The gate to the house whined as she followed Kane through it but as they reached the porch, she turned and searched the misty sidewalk. Her heart pounded in her chest. Someone was watching her, someone in the mist.

FORTY-ONE

After visiting her dog at the vet, Wendy drove home. She spent time with the little dog before and after work. The long-acting poison was slowly working its way out of the dog's system and hopefully a few more days in the care of the veterinary surgeon would see her coming home. She pulled up outside her house, opened the glovebox, and pulled out the Glock. Since the scare, she never walked inside her house without the pistol in her hand.

Even after taking an earlier shift, she still arrived home in the dark, and with the river so close, the front door was obscured by heavy mist. Swallowing her fear, she swung her purse over one shoulder, and with her keys in her right hand and gun in her left, took a deep breath and dashed for the front door. Inside with the door bolted, she reached for the light. It was warm inside and the smell of smoke tainted the air. She pushed her keys into her pocket and holding her Glock out in front of her, moved slowly into the family room. In the hearth, the embers, which she'd swear she'd left cold, glowed red. Agreed, she'd used large logs the previous evening to save on the heating bills, but she'd been sure there'd only been gray ashes there this morning. Fear rose the hairs on her arms and goosebumps prickled over her. Momentarily frozen, she kept her back to the wall and, switching on lights as she went, moved along the passageway and into the kitchen. Her gaze swept over the kitchen table and to the neat stack of mail. She blinked and keeping the kitchen door in sight, eased her way to the back door and turned the knob. It was just as she'd left it, with the key in the lock.

Breathing a sigh of relief, she went back to the kitchen. Had she collected the mail before leaving for work? She had been in a rush to see Lola, so maybe it had slipped her mind. She sorted through the mail, finding the usual bills and flyers. She narrowed her gaze at a flyer for the Halloween Ball and smiled. This year would be fun. It would be good to meet up with all the people she'd gotten close to in town. The house creaked and the sound of nails running down a chalkboard spun her around. She moved swiftly from the window. If anyone planned to frighten her tonight, they'd picked the wrong girl. Gathering her courage, she retraced her steps and headed for the bedrooms. She went into each one, checking all around to make sure no one was hiding. When she reached her own bedroom, she opened the closet doors and peered inside. Feeling a little stupid, she went into the bathroom. It looked just as she'd left it. She'd wiped down the vanity and placed her makeup bag into the cabinet above the sink. Something touched her toe, and she glanced down to see a lipstick on the tile. It wasn't one she usually used and frowned, wondering how it had gotten there. She bent to pick it up and opening the cabinet placed it back into the makeup bag. A chill went through her—the fire, the mail, and now the lipstick. Had someone been inside her home? It wasn't possible, was it? She'd taken every precaution by locking all the doors and windows. The scary guy in the

Halloween mask had really upset her and after hearing Sheriff Alton tell Susie about an actor scaring people, she'd realized she'd become the brunt of a joke. She closed the cabinet and looked at her reflection in the mirror. "Wendy. You need to get a grip."

FORTY-TWO

FRIDAY

The morning was eerily still as Jenna walked from the kindergarten with Kane at her side. The mist still swirled along the sidewalk as people walked by. The sinister laughs and chuckles of the Halloween displays drifted toward her and she turned and scanned Main. It appeared so different in the daylight. It was festive with all the brightly colored bunting hanging over every available space. She turned to look back at the kindergarten. It gave her a pang of regret parting with Tauri each morning and she wondered how she'd cope if they ever had a baby and with her working full-time. She climbed into the Beast and waited for Kane to slide behind the wheel. "It's hard walking away and leaving Tauri, but if I have a baby, how can I leave and rush off on a case?"

"Don't worry, we'll work it out together. We have Nanny Raya and room to build a nursery suite in the office. It's not like you'd be away for hours at a time. I figure we'd work it out fine, most parents do." Kane looked at her and raised one eyebrow. "Is there something I should know?"

Jenna shook her head. "I wish, but no."

"Tauri loves playing with the other kids and he looks

forward to going to kindergarten." Kane turned the Beast toward the office. "It's tough for him at the weekends if we need to work, but Blackhawk has been using those times to spend with him at Nanny Raya's. Tauri is smart enough to understand we have weeks like this when we're busy and weeks when we have time as a family. It's the mothering instinct, Jenna. No one is good enough to care for your child. I figure it's normal because I feel the same way." He pulled into his parking space at the office. "It looks like the gang's all here."

Not wanting to discuss the case with Jo and Carter over dinner the previous evening, when Tauri was awake they'd eaten, and Jo and Carter had gone back to the cottage. It had been a relaxed evening after days of stress. Rested and alert, Jenna bounded up the steps and pushed into the office. The smell of fresh coffee filled the room and she smiled at Maggie behind the counter. "Where is everyone?"

"They've set up the conference room, seeing that there's so many of you on this case." Maggie pointed toward the stairs. "Have you made any headway?"

Shaking her head, Jenna shrugged. "Nothing substantial. We're trying all angles, but so far we haven't found a potential suspect who looks right for the crime."

"There's been nothing of interest on the hotline." Maggie rolled her eyes skyward. "Sometimes I figure people call in for an excuse to chat. Halloween has the townsfolk's imaginations running riot. One woman called who swore she'd seen a unicorn running along the middle of Main late last night, but she wasn't sure if it was a zebra with a horn. When I explained that unicorns were usually white, she admitted she'd made a mistake. Like I said, people's imaginations get the better of them over Halloween."

"People see many strange things in the mist at night." Kane smiled. "Add a good sprinkling of weird whines and cackles from the local displays and anything is possible."

"They do indeed." Maggie turned as the phone on the desk rang. "Ah... another report of a headless horseman no doubt."

Laughing, Jenna headed for the stairs and walked to the conference room. The sound of voices drifted toward her as she pushed open the door. Jo, Carter, Rio, and Rowley all sat at the long table. The whiteboard had been brought up to date and she recognized Rio's neat handwriting, listing victims of the cold cases on one side and the missing women on the other. Suspects and information on each set up in a bulleted list. They must have arrived early or worked late to have correlated all the information on both cases. On the bench both coffee machines gurgled, filling the glass jugs with a rich aromatic brew. The pod machine was a luxury she enjoyed, but she'd noticed most of her team preferred the filtered variety. She placed her things on the table and glanced around the room. "Morning. You've been busy, Rio. Thanks for all the information. It's good to see everything at a glance."

"It was a joint effort." Rio leaned back in his chair. "After searching through hours of drone footage without a result, we spent the rest of our time piecing together all the information everyone had gathered to date."

Jenna nodded and sat down to bring everyone up to speed with her trip to Twisted Limbs Trail and the strange Hank Maxwell. She grimaced recalling the smell and the overconfident man. "Could he be a serial killer? Yeah, in my opinion he is more than capable. He lives in the forest, already has a house that stinks of death, and was over-cooperative."

"Hmm, burning potential evidence makes him suspicious." Carter frowned. "If he moves around on horseback, he knows the forest well. I wouldn't discount him. He could be moving bodies in his horse trailer and transporting them on his horse to a burial site."

"His behavior would suggest he's a person of interest." Jo made notes on her iPad and glanced up at Jenna. "We don't know if he collects roadkill or he's butchering animals for fun. Many psychopaths begin their killing sprees by mutilating animals. We've already agreed the MO of this killer is well rehearsed. He's either been killing for longer than we realize or he's practiced on animals."

"I'm confident he's the same man who murdered the women seven years ago." Kane rested both hands on the table, his fingers loosely interlaced. "The crime scenes match. This guy is re-creating a scene, replaying something that happened to him a long time ago. We all agree he's following a ritual and we also know that some psychopaths can go through periods of not killing as they plan a multiple murder. It seems this particular type of psychopath is content with a series of killings once a year. I would imagine he spends the rest of the year selecting his victims."

Jenna glanced at the whiteboard and nodded in agreement. "They all have the transport and types of occupations where they can move bodies around, plus they move around without people noticing them because they're seen regularly." Her attention moving to Jo and Carter. "I'm glad you found Duane Warner. What is your opinion of him?"

"Same as the others." Jo stood and poured a cup of coffee and then turned back to look at her. "Smooth as silk, with just the right amount of indignation at being questioned."

"I'd keep him on the list." Carter tossed his toothpick into the trash and stood. "I'll pour the coffee. I figure the interview with him was routine."

After listening to their encounter with Duane Warner, Jenna rubbed her temples. "So, we have another possible but only circumstantial evidence. Do you figure we need to bring him in for questioning and hope he incriminates himself?"

"It would be pointless unless we have some shred of evidence to point to him being involved." Carter handed out cups and slid the fixings on the table. "I figure Warner, Stark,

Cummings, and Maxwell are all possibles." He dropped into a chair and looked around the table. "We have Kalo checking them out again, but we come up against the same background with all of them. It's like they're facsimiles of each other. They all drive vehicles suitable for carrying a body and that blend into daily life. They were all in town around the time of the murders, although we can't prove it. They move around and work odd hours." He stirred his coffee and tapped the spoon on the side of the cup. "The one I'd have at the top of the list is Stark. The rest are close behind, but he's the only one of them who we have saying he'd been actively interested in Freya Richardson and we know he spoke to Daisy in the pizzeria."

Making a note on her "things to do" list, Jenna met his gaze. "Okay, I guess we haul him in for questioning. He's a postal worker, so we should be able to locate him." She thought for a beat. "Not that we'd be able to hold him as we only have an assumption of a crime. For now, both our victims are missing persons." She turned her attention to Rio and Rowley. "Rowley, call all the local departments of the Montana Department of Fish, Wildlife and Parks for here, Louan, and Blackwater and ask them to notify all their wardens that we're searching for missing persons and, more likely, bodies. They know the signs to look for if our victims have been dumped anywhere." She turned to Rio. "Do the same for the tour guides, hikers clubs, and all the hunting clubs. Also update the media release, reminding people to be on the lookout for the missing women and to call in about anyone acting suspiciously, including any vehicles parked late at night."

"Okay." Rowley stood, picked up his coffee, and headed downstairs.

"Do you want me to include prowlers on the list?" Rio frowned. "I know it's Halloween and all, but maybe if we make it clear that, Halloween or not, prowlers set on frightening people at night won't be tolerated?"

"Maybe you should tell them to shoot on sight?" Carter grinned at Jenna over the rim of his cup. "It would save you the trouble of hunting them down."

Shaking her head, Jenna gave him her best disparaging glance. "I guess it's within their legal right to do so if they feel threatened, but so far our townsfolk haven't descended into the mentality of the Wild Westerners." She looked at Rio. "Mention being aware of prowlers, but leave out the shoot-to-kill advice."

"Okay." Rio's lips lifted in the corners as he fought back a grin. "Aw, and just when the media releases were getting interesting." He collected his things and, shaking his head, strolled out the door.

FORTY-THREE

Getting nowhere fast in the investigation, Jenna turned to Jo. "We've exhausted all avenues of the investigation. We have a guy slaughtering women and I need to stop him before he strikes again." She ran both hands through her hair and stared at the table. "Why can't we locate the bodies? Where the heck is he hiding them?"

"It would sure help if we could locate them." Kane finished his coffee and collected the cups and took them to the sink. "I've looked over the search areas that Rio and Rowley have covered with the drones and the problem is, if he's covered the graves with leaves, they're undetectable. He'd need only see the drones flying around to keep well away from that area during the daytime. This guy knows the forest. It's an angle we might explore."

"I'm not sure how much we'll get out of reinterviewing the suspects." Jo leaned back in her chair and crossed her legs. "If one of them is the killer, and I'll say 'killer' because it's obvious no one could survive the blood loss we witnessed at the crime scenes, then he knows we haven't found a body." She twirled a pen in her fingers. "The media release will let him know we have no idea where he's hidden the bodies. The women are being spoken about as 'missing,' so why do you figure he'll falter in an interview? In my opinion, it will make him super confident. Right now, he thinks he's untouchable." She shrugged. "Which it seems is correct."

As usual Jo was right and Jenna lifted her chin. "This is the reason I want to bring Stark in for questioning. You and Kane have a knack for asking questions that dig right into a person's psyche, and maybe he'll let down his guard." She shrugged and swept a gaze over each of them. "Right now, I'll take any suggestions going forward because we're getting nowhere. Sure, we have suspects, but I could pick out ten people in the line outside the pizzeria and drag them in for questioning and chances are they've all had contact with both victims at one time or another. We know it's a hangout for the younger set. It's there, Aunt Betty's Café, or Antlers. I'm not seeing many out at the Triple Z Bar or having the cash to splash at the Cattleman's Hotel." She sighed. "Unless there's sporting events going on, the age group between leaving college and settling down has limited places to meet in town."

"You mean since they closed the drive-in movies?" Carter popped a toothpick into his mouth and grinned. Trust me, there are plenty of meeting places in town. You see, not being single, you don't have the need to be hunting a mate. The Turf and Surf is one. The ski resort is open even during summer on weekends. Single people go there. The showgrounds have things going on all weekend—markets, car shows, animal shows—and there's the art show at the town hall. There are a ton of places to meet people in Black Rock Falls."

Raising both eyebrows, Jenna stared at him. "Well, I'm sure you'd know. Have you had any downtime of late to spend in your fishing cabin?"

"Not for a while." Carter's eyes sparkled with amusement. "But I drop by from time to time to unwind."

"We've been sitting jawing for an hour or so." Kane stared at Carter. "I figure discussing your downtime exploits is a waste of valuable time. I'm with Jenna. We get Stark in and shake him down. I want to find out more about him. He's acting like a creep, and from what we've been told, seemed to have an obsession with Freya. It's all we have for now and I suggest we run with it."

Glad of the support, Jenna smiled at him. "That works for me."

"I'll call Kalo and he'll locate Frank Stark." Carter pulled out his phone. "He'll be able to access the postal service computer and pinpoint where he is at any given time. As luck would have it, the postal workers run to a tight schedule." He made the call.

A few minutes later Kalo returned the call and Carter made a few notes before disconnecting. Jenna looked at him. "Any luck?"

"Oh yeah, better than you imagine." Carter smiled and pushed to his feet. "He's due back at the receiving dock in twenty minutes."

Nodding, Jenna heaved an inward sigh of relief and looked at Kane. "Go in the cruiser with Carter and bring in Stark for questioning. Make some excuse to his boss. If he's innocent, I don't want him losing his job because we hauled him in."

"I'll think of something." Kane shrugged. "Maybe we need him to identify someone seen on his run?"

Pushing to her feet, Jenna went to the sink to rinse the cups. "Okay, I'll be in interview room one when you get back. No cuffs. Make it friendly, okay?"

"Sure." Carter smiled at her. "I can be nice too." He followed Kane out of the door.

"He likes it here. He loves working on motorcycles with Dave and fishing." Jo took the cups that Jenna washed and dried them before setting them back on the shelf. "He's here more than you imagine. I figured he'd found someone but now I'm not sure. I know he likes solitude and misses his cabin in Snakeskin Gully. He has a one-bedroom shack in town. It must be suffocating. I invite him around for Sunday lunch most weekends, but he's like a cat on a hot tin roof. If he's not working a case, he's bored out of his mind."

Jenna dried her hands. "This worries you?"

"Well, I have Jaime, and as you now know, a child takes up all of our spare time, so I don't get lonely, and I have our nanny as well. I mix well with the locals and enjoy my downtime. Carter is a young man; he needs someone in his life. All this bravado about loving the single life is a lie. He wants a wife, a ranch, and a bunch of kids but just won't admit it." She shrugged. "He's been working too long with me. He knows about my cheating husband and messy divorce. I guess it makes him gun-shy."

Finding it hard to believe there was another side to Carter, Jenna nodded. "Maybe he just hasn't found the right woman yet? She'd need to love fishing and be happy to sit at home while he travels all over the state solving crimes. It wouldn't be easy to keep a relationship going with the strange hours we all work."

"I guess." Jo straightened. "So how do you want to handle the interview?"

Jenna thought for a beat. "I've already spoken to Stark. I think we all go into the room. You take the lead with Dave and see how it goes. Maybe you can dig something out of him. Carter is good at leaning on suspects, so it might just work. He was on Main when Freya left work. Maybe he saw something. That's an angle we can pursue."

"Okay." Jo collected her iPad and notes. "Let's do this."

FORTY-FOUR

Walking into the postal building, Kane went to the desk and asked to see the postmaster. He introduced himself to a woman in her thirties and gave' her his best apologetic expression. "Sheriff Alton would like Frank Stark to come down to the office to identify someone. It may take some time. Is he due out again this morning?"

"Not until two, so he needs to be back to have his truck loaded no later than one-thirty." The woman checked her computer and looked up at him. "On his break, he usually grabs a meal and rests up before he heads out again. We don't like our drivers to fall asleep at the wheel."

Kane nodded. "Oh, not a problem. This shouldn't take that long." He had a thought. "Does he drive the same mail van every day?"

"Yes, he starts early. We have a few drivers who start early and finish late. He has to be here before dawn, which means he needs to make sure he has gas in the truck. It works out better for all of us if they take the trucks home. Having their own gives them pride in their van. They look after them better this way."

She sighed. "I know it's not the way it is in other towns, but it works for me."

The story matched what Stark had told them. He touched his hat and headed out back to the delivery and dispatch bays. A white van was backed in and he made out Stark tossing bags to men in the loading bay, who placed them onto carts and wheeled them inside. He nodded to Carter, who was leaning casually against the wall, and then peered into the back of the van. "Need some help?"

"Sure." Stark frowned. "What, don't you have any crimes to solve today, Deputy?"

Kane's invitation to get inside the van was all he needed to make it legal. He climbed inside and walked to the back, scanning the bags, walls, and floor of the interior for any signs of blood. He inhaled, trying to catch a whiff of death, and lifted a bag from the back and tossed it to Stark. After moving each bag without finding anything of interest, he jumped down. The van was spotless, as if it had recently been washed down, the outside as well. Maybe he'd taken it to the car wash? He nodded to Stark and he closed the back doors. "The sheriff needs to speak to you. It's a follow-up to the interview we had recently. You might have seen something and not realized it. Do you mind coming down to the office with us? We'll drive you back when we're done."

"Mind if I drive there myself?" Stark moved his feet restlessly. "I need to eat and get back here to load my van."

Kane nodded. "Yeah, I'm aware. I spoke to your boss. I didn't want anyone getting the wrong impression about why we need to speak to you. I'll ride with you and explain."

"Okay, sure." Stark climbed inside the van.

After signaling to Carter to follow them, Kane climbed into the passenger seat. He could be sitting beside a serial killer, but if so, Stark had no idea of his skills. One chop to the neck and he'd likely kill him outright. He smiled to himself. It was just as well he stayed on the right side of the line. With his skills, if he turned rogue, people would die and nobody would be able to take him down.

At the office, after frisking Stark, Kane showed him into an interview room. He noted the surprise on the man's face when he was confronted with two FBI agents and Jenna. "Take a seat and we'll get this over with so you can get back to work."

"This interview is being recorded." Jenna switched on the recording device. "For your protection, I'll read you your rights." She Mirandized the startled man. "Do you wish to have a lawyer present?"

"I haven't broken the law, so no, I don't need one for routine questioning." Stark looked from one face to another. "I do know my rights and I can ask for a lawyer at any time, right?"

"Yes." Jenna sat down. "When a law officer reads you your rights, it's to protect you, Mr. Stark. This isn't a witch hunt."

"We've spoken to you about the night you watched Freya Richardson as she worked in the beauty parlor." Jo's pen was poised over a legal pad but her face was expressionless. "We need you to expand on what you saw that night." Her lips offered a small smile. "I know you believe you've told us everything about that night, but it's normal to miss things, so I want to go through it step-by-step and see if you can remember anything we can use to find Freya."

"I told you everything, I recall." Stark shrugged.

"Let's start with inside the pizzeria." Jo leaned back, twirling the pen in her fingers in a casual way. "You're sitting there eating your pie and looking into the street. What do you see?"

"Traffic, people moving through town, nothing unusual." Stark pressed both hands flat on the table, the index finger of the right hand tapping.

"Was Freya cleaning when you arrived, or was that later?" Kane leaned forward in his chair.

"No, Freya was in front of me, collecting a slice." Stark closed his eyes. "She was saying her truck was in the shop and she was on foot. She told the guy behind the counter she lived on Elm and hated walking home in the dark." His eyes opened. "I got my pie and took a seat alongside the window. She walked across Main and into the beauty parlor. She must have eaten her slice before she started work because it was ten minutes or so before I saw her inside. She arranged some Halloween decorations in the front window and came back outside to look at them. All the lights were on and she stripped off her jacket and started to clean. She worked hard, sweeping and wiping down, washing floors and the basins. She finished about the same time as I drank my soda. I checked the time and decided to walk to the dispatch bay and see if my truck had been loaded."

"Did you see anyone else on the sidewalk?" Jo made a few notes.

"Yeah, this time of the year people are out and about taking in the Halloween displays. It's spookier at night with the mist and all." Stark shrugged. "I don't recall anyone specifically, just regular folks, are all."

"So you followed her for a time?" Kane looked at him and raised one eyebrow in question. "As you were both traveling in the same direction?"

"Yeah, I went to pick up my truck." Stark blew out a breath. "I already told you all this."

"You mentioned it wasn't ready to leave, is that correct?" Kane checked his notes. "So what is it, you picked up the truck or waited for the truck and for how long?"

"Not long, five, maybe ten minutes or so." Stark's eyes flashed in annoyance. "What difference does it make?"

Jenna watched the questioning closely. Jo and Kane had

jumped on an inconsistency in Stark's memory. Intrigued, she leaned forward listening intently.

"You mentioned having a midnight delivery, but we've made inquiries. There weren't any late consignments on that night." Jo had mentioned a fact that Jenna wasn't aware of. Had Kalo found Stark's schedule on the net and only recently sent the information?

"You must have misheard me. I often load my truck late at night, so I can leave first thing in the morning." Stark stared at her. "That's what happened."

"You took mail home?" Carter barked a laugh. "I'm sure that's against the law."

"They make an exception for a few of us trustworthy guys." Stark glared at him. "Haven't you seen mailbags, Agent Carter? They have seals to prevent tampering. Only the receiving office can remove them and each one is recorded. I couldn't tamper with the US mail even if I wanted to." He rubbed both hands down his face. "You sayin' I took something from the mail?"

"No." Jo stared at him across the table. "It's the timeline, Mr. Stark. You were seen leaving after Freya set off for home. We know how long it took her to walk home and you could have easily caught up in your truck." She paused for a beat. "Did you follow her home? It's obvious to more than one witness you had more than a passing interest in her. Witnesses tell us you didn't take your eyes off her for a second from the minute she walked out of the pizzeria. Now she's missing. You didn't take her anywhere in your van, did you, Mr. Stark?"

"No, I didn't see her after I walked back to the depot." Stark had paled significantly. "If you figure I had something to do with her disappearance, then think again. Fingerprint my van if you want. Go ahead and forensically test it, but you won't find nothing." He huffed out an angry sigh and glared at them. "I ain't answering any more questions without a lawyer. I'm not being railroaded into something I didn't do."

Nodding to the others, Jenna noted the time and the conclusion of the interview. She looked at Stark. "That will be all for now. Thank you for your cooperation. You're free to go." She stood, flashed her card, and opened the door.

"Don't try and make me your scapegoat. I have rights." Stark stood and his eyes flashed with malice as he pushed past her and moved quickly along the passageway.

Jenna turned, allowing the door to click shut behind her. "What do you think?"

"I figure he's using the mail pickup as an alibi." Carter tossed a toothpick into his mouth. "He drove to her house, parked in the alleyway, and murdered her." He let out a long sigh. "We've been over the statements of all the potential suspects so many times my eyes are crossed. This has to be our guy. Proving it is another thing entirely."

"He does have a pile of folded mail sacks in the back of his van, I saw them before." Kane leaned against the wall. "Easy enough to put Freya inside, the other mailbags could cover the body if anyone stopped him. He took her home and somehow got her into the forest for burial." He looked at Jenna. "Same for Daisy. He had contact with her. We know this for sure. He admitted it. Who looks at a delivery van, especially a postal van? It's invisible, forgettable. He could park out back of Daisy's house and no one would see him. It's like a jungle out there."

Nodding, Jenna looked at Jo. "Is he capable of murder?"

"Yeah, he has an aggressive streak a mile wide." Jo collected her things from the desk. "The thing is, all we can do is watch him. There's not enough evidence against him for an arrest warrant. All we have is circumstantial, at best. Looking at Freya won't hold up in court for a murder conviction. We'll need to catch him in the act."

"Then we'll watch him." Kane folded his arms across his chest. "We know where he lives. We'll go by and install trail cams in the forest. Perfectly legal. If we make sure they watch only the road and forest, they won't invade his privacy. Ours have motion sensors. If he steps one foot out of his cabin overnight, we'll all get a notification via our phones." He smiled. "Then we follow him. He'll never see us coming." He looked at Carter. "Will he?"

"No way." Carter grinned around his toothpick and looked at Jenna. "Use of deadly force, Sheriff?"

It was an order she never ever wanted to give. "I'd prefer to find the other bodies and the motive behind years of murders at Halloween than see him dead." She looked from Kane to Carter. "I don't need dead heroes. Use your own judgment if you confront him."

"Okay, I'll go with Carter to scout out the forest around his cabin and set up the cameras. We'll discuss a plan of action, if and when Stark makes his move. I'll have the details by the time we get back. It might mean having two teams on the ground, one in the forest and one in town. We can't show our hand at any time if you want to catch him in the act."

As usual, Kane's field experience was an asset. Being sheriff, Jenna could never hope to have the versatile depth of knowledge of individual team members. Using the expertise of experts was the key to success. "Okay, let's make this happen. We know he is due out at two, so that gives you a couple of hours to set up the cameras before nightfall. We'll take a break now, and once we've set the cameras, we'll head for home to wait and see what happens. With Wolfe and Rio in town and Rowley to the north and us to the south, we'll have the area covered, whichever way he goes. Once he makes a move, we'll be on him. Time is getting short. He's going to strike tonight. I feel it in my gut."

FORTY-FIVE

It's late afternoon and I'm at Aunt Betty's Café. I needed a break, and sitting and watching Wendy go about her work was soothing. My hand trembles around my cup, and the distorted refection of my eyes in the rich brew is an insight into my mind right now. I know by my third offering I'm reaching my peak. I'm living on one long adrenaline rush and loving it. Right now, keeping calm and in control as time ticks by so slowly is torture. The sun is dropping low in the sky, the shadows creep across the sidewalk, and the mist rises. I'll be appeased soon but I wish it were now. The need to smell blood, feel the racing heart like a small bird's beneath my palms before it slows, jitters, and stops is like craving for an illegal drug. I press my hands around the hot cup. It burns my flesh but turns my mind away from the delicious images flooding my mind.

I stare at the hideous spider over the entrance. The red-eyed babies scattering when anyone walks past and the hissing is annoying. The entire town has gone mad, each store littering the sidewalk with bleeding corpses, skeletons, or other hideous debris, but with everyone's attention on the decorations, I can move around without one single person registering I was there.

Here at Aunt Betty's, I know where the CCTV cameras are located. They're aimed at the front counter. At Aunt Betty's you have choices: order at the counter or sit and wait for a server. I avoid the camera by sitting at a table. It's not rocket science.

The local kids are out and about taking in the sights. They seem to revel in the freezing temperatures and love the swirling mist. How easy it would be to pluck one from the sidewalk and drag them into an alleyway for some Halloween fun. I'm smiling but if I started killing kids, there wouldn't be a future generation.

Wendy, Wendy, Wendy, her name has been buzzing around my head for a time now. Last night I dreamed about her, hair wet from the shower, seeing my reflection in the mirror. It was just like being there and I woke with my heart threatening to leap from my chest. Even now, some hours later, I can see Wendy clear in my mind, her eyes pleading for me to stop as her life's blood pools on the white tile. I can see my reflection in her eyes as she takes her last breath. The vision is tantalizing. It's like the gift under the Christmas tree. You see it all wrapped in glossy paper with a fine bow on top but can't quite read the name on the label. You want so much to reach out and tear it apart to enjoy the contents, but a voice tells you it's not yet time. What is time anyway? A manmade invention to keep everyone at the right place? Like sheep we must all rise and be some-where because we follow time. Our lives are destined by age, when we all know age is a state of mind. I have no age. I refuse to acknowledge it because I'm going to live forever.

The clock on the wall ticks by another five slow minutes. This is what time does to a person's mind. Some days it drags along and other times it speeds like an out-of-control locomo-tive. Why is this? Are we really following the same time or are some of us moving faster than others? I finish my coffee and place the cup down. As if reading my mind, here comes Wendy to refill my cup and bring me a slice of pie. She remembered my favorite and gives me a wide wedge. Her smile lights up the room and I return it. I sigh, but she had her chance. I did ask her to go to the ball with me. If she'd agreed, I would have removed her from my list. It's a shame that she has someone else in her life... but not for long. Soon she'll be mine.

FORTY-SIX

"He's on the move." Kane stared at his phone and then lifted his gaze to Jenna.

Jenna's phone signaled a message. "Rio's on it." She looked at Kane. "I just knew something was going down tonight."

They'd eaten dinner and, with Tauri sound asleep, had retreated to the family room to drink coffee. No one wanted to retire early. Everyone's nerves were on edge.

"His schedule doesn't have him leaving town until five in the morning." Carter scrolled through his phone. "I wish we could have placed a tracker on his van. It would've made life easier."

Glancing toward the bedroom, Jenna's stomach gave a roll. She didn't want to wake Tauri and drag him over to Nanny Raya's at night, but if something went down, it would take valuable time to move him. She looked at Kane. "We'll need to take Tauri to Nanny Raya's before this explodes in our faces."

"Okay." Kane nodded and squeezed her arm. "We knew this would happen from time to time and so does he. Look at Jo's daughter. She accepts her mom is away for days at a time. Kids are adaptable."

"I'll stay and care for him." Jo looked from one to the other. "My expertise is in profiling criminals; yours is taking them down. The five of you will cope just fine without me. I'll act as the command center." She smiled.

Relieved, Jenna nodded. "That would really ease my mind. I want Tauri to have a stable upbringing. If I could have Nanny Raya living with us, I would, but it's impossible."

"How so?" Carter raised one eyebrow. "This place is like Fort Knox. She'd be safe living here."

"First up, we'd need to build her a separate dwelling. We can't use the cottage because we need that for visiting FBI agents. Since they've expanded the Rattlesnake Creek field office, we never know who will be dropping by." Kane shrugged. "Secondly, we didn't discover anything nasty when we did background checks, but sometimes we talk about cases at home, and you know darn well I have military information that's need-to-know, same as you. She doesn't have that level of clearance, so she remains in town. The house we bought for her is secure. It's just inconvenient when we need to be away on a case."

"I actually know a couple of FBI agents who retired without having kids. They missed having a family and became nannies." Jo nodded to Kane. "Maybe you need someone like that, who has clearance?"

Jenna's phone chimed a message, she swiped her phone and looked at it. "Rio said Stark is heading toward Stanton. We need to go." She looked at Jo. "He sleeps right through, so you won't have a problem. We'll leave Duke here." She looked at Carter. "Is Zorro staying here?"

"Yeah, he'll be fine with Duke." Carter looked at Kane. "I'll ride with you and Jenna. We'll need to leave a vehicle for Jo, for emergencies."

"Well, that's a relief but I could always try my hand at riding a Harley." She winked at Kane. "You wouldn't mind, right?"

"Well... maybe." Kane pulled on a liquid Kevlar vest from the pile he'd just dropped on the sofa and handed one to Jenna. "Need ammo?" His gaze moved to Carter as he went to the gun safe and unlocked it before filling his pockets. "Help yourself." He tossed a clip to Jenna.

Jenna pulled on her jacket. "We need to move it. Go, go, go." She waved the men toward the door and looked over one shoulder at Jo. "I'll call you if anything goes down." She hurried after Kane.

As the Beast roared along the highway, Jenna call Rio. "What's your position?"

"I'm not far from my house, tucked in the shadows facing Stanton. He hasn't passed me yet and he was heading this way." Rio sighed. *"The fog is really bad here, but I figure he'll spot my vehicle the moment I pull onto the road. What do you want me to do?"*

A message chimed and Jenna cleared her throat. "Wait up, I have a call from Rowley."

She took the call and listened. "Okay, Rio is heading your way and we'll be there in five. Use your comm from now on, so everyone hears what's going down." She disconnected Rowley and switched her phone back to Rio. "Rowley is on Main. He's driving Sandy's gray pickup. He's parked between the pizzeria and Aunt Betty's Café. Stay back and allow a few vehicles to go past before following Stark. Maybe take Maple and travel parallel with him. We're coming in hot. We've just made the highway into town now. Use your comm. We'll need hands-free communication if we're going to take this guy down."

"You got it." Rio disconnected.

Excitement shimmered through her as she reached into the glovebox and pulled out the comms, fitted hers, and then turned to look at Carter. "I have spares."

"I have my own. I just need to change it to your frequency."

Carter adjusted the control on his battery pack and clipped it to his belt. "I'm good to go."

"People are used to seeing us in Aunt Betty's." Kane glanced at Jenna. "I figure we wait there and let Rio and Rowley track Stark's movements. If we're seen holed up in the Beast, Stark will know he's under surveillance."

"Well, best we keep our jackets zipped." Carter barked a laugh. "The liquid Kevlar vests are a dead giveaway something's up."

Startled by the waves of white mist rolling across the blacktop and almost obliterating the traffic, she glanced at Kane. "I've never seen it this bad. How are we going to get through that and see Stark in a white van? He'll be invisible."

"I have fog lights." Kane shrugged. "We'll be fine. It's probably patchy, and with five of us searching for him, he won't slip by."

As Kane pulled up some ways from where Rowley had parked, his gray vehicle hardly visible in the white cloud surrounding it, Jenna tapped her comm. "We're behind you. We'll take a walk and take in the displays nice and casual and then go into Aunt Betty's. Have you had eyes on Stark yet?"

"Nope. I can't see much at all, but if he drives by, I'll see him." Rowley sounded as if he were standing beside her.

"He's just driven past me." Rio's engine rumbled. *"I'm taking Maple. If he stops in town, I'll park somewhere and come in on foot. I'm not in uniform, so he won't notice me."*

Jenna nodded. "Copy." She climbed out of the truck and as the mist swirled around her legs, she waited for Kane and Carter to join her on the sidewalk. The foggy night distorted the view and played tricks with her mind. Things moved and people seemed to emerge out of nowhere. She swallowed hard. She had a job to do and straightened her spine. For a few seconds the swirling clouds swallowed up Kane and Carter. Weird noises from the displays drifted to her as people walked by. Heart thumping, Jenna turned around as screeches and sinister laughter surrounded her. Taking a firm grip on her nerves, she fought hard to push back her Halloween jitters. As Kane and Carter came to her side, she took a deep breath but blinked hard. Not a stone's throw away from her, as people strolled along the sidewalk swirling the mist, they became almost transparent at times as rolling clouds engulfed them. Even with so many people milling around, Jenna couldn't shake off the surreal creepy feeling that something malevolent was out there, waiting to strike. She ignored the icy chill slithering down her spine and smiled at Kane. "Look interested in the displays. Laughing is good." She took Kane's hand and squeezed. "Don't look so serious."

"I'm finding it difficult to see anything." Kane peered into the fog.

As they moved closer to Aunt Betty's Café, Wendy stepped out pulling her hoodie over her long hair. Jenna smiled at her. "Heading home?"

"If I can find my ride. It's not far but I can't see a foot in front of my face." Wendy smiled at her. "They said the fog would be bad this week. Apparently the river is warmer than usual and the nights are colder, and that causes the mist to rise thick like this." She looked around nervously and shivered. "It's darn right spooky out here tonight. I had planned on being home by now, watching TV in front of the fire."

"I'll walk you to your ride." Carter smiled at her. "I can't have a lovely lady being spooked now, can I?"

"Oh, who could say no to an FBI agent?" Wendy smiled. "Thank you, Ty, that's very kind of you."

Jenna turned to look at them walk away. "We'll wait here for you."

"Okay." Carter's voice came out of the fog.

"Come and look at the display over here." Kane tugged at

her hand. "The severed heads look so real apart from the eyes moving back and forth."

Swallowing hard, Jenna stared at a blood-soaked table with four severed heads, each with a hand of cards before them and a stack of chips. Their eyes moved back and forth as if contemplating a bet. "I don't know where people come up with his stuff."

"My favorite is the one with the Wild West cowboy skeletons playing cards and smoking cigars. One of them has eyebrows and they go up and down." Kane chuckled. "The honkytonk saloon music is great."

"*I see him.*" Rowley's voice came through Jenna's earpiece. "*He's heading into the pizzeria.*"

Jenna tapped her earpiece. "Copy, just watch him. Rio, do you copy?"

"*Yeah, I'm parked in an alleyway. Want me to go and buy a slice and eat it there?*" He cleared his throat. "*I do drop by there often on Friday nights, so I won't look out of place.*"

Jenna looked at Kane and he nodded. "Yeah, good idea. We'll be inside Aunt Betty's. Let me know the second he makes a move to leave." She noticed Carter emerging from the mist and they headed toward Aunt Betty's Café. "Rowley, are you in uniform?"

"*Nope.*"

"Okay, join Carter in the pizzeria. People see you around together all the time. Buy a pie and take a table. No good sitting out in your truck when it's so foggy."

"*Copy.*"

Breathing a sigh of relief that they had everything under control, she looked at Kane. "Now we wait."

FORTY-SEVEN

As Wendy's headlights pierced the thick white cloud engulfing her home, her first instinct was to turn the Jeep around and head for a friend's place and beg a bed for the night. After being spooked twice, the last thing she needed was to walk from her vehicle to the shadow-shrouded house. Darn it, she should cut down the trees around her home, but in daytime they made the place look so pretty. At night they cast twisted shadows, like long gnarled fingers in all directions, scratched at her walls at the slightest breeze, and could hide any type of malignancy hiding there just waiting to do her harm. After taking out her Glock—it had become her constant companion of late—she stared at the swirling mist getting thicker by the second. She needed to get inside and pushed open the door. Cold seeped through her clothes, raising goosebumps all over her flesh the moment she stepped outside. The fog closed around her and the tiny water droplets brushed against her cheeks in an icy caress. Did the kiss from a ghost feel the same?

With her keys in one hand, the Glock in the other down by her side, she moved as fast as possible to the front door. In darkness, she fumbled for the lock but under her hand the door swung open. She froze, gaping inside the black maw that was her family room. Had she left and not locked the front door? Was she losing her mind? Leaving the fire burning was one thing, but going out in Serial Killer Central without locking the door? She swallowed hard and ran her fingers along the wall for the light switch. When the room flooded with light, she stood transfixed, too afraid to go inside and too scared to risk running back to the Jeep.

The house appeared to be undisturbed. If someone had broken in, surely there would be signs? She pushed her keys inside her pocket and holding the Glock out in front of her with both hands, moved through the house. Everything seemed normal. She'd locked the back door when leaving and it was still locked. No drawers hung open, no one had riffled through her things. She turned back around and walked to the front door, turned the deadbolt, and collapsed against it, heaving a sigh of relief. No one had been there and her home was safe. It had been a long day. She'd eaten at Aunt Betty's and needed to take a long hot shower and relax for a few hours. Maybe she'd watch TV in bed.

Heading back to the kitchen, she dumped her purse, Glock, and keys on the kitchen table and went to the mudroom to remove her coat and shoes. Returning she stared at the fog pushing hard against the kitchen windows. A wave of fear gripped her as something moved deep in the misty depths. Was the breeze from the river swirling the mist into strange shapes or was someone out there watching her? Had the fool with the Halloween mask returned to play a cruel joke on her again? That had been the most embarrassing thing ever. After calling Zac Rio for help and then having Jake Rowley assume she was hitting on Zac had made her blush for days just thinking about it. As if she'd do such a thing? She had to work in close proximity with the sheriff's department all the time and she didn't need any kind of awkwardness. Next time she needed help, she'd call 911.

She went to her bedroom after pulling her phone from the top pocket of her shirt, tossed it onto the bed, and undressed. After pulling on a robe, she went back to the mudroom, to drop her clothes into the washer. The smell of cooking lingered on them and she could almost scrape the feel of oil from her skin. As she walked along the passageway to her bedroom, a familiar grinding creak sounded behind her. Heart pounding, she stopped midstride and looked over one shoulder. The one place she hadn't checked was the cellar. She always kept the bolt across the door and never went down there. It was filled with storage boxes and some old furniture, spiders, and cobwebs. In her mind it was a no-go zone but she recognized the whine of the old hinges and every hair on her body stood to attention. It wasn't her imagination this time. Floorboards creaked. Someone was inside the house. Trembling with fear, she moved into her bedroom. She'd left her Glock on the kitchen table and frantically looked all around for a weapon. Rushing into the bathroom, she grabbed a can of deodorant and went back into the bedroom and snatched up her phone. She called 911 and the call went straight to Rio. "It's Wendy. There's someone inside my house."

"You sure it's not your imagination again?" Rio let out a long sigh. *"It's foggy outside and spooky. Maybe it's just the trees scratching against the house again."*

Wendy wasn't imagining the sound of footsteps moving through her house. Someone was looking for her. "I can hear footsteps, Zac. I'm stuck in my bedroom and my gun is downstairs. I need help."

"Okay, I'll call it in. I'm on a case right now." He disconnected.

Panic gripped her and she stared at the blank screen in her hand. Would anyone come and help her?

FORTY-EIGHT

When Rio's voice came through Jenna's earpiece, she tensed ready for action. "What happened?"

"It's Wendy from Aunt Betty's. She called again about a prowler. What do you want me to do? I figure she's just lonely and seeking attention."

Annoyed, Jenna glanced at Kane. He could hear the conversation through his comm. "What prowler? You've never mentioned it before."

"Twice now. Once, she saw someone in a Halloween mask outside her window; second, she said someone had been inside, set the fire, and filled the coffee machine. I did report we went by her house to check it out but not about a prowler because there wasn't anyone. It's her imagination, is all. We searched all around, did a drive-by later that night as well, but there was nobody there."

Shaking her head and dialing her phone to speak to Wendy, Jenna sighed. "Do you have eyes on Stark?"

"Yeah, he's right here."

"Watch him." Kane's chair scraped along the floor as he stood.

Dragging on her coat and heading for the door with Kane and Carter on her heels, Jenna waited for Wendy to pick up. "It's Jenna."

"*Someone's in the house.*" Wendy was breathing heavily. "*I just got home and heard the cellar door open. I hear footsteps like someone is searching around.*"

Jumping inside the Beast, Jenna kept the phone pressed to her ear. Panic for Wendy's safety gripped her, but she needed to sound calm and in control. "We're on our way. Where are you right now?" She switched the phone to speaker.

"*I'm in the bedroom. I shut the door, but my Glock is in the kitchen with my purse.*"

Jenna glanced at Kane as he hit lights and sirens and pushed his way through the dense fog along Main. "Okay, do you have anything to push across the door? If so, do it now." In the background she could hear grunts of effort and furniture moving.

"*I've put the bed across the door but I don't think it will stop anyone coming in. Just a minute.*" She grunted and heaved. "*Okay. I've turned the nightstand around so one end is butted up against the bed. I figure it will hold for a short time.*"

Heart thumping, Jenna bent to switch off lights and sirens as they turned onto Maple. If this was the killer, they could sneak right up on him in the fog. She kept her voice steady. "We're close by, whatever you do don't go into the shower. If this is who we think it is, he likes to strike in the bathroom."

"*I hear someone in the passageway.*" Wendy's voice was just above a whisper. "*He's here right now. Oh, my God the doorknob is turning. He's trying to get inside.*"

"Do you have a two-way lock on the bathroom door?" Kane took his foot off the gas and rolled onto Maple.

"*Yes, it has an inside lock and outside I can lock it with a key. The key is always in the lock.*" Breathless, Wendy was trying so hard to keep calm.

"Okay, go and lock the door, take the key, and then hide in the closet. He'll think you're in the bathroom. We're two minutes away. Stay on the line, but don't say anything. We're sneaking inside." Kane's voice was low, controlled, and calm, and his eyes were as cold as ice.

The Beast came to rest about twenty yards from Wendy's house. Jenna muted her phone and tucked it inside her top pocket, she glanced at Kane. "She has a deadbolt on her front door, how did he get inside?"

"Not sure." Kane looked at Carter. "Can you get through a deadbolt without making a sound?"

"Can you tie a shoelace?" Carter slipped away into the fog.

Running, Jenna led the way along the back of the house and stood to one side as Kane turned the handle to the back door. It turned with ease and they drew their weapons and slid inside. Thumping sounds came from along the passageway. The intruder hadn't made it inside the bedroom yet. Moments later, Carter came through the front door and met them in the family room. The next moment wood splintered and terrified screams shattered the silence. Heart in her mouth, Jenna ran toward Wendy's bedroom, and raised her voice. "Sheriff's office. Drop your weapon."

The door to the bedroom hung in jagged pieces. Jenna moved forward, her back to the wall, and peered inside as a naked man wearing a Halloween mask dragged Wendy by her hair screaming and fighting from the closet with one hand. In the other he brandished a hunting knife. Behind Jenna, Kane took the high position and Carter ran past the door and took the other side. Without hesitation, Jenna pointed her M18 pistol at the intruder. "I said put down your weapon. I will not hesitate to shoot. Put down your weapon."

"You don't understand." The masked man pulled Wendy in front of him, one arm wrapped around her chest and a glistening hunting blade at her throat. "She must die, so I can live."

"No one is dying today." Kane eased inside the room and pushed the bed away with one foot, his gun never moving from the intruder. "Let's talk about this. Wendy is our friend, so we'll use deadly force to save her. You know that, right?"

You can't negotiate with a psychopath. Confused, Jenna stared at Kane. It was their mantra, so why was he employing a useless tactic? Panic gripped her and she sucked in a breath as the knife pricked Wendy's stretched neck and a trickle of crimson welled up and spilled over the collar of her robe. Behind her, Carter had his weapon aimed and his back against the wall. They were at an impasse: shoot and Wendy would die; do nothing and Wendy would die.

"You can't kill me." The man pressed the knife harder and Wendy whimpered. "I have another nine years."

"The goddess wouldn't want this one." Kane shrugged. "You know the rules. The offering must be fresh from the shower."

Jenna's trust in Kane surged. He was using the man's MO against him. This guy only killed women fresh out of the shower. Stomach churning, she kept her aim steady and waited.

The eyes in the mask blinked and stared at Kane as if trying to look right through him.

"You can't know that. How can you?" The man shook his head as if to dispel a thought. "The goddess only speaks to me."

"Well, then we have a problem." Kane shrugged nonchalantly. "You see, I happen to know unless the offering is bathed before the sacrifice, she takes it as an insult." He smiled. "She'll remove all those years you've accrued. Make a mistake now and you might not see another sunrise."

"I don't care." The man gripped Wendy so tight, she was gasping for breath. "She deserves to die."

Wanting this to end now, Jenna stepped over the broken wood and moved into the room. She could play this game and stared at the hideous face. "Put down the knife. The night's still young. We'll take you back to the office and charge you with a break-in, is all. You'll walk on bail and still have plenty of time to find someone else. We only care about Wendy."

"Oh, do you now?" The man chuckled. "Too bad, huh?"

The knife in the man's hand slipped a couple of inches, and Kane moved so slowly to her side, she only sensed him there. Fire now or move forward to disarm him was out of the question. He'd slice so deep, Wendy would die in front of them. When the man lifted the knife from her throat and used the flat of the blade to caress Wendy's cheek, her terrified eyes swiveled to Jenna, pleading for her to do something, but there was nothing she could do to save her.

FORTY-NINE

Desperate to save Wendy, she glanced at Kane and they exchanged a meaningful glance. After years of working together, she didn't need to spell it out for him. When he gave her a barely perceivable nod, Jenna sent up a prayer to keep Wendy safe. The next few seconds could mean life or death.

"I'll cut her up piece by piece just because she's a friend of yours." The man chuckled. "Seeing the fear in your eyes as I take away little slices would make up for her not being cleansed. Pain and suffering will make up for a little sweat." His eyes met Jenna, black intense emotionless coals. "What are you gonna do, Sheriff? Shoot me and the girl dies; don't shoot me and the girl dies. You can't beat me. I never lose."

With her arms pinned to her sides, Wendy couldn't do anything to save herself, but the moment he moved the blade away from her cheek, she slumped forward as if she'd fainted. It was a move Kane had taught the locals during a recent self-defense class. The next instant, a gunshot shattered the silence, followed by screams. On Jenna's left, Wendy was on her hands and knees, scampering across the carpet toward her. On the floor, the intruder's streams of abuse cursing Kane to hell, thundered in the small space. He'd dropped the knife and was rolling on the floor cradling a smashed knee. Beside her, Carter scooped up Wendy and carried her outside. Without a second thought, Jenna ran forward and kicked the knife away.

Ignoring the man's wails of agony, she glanced at Kane and, when he nodded, she grasped the mask and pulled it from the man's head. "Well, if it isn't Duane Warner. What's with being naked? Is it part of the ritual?"

"What would you know?" He fell forward, reaching behind him and drawing a blade. It had been stuck to his back with tape, and the long sticky strands trailed from the hilt.

As he lifted the blade with his cold gaze fixed on Jenna, another shot almost burst her eardrums. She gaped in horror as the man's hand, still holding the knife, tumbled over and over before dropping into one of Wendy's slippers. It all happened so fast, as if between two heartbeats. Screaming, Warner was staring at the gushing wound, disbelief etched on his face. Swallowing hard, Jenna looked at Kane's stern expression. He'd blown off the man's hand and nearly severed his leg at the knee. She moved forward to give first aid, when Kane stepped in front of her. She glared at him. "Duty of care."

"Sure, but he's still dangerous. If you keep your weapon on him, I'll stem the bleeding." Kane pulled zip ties from his pocket and kneeled beside Warner. "Don't try anything stupid. The next one will be between your eyes." He tapped his comm. "Rowley, call the paramedics to Wendy's house. We have our man. Get here ASAP." With swift efficiency, he slid the zip ties around the injured limbs to create a tourniquet and then glanced at Jenna. "He was aiming that knife at you. He telegraphed his move. I had no choice. I can't move as fast as a bullet."

"You've crippled me." Warner was rocking back and forth wailing and sobbing. "You'll pay for this."

Stomach churning, Jenna swallowed hard at the sight of Warner's injuries. She had him at a disadvantage right now and maybe he'd let slip about where he'd buried Freya and Daisy. "Were you planning on burying Wendy beside Freya and Daisy? You like burying the women in threes. It's part of the ritual, isn't it?"

"Argh." Warner glared at her, cradling his ruined arm. "What would you know about ancient rituals?"

Shrugging, Jenna stared down at him, wondering how he felt now, suffering like his victims. "We know more than you realize. You see, the moment you started killing in threes, we researched all the rituals right back to the pagans. We needed to discover what you thought you hoped to achieve." She kept her gun pointed at his chest. "I'm interested to know how you decided which woman to kill? You planned everything, so why Freya, Daisy, and Wendy?"

"I have a long list." Warner swayed as if close to losing consciousness. "I got close to them and they all knew me. I'd ask them out for a cup of coffee or dinner, and if they refused, they made it to the top of the list. They chose themselves." He gave a slurred chuckle and his head dropped to his chest.

"Hey, wake up." Kane bent and shook him by the shoulder.

"Argh! I need pain meds. Cops carry morphine, right?" Warner glared at them. "I'm so gonna make you pay for doing this to me."

Shaking her head, Jenna stared at him, wishing they could cover him up. He resembled a blood-splattered corpse and the sight sickened her. "I don't think so. I figure the paramedics will give you something. In the meantime, you could make your life easier by answering some questions."

"When we found the graves at Bear Peak and the recordings, we knew that the moment you murdered Freya Richardson, you'd returned to Black Rock Falls." Kane's face held no compassion as he looked at the man at his feet. "An FBI agent is here. You know if you come clean about where you've buried their bodies, I might be able to persuade him to talk to the DA on your behalf. I could be real nice and go get a bucket of ice to preserve your hand so the hospital can reattach it. Right now, it's just sitting there going bad."

In the distance the sound of sirens blasted through the still night. Jenna looked at Warner. "You don't have too much time. Once the paramedics arrive, the deal is off the table."

"Cops are stupid." Warner gritted his teeth in a grimace of pain. "If you knew about the rituals, you'd know they form triangles. How many triangles are in a circle? Everything fits into the circle of life. Work it out. It's not brain surgery."

Frowning, Jenna glanced at Kane and then back at Warner. "That's not much help, is it? A circle contains an infinite number of triangles."

"Unless you already know the size and angle of some the triangles within the circle, and I presume, they're all the same size? In a ritual the size and placing are crucial." Kane rubbed his chin. "We already have three triangles."

Warner was trying to control the situation and had managed to confuse them in a few words. Refusing to be beguiled by a psychopath, Jenna lifted her chin. "Last chance. Where did you bury the bodies?"

"Directly under the bear." Warner moaned and leaned back. "Satisfied? Now, at least cover me with a sheet before anyone else comes by."

"Nah, I don't think so." Kane shook his head. "The paramedics will have something to cover you, but it's going to be a cold ride to the hospital."

Jenna turned as Carter walked into the room. "Ah, there you are." She followed him into the hallway. "Kane is going to read Mr. Warner his rights. He's under arrest for the attempted murder of Wendy and a ton of other offenses we witnessed, but he's given us the place where he buried the other two victims. I'll call the DA and get the paperwork underway for his arrest, but I figure he's going to be in surgery for a time."

"Once he's officially charged and out of surgery, do you want me to arrange transport to County? You can interview him there." Carter met her gaze. "Or they can send guards to watch over him in the security wing at the hospital?"

Thinking for a beat, Jenna nodded. "He's not going anywhere anytime soon. We'll keep him in the secure ward, and by all means, if they can spare prison guards to watch him around the clock, that would be good. I figure we need to discover the extent of the murders he's committed. With Jo here, we might be able to get him to talk. If he lawyers up and refuses to give us any information, then County can have him. One thing for darn sure, he's not spending time in our cells."

"I sure hope he talks. It would be good to know the extent of his killing fields." Carter glanced over one shoulder. "Wendy is in the kitchen. She seems okay. A little shaken, and she has a few nicks on her neck. We'll get the paramedics to check her out. She wants to go and stay with relatives but needs some clothes."

Jenna nodded. "Okay, thanks. I'll make sure she packs a bag once the prisoner is out of here. Can you stay with Kane? I need to go and get some ice."

FIFTY

SATURDAY

Jenna paced up and down outside the hospital room in the secure ward at Black Rock Falls General. They'd spent every minute since sunup using Duke to follow Warner's scent from the fire road that ran to the forest below Bear Peak, hunting through the forest for the graves of Freya Richardson and Daisy Lyon. They'd finally found them directly under the craggy rock-face depicting a bear that the peak had been named after. The bodies were well hidden and covered with dead branches and leaves, and Wolfe and his team had set to work exhuming them. Both were wrapped in the missing bedding from their rooms and buried along with a phone containing every second of their horrific deaths. They'd been taken with dignity back to the morgue and autopsies would follow, but as the bodies were so fresh and preserved at near freezing temperatures, Wolfe had completed an initial examination and considered they'd both died by the same means as all the others in the previous graves.

The seven years between the murders concerned Jenna. There had to be many more graves out there containing murdered women missed by their families. She needed to know where they were located, so that their loved ones could find closure. Right now, nothing was happening and the investigation had ground to a halt. Duane Warner wasn't talking. He'd asked for a lawyer, which was his right, and Sam Cross had been called to defend him. Sam being one of the toughest defense lawyers around hadn't been too pleased about Jenna offering a deal to his client without representation. When he stepped out of the hospital room, Jenna followed Kane over to speak with him. "Is he going to talk?"

"My advice is for him to say nothing." Cross shrugged. "You do understand I must advise my client not to incriminate himself. Although, he does admit you did read him his rights and he's unclear if this was before or after you questioned him." He gave her a long look. "Which was it?"

Jenna shrugged. "You know I'm not going to answer a leading question like that. We read him his rights. He told us where he hid the bodies. He could hardly deny trying to murder Wendy, could he?" She sucked in a breath. "We really need to know about the other women. The six graves we found in the forest dating back seven years. We know it's him. The MO matches exactly and now we have proof. There are more out there. We need information."

"He's refusing to talk." Cross leaned against the wall and folded his arms across his chest. "End of story."

"One question." Kane looked at him. "You'll be right there."

"Okay, one question." Cross pushed open the door and walked inside.

"What are they doing here?" Warner sat propped up on pillows, one leg suspended and his arm in a sling. "You said I didn't need to speak with them."

"You don't." Cross pulled up a chair beside the bed.

"We've found the graves of Josephine Wade, Lydia Ellis, Sadie Bonner, Cora Griffin, Daphne Cotter, and Esther Cary." Kane stared at Warner. "What you don't know is that we found a thumbprint on one of the phones you buried with the bodies and it's a match. You're going down for all six cold case murders. Up to now, we didn't have a matching print and now we have yours."

"Well, you can't put me away for more than life, can you?" Warner grinned at them. "It's not so bad in jail, I hear. Three squares a day and TV, what more could I want?"

Jenna kept her distance, although one of his legs was shackled to the bed, she didn't trust him. "There will be more than one life sentence. The thing is, we know about the rituals now. We could persuade the next of kin to bury the remains but many have requested cremation and I know that would negate your offering. They have to be buried as far as I'm aware but before I ask them if they'd be willing to do this, I need to know what happened during the seven years between the last murders and these recent ones. How many did you kill and where?"

"You know, I can't recall, and once they're buried, the offering is complete. Lying to me doesn't work because I can outsmart you, even lying here high on morphine." Warner stared at her and a strange darkness crept over his expression. "I moved all over but one thing's for sure: I enjoyed every minute."

EPILOGUE

HALLOWEEN

The last few days had to be the most frustrating of Jenna's career. With Warner refusing to talk and Norrell's morgue filled to capacity with the tragic remains of women slaughtered by him, she needed to know what had happened in the seven years Warner had left Black Rock Falls. The breakthrough came after the warrant to search his home uncovered a wealth of information. Like most serial killers, Warner kept trophies but his came in the form of recordings made during the murders of his victims. He'd recently transferred his complete collection to a large-capacity thumb drive. Killers always make a mistake sooner or later, and Warner, being supremely confident that no one would ever catch him, had carried the small metal thumb drive on his keychain. At his home, he'd left three older data storage units on a desk with his laptop. When these items were seized and analyzed, the dates the recordings were stored were retrieved. As Warner's occupation as a driver took him all over the state, he was traceable through his employment record.

From hours of listening to horrific recordings, the combined teams had been able to give Jenna a list of names and dates. This information Kalo ran through all missing persons files and came up with hits. Twenty-one women who went missing over the seven years Warner was away from Black Rock Falls could be linked to him. He'd been working in the areas where the women vanished. All local law enforcement agencies had been notified. The six young women in Norrell's morgue, and Freya Richardson and Daisy Lyon, would be returned to their families for burial. It had been a heart-wrenching time notifying loved ones. The discovery of six more recordings preceding the first Black Rock Falls murders had given her the extent of the killing spree. Warner had begun his Halloween rituals two years previously in Blackwater and the victims totaled thirty-five. The hunt for all the graves would continue for many years to come.

One thing was for sure, with the evidence and long trials ahead, Duane Warner would never leave jail. As she closed the file, Jenna leaned back in her chair and huffed out a long sigh. She'd dropped by where Wendy was staying and found her to be her usual bubbly self, although discovering the remark Rowley had said to her suggesting she was crying wolf to get to see Rio had outraged her. The town had gotten behind Wendy and after an online fundraiser, her beloved cabin by the river would be getting a makeover and fitted with a full security system. Wendy would return to her home, with her now fully recovered dog, and her cousin would be her housemate.

Jenna looked at Kane. "Could you call Rio? I want to speak to him alone."

"Yeah, sure." Kane frowned. "He's a good cop and made a judgment call. Don't be too hard on him."

Glaring at him, Jenna shook her head. "His mistake almost killed Wendy. I'm speaking to him, not firing him, and doing it one on one."

"Okay." Kane stood and headed for the door.

A few minutes later Rio walked into the office. Jenna looked at him. "For a gold shield detective, I figured you'd have more sense. Why didn't you immediately inform me that Wendy had called in a prowler?"

"You were knee deep in a case." Rio shrugged. "I dealt with the situation. I went out to her house with Rowley. We found no evidence of a prowler or a break-in. Not as much as a footprint. Over Halloween people get spooked. I followed procedure, checked it out twice, we did drive-bys, which usually dissuade prowlers. I did mention this to you at the time. The moment she called it in again, I notified you."

Nodding, Jenna lifted her chin. "I don't want to know about every ticket you write, but prowlers or strange happenings are pertinent. They are need-to-know, especially during a murder investigation. Next time, keep me in the loop."

"Yes, ma'am." Rio nodded, his expression serious, and turned and headed for the door.

Jenna relaxed. "Now that is over, I hope you and your family will join us for Halloween as usual? It wouldn't be the same without you."

"Thanks, and yeah, we'll be there." Rio's lips twitched into a smile. "We wouldn't miss it."

"That's good." Jenna lifted her chin. The next part would be difficult. "Send in Rowley."

When Rowley came into the office looking sheepish, Jenna stared at him. "I figured I'd taught you better. Never, ever presume a woman is hitting on one of our team if they call for assistance. You take the report and come to me. Never ever dissuade anyone who needs assistance from calling 911. Do you understand?"

"I misinterpreted the body language and I've already apologized to Wendy." Rowley hung his head. "We'd checked out her place twice and driven by three times to make sure she was okay. I figured she was safe."

Seeing his remorse, Jenna nodded. "Okay." She smiled at him. "I hope we'll see you and Sandy and the twins tonight? I wouldn't want to miss our family trick-or-treating. Rio will be there with his family as well. I know Wolfe is coming with Norrell and the girls."

"Yeah, we'll be there." Rowley's face split into a wide grin. "Although, no ball for us this year. We're staying home with the kids. We'll meet you at the top of town as usual?" Smiling, Jenna looked at him. "Wouldn't miss it."

When he left, Kane walked back into the office. "How did it go?"

Sighing, Jenna stood. "It went okay." She went to the coffee machine to pour two cups and, after adding the fixings, passed one to Kane. She sat down and looked at him. "Do you recall going trick-or-treating with your parents?"

"Yeah, the best part was going home, tipping out the buckets, and sorting the candy." Kane grinned. "It was a time when we all laughed and had fun together. Why?"

Recalling the same happy memories with her parents, Jenna smiled. "Yeah, me too. I'd like to miss the ball this year and enjoy Halloween with Tauri. He's never had a real Halloween with a family."

"He'll have a great time with the other kids." Kane grinned. "He's so fascinated with the displays and he made a basket in kindergarten to collect candy. Well, it's a plastic bucket with things stuck on the outside. He told me about it this morning when you were in the shower."

Jenna glanced at her watch. "Can we organize a Halloween party at our house by this afternoon? Is it possible?"

"Yeah, we have everything tied up here." Kane shrugged. "I'll get the refreshments organized and the ranch is already decorated."

Laughing, Jenna picked up her phone. "I'll call everyone."

A knock came on the door and Jo and Carter walked inside. With Jo was her daughter, Jaime. They always came for Halloween.

"Hey." Jo sat down with her daughter beside her. "Jaime is so excited to see Tauri again. They'll have fun tonight."

"More fun than you figure." Kane chuckled. "We're dumping the ball this year and holding a Halloween party so the kids can have a special time."

"Oh, that sounds like fun." Jo looked at Jenna. "What can I do to help?"

"We'll organize everything before we leave tonight to go trick-or-treating." Kane stood. "I'm heading out to get supplies now." He patted his leg. "Come on, Duke."

"I'll help." Carter stood and looked at Jenna. "This is a good thing you're doing for Tauri for his first Halloween with you."

Jenna stared at the photograph on her desk of Tauri with his arms wrapped around her and Kane. Her heart overflowed with love for her men and she nodded. "Yeah, a special Halloween for our special little boy and we want to make it one to remember forever."

A LETTER FROM D.K. HOOD

Dear Reader,

Thank you so much for choosing my novel and coming with me on another of Kane and Alton's chilling cases in *A Song for the Dead*. If you'd like to keep up to date with all my latest releases, just sign up at the website link below for my newsletter. An email from me will arrive about my latest release. I will never share your email address or spam you, and you can unsubscribe at any time.

www.bookouture.com/dk-hood

I love writing Halloween stories and this story was extra fun because this time I brought along some of my readers as extras. Not in any sinister way, of course, but as managers of stores and the like. I posted on Facebook and asked for names and was very happily surprised with the response, so I'll do it again soon. I often use the first names of family members and close friends as well in my stories, just so they know I think about them when I write.

If you enjoyed *A Song for the Dead,* I would be very grateful if you could leave a review and recommend my book to your friends and family. I really enjoy hearing from readers, so feel free to ask me questions at any time. You can get in touch on my Facebook page or X (formerly Twitter), or through my webpage.

Thank you so much for your support.

D.K. Hood

Keep in touch with D.K. Hood

http://www.dkhood.com/
dkhood-author.blogspot.com.au

ACKNOWLEDGMENTS

To the amazing #TeamBookouture and my very supportive editor Helen, many thanks.

I must thank my wonderful readers who are always there to support me. Writing is a very isolated occupation, and the feedback and encouragement I receive from my readers, many who have become friends, is second to none.

To Gary, my rock. You help me climb mountains.

PUBLISHING TEAM

Turning a manuscript into a book requires the efforts of many people. The publishing team at Bookouture would like to acknowledge everyone who contributed to this publication.

Audio
Alba Proko
Sinead O'Connor
Melissa Tran

Commercial
Lauren Morrissette
Jil Thielen
Imogen Allport

Data and analysis
Mark Alder
Mohamed Bussuri

Cover design
Blacksheep

Editorial
Helen Jenner
Ria Clare